AN UNLAMENTED DEATH

A Dr. Adam Bascom Murder Mystery

WILLIAM SAVAGE

First published 2015

This edition published in paperback 2016.

ISBN: 978-1-5272-0016-6

Ridge & Bourne

PUBLICATIONS

HOLT, NORFOLK, ENGLAND

For Jenn

AN UNLAMENTED DEATH

Chapter One

An Inconvenient Corpse

Around 8:00 am, Tuesday, 10 April 1792, Gressington, Norfolk

SO FAR, APRIL HAD SMILED AND WEPT and smiled again, exactly as it should, but this morning the sky was clear in the first frail light of dawn. Adam's brother was used to him leaving the house for walks at such an early hour and would not fret to find him gone. His breakfast would be awaiting his return, thanks to the housekeeper.

Adam Bascom was still, he supposed, counted as the 'new' doctor in the small Norfolk market town of Aylsham. He had been in practice there for nearly two years now. Still, the local people were slow to accept newcomers and he suspected he would still be "the new doctor" in ten years time. It was not an ideal town for a new practice. It was small and somewhat isolated near the northern coast of the county, but beggars could not be choosers. If his dear father had not died and left him a small—a very small—inheritance, he could not have established

1

a practice at all. Aylsham would do for now, even though there were few of the professional people of the middle sort and the local gentry on whom doctors' practices depended. The poor had the greatest need, but the least ability to pay. Philanthropy pleased the conscience, but would not put meals on the table.

Shaking himself free of these thoughts, Adam brought his mind back to enjoying his walk. He found the early cold invigorating. His shoes might be soaked with dew, but his heavy petersham and tarred Monmouth cap were proof against any weather. There was so much to raise the spirits at this time of year. Turning his head this way and that, he caught the fleeting scents of apple blossom and cowslips. On all sides, pale blooms caught the early light. First he inspected the delicate flowers on the blackthorn. Then he bent to sniff a few early bluebells hiding under the hedge with the cowslips. A moment later a robin was singing ahead of him, and a thrush replying to his left, caught his attention. He still had much to discover of the world of nature and much to love. Presently he lacked the means to indulge himself in walks like this too often. A new doctor cannot afford to be out when any patient calls or summons him. It would not always be so.

Adam would not even have been here today, had not his niece Mary suffered from another bout of bronchitis. The cold east winds that blew along this coast were not ideal for anyone who had a weakness in the chest. After Adam's father's death, his elder brother Giles inherited the family estate at Trundon Hall. It contained good land and a mansion neat enough. The position was a fine one as well, for it lay just below a ridge plunging down from Holt towards the River Glaven and the sea. Yet Trundon was a troubled inheritance. Giles senior had been improvident, feckless and hopeless at any sort of business. His expenditure so exceeded his income that he had left his elder son an estate much burdened with mortgages. It also needed significant capital expenditure and much better management to produce higher rentals. Giles could supply the management. The expenditure would have to wait.

Adam had long known he could expect little in the way of a personal inheritance. Like most younger sons, his lot in life must be to find his own income. Yet there were few acceptable options. Adam had no wish to enter the church. The dullness and diligence needed to be a lawyer were not part of his nature either. Nor were the courage and daring needed to be a soldier. Of business, he knew nothing. At length, to his family's surprise, he had chosen to qualify as a physician, even though the task was hard and he had to finance his studies himself.

Still, that was in the past. Now he was qualified, he could at least bring help and solace to his brother's family when any fell ill. Mary would recover, he was sure, with careful tending. Indeed, he could have returned home yesterday had not a thick fog rolled in from the sea. This was an isolated area and the roads were poor at the best of times. Riding along them alone and in fog was reckless in the extreme, so he had stayed the night with his brother. Now, needing to smell the morning air and stretch his legs, he had taken an early walk.

Adam's choice of route lay alongside the river towards the coastal village of Gressington. He could just see it now. He recalled it had but one or two large houses, principally the vicarage and the home of the most prosperous farmer. There was a single inn—somewhat weatherbeaten when he last saw it—and a group of smaller homes for tradesmen. For the rest, it was simply a cluster of fishermen's cottages and shacks, which stood at all angles to the roadway. Most of the buildings still seemed neglected or in need of repair. A stranger would have judged some of the cottages deserted, had he or she not been able to see the thin columns of smoke rising from their sagging chimneys. Gressington had for many years been one of the poorest villages in the locality. It had not always been so, for what lay before him was all that the sea had left of a once-thriving port. Centuries of storms and the shifting of the shingle had destroyed the rest. Now only the large and handsome church still showed the place's past prosperity. Yet even there the south aisle was just a ruin.

Adam sighed and opened the gate to the churchyard, looking towards the sea, calm and silver in the pale light of the new dawn. The fog had left during the night, though a few drifts of mist still clung to the river itself and the water-meadows that bordered it.

On an impulse, Adam decided to walk in the churchyard a little, looking for signs of spring. He was not disappointed. Here shy violets peeped from near the wall. There were the first leaves of the primroses that would soon spread themselves between the grave markers. Soon there would be daisies, wild carrot and all manner of other flowers to delight the bees. What men designated a place of death, nature ever filled with abundant life. There was a lesson there.

Just then, his foot struck something and he came close to losing his balance. It was a man's leg. Looking down, he saw where it protruded from behind a headstone near the churchyard wall. Not just any man's leg either. This leg wore a fine silk stocking and had an elegant shoe at the end of it, adorned with a silver buckle.

Adam bent to look closer, then straightened as he saw that a well-dressed man was lying just out of sight from the pathway. There was no need for haste. Adam was doctor enough to know at his first glance that the man was far beyond mortal help.

Resting his backside on a convenient table-topped tomb, he considered the situation with care. A man of perhaps five-and-forty years was lying dead in this churchyard. How had he come to be lying thus? How had he met his death? Neither question seemed to offer a route to an answer.

Here was a man dead. Perhaps reason and observation might point beyond facts to the cause, as they did so often in identifying the nature of a patient's disease.

It was not a robbery. The man's coat was open, showing a silver pectoral cross still in place. A clergyman then. There was also a gold ring visible on one finger, and no sign of the general disarrangement of clothing made by a cut-throat looking for a purse. He was lying in grass soaked with early dew, yet there were no footprints to be seen. If it was murder, where were the wounds? Adam could see no sign of a weapon. Indeed, from the mottling of the skin on his face, and the pinkness in his eyes from blood congesting there, he might as easily have had an apoplexy or a seizure.

The sensible course of action was to summon the local clergyman and leave matters in his hands. Adam was not sure of the current pastor's name, but he did know where he lived. That house to the left of the churchyard, somewhat larger than the others, had been the vicarage since his childhood and before. Now … should he leave the body lying where it was? He decided this was best. Once he had found help, he could, if they wished, make an initial examination. Then it would be up to the local coroner and magistrate. They would decide what further enquiry should be made into the cause of death.

The Reverend Mr. Flather turned out to be a man of dispatch. Adam waited scarce two minutes for him to ready himself to leave his house. Like Adam, he had dressed for a chilly morning. Together, they hastened across the churchyard to the place where the body lay. As they went, Rev. Flather told Adam what he planned to do.

'We must take the body to a suitable resting place to await whatever examination the coroner and magistrate may wish to make. Only then can he be handed over to his family for decent Christian burial,' he said. 'However, I see no reason why we should not make use of the gift of Providence in sending us a physician to find the body. If you are willing, I think it proper that I ask you to make a preliminary examination to establish cause of death. We will go to the body, so that I may say a brief prayer for the soul of the departed, then fetch the sexton. Together, we should be able lift the poor man onto the parish bier and take him into the small chapel off the north aisle of the church. There we may lay him out in a fitting way and you can make your examination away from prying eyes.'

Adam nodded his agreement. He kept his eyes fixed on the ground as they walked, in case there should be any indications there of what had taken place. But there was nothing. The dew lay undisturbed on the grass all around.

Arriving back where the corpse lay, Adam stood aside to allow the pastor to see the man and make his prayers undisturbed. Mr. Flather started at once in alarm and gave out a hoarse shout. 'Oh, my Good Lord,' he said. 'It is the archdeacon!'

'The Archdeacon of Norwich?'

'Indeed so. Dr. Nathaniel Ross. An important man in the church. What on earth is he doing here?'

'He had not come to see you?' Adam asked.

'No. His last visitation to this parish was some weeks ago. He is most diligent in his duties of inspection and correction. Yet he has always informed me by letter of his attending on me. I have heard nothing. He had no reason to be here, yet here he is—and dead as well. I must fetch Tom, my sexton. We must not allow Dr. Ross to lie on the wet ground any longer.' It occurred to Adam that the state of the ground would be of no concern to a corpse, but he held his peace.

'And the constable and magistrate?' he asked. He kept his tone low since it was clear this discovery had greatly shocked the pastor.

'I sent one of my servants to fetch the parish constable before we left', Rev. Flather said. 'His name is Garnet—John Garnet. He is a longshoreman, I suppose, for he owns a boat and sometimes goes fishing. He also hires himself out as a local pilot to such few ships as now trade to the port of Blakeney nearby. What else he does, I think it best not to ask. There are many on this coast whose dealings are a matter of concern to the Excise. For poor people scraping a living from the sea, the smuggling trade is a lifeline.'

Without more words, the pastor hurried off to fetch sexton and bier. Adam stood alone once again with the mortal remains of The Venerable Dr. Nathaniel Ross. What an intriguing puzzle! For anyone to have been out alone in the churchyard in the cold, wet fog last night was strange enough. For that person to be the Archdeacon of Norwich seemed almost past belief.

After several more minutes, the pastor returned, now accompanied by a man of indeterminate age whom he introduced as Sexton Hart. The three of them lifted the archdeacon's body onto a bier which the sexton had brought. Then Hart wheeled the body towards the church, while Rev. Flather lead the way, chanting some prayer or psalm in a low voice. For a few moments, Adam hung back to examine the ground where the corpse had been lying.

Aside from the dry depression in the grass caused by the body itself, there was nothing to see. No marks on the dew from any footsteps, other than his, the pastor's and the sexton's. No weapon thrown aside. No signs on the ground of any struggle, nor where men might have gathered around. Below the head, there was a darker mark on the grass leaves that might have been blood. Adam touched a finger to the stems and it came away stained with a pale pink. Not much blood then; or the dew had washed it away. The man must have been on the ground since early yesterday evening.

AN UNLAMENTED DEATH

Chapter Two

Preliminaries

The same morning

WHEN THEY HAD LIFTED THE BODY, they found it stiff and uncoop-
erative. Rigor mortis was well advanced. It might begin within a few
hours of death, perhaps three to six, depending on the age, bulk and
gender of the corpse, as well as its muscularity. Temperature too. Last
night had been cold and this might have slowed the process somewhat.
Whatever else, the body was stiff now and this state might last for
twelve hours or more. All Adam could guess was that the archdeacon
had died in the early evening and had lain outside all night. Seeing
that the others had now entered the church porch, he rose and hurried
after them.

The sexton wheeled the body on its bier into a chapel off the
north aisle of the church. The pastor bent his head again in prayer, then
stood back to allow Adam to begin his examination. Adam peered first
at the archdeacon's throat, but could see no marks on the flesh of hands
or a string. No cut such as a knife would have made. Nothing. No cuts

9

to his clothing that he could see. No sign of a bullet wound. He would have to remove the clothing to be sure of that, but to do so would go beyond the bounds of propriety.

The archdeacon's eyes were closed, yet his features were fixed in a grimace of fierce anger. Had he confronted his killer? Still, Adam had seen odd expressions on the faces of many corpses and put little store by them. He had seen executed murderers who looked peaceful and serene. Those who had passed away surrounded by a loving family, often looked surprised that death had come.

Lifting the head as far as he could, Adam looked at the skull and slid his hands over the thinning hair. Ah, there was something. A dent, a depression in the skull, most likely from a heavy blow. Taking his hand away, he examined the palm. A little blood, not much. There must be only a small cut there, for head wounds of any size usually bled a good deal.

At length, Adam straightened up and addressed the others. 'There's a depression on the back of the skull and a cut across it, I believe. Look. Blood on my hand. I suspect his skull was broken by some heavy blow. His neck is so stiff I cannot raise his head to take a decent look, but I reckon he has a small wound where the blow fell.'

'Murdered?' Rev. Flather asked.

'There's no way to tell, sir. Without a weapon or signs of violence on the body, all I can say is that the man suffered a severe blow to the back of his head.'

'Enough to cause his death?'

'Again, I cannot be sure. It may be so. To be clearer on the subject it would be necessary to cut the scalp and examine the nature and depth of the depression beneath. I expect the coroner or the magistrate will order that, but it is their decision. I can see no superficial signs of violence. I do note the dark colour of the skin on his face. Without the wound, I might have guessed at an apoplexy, but that bump on the head changes everything.'

While he was talking, a young man had entered the church and whispered something to the pastor. The response was immediate. 'Why is he not coming yet? Speak out, boy.'

'I found Constable Garnet with his nets and boats, sir. The tide is just on the turn. Too far out to launch, so the men are readying their tackle for the next high water. The constable had his boat upside down on the shingle and was painting something on the hull. It smelled terrible, it did! Anyhow, I told him about this corpus, as you said to, and he said he would come when he could.'

The pastor's face was a picture of astonishment and anger. 'Was that all?' he said. 'He would come when he could? The man is a fool!'

The young man hesitated, afraid to cause his master to become angrier still. 'He said he reckoned as how the body would keep until he finished his task, master. He promised to see to matters after that. When that might be, he did not say.'

Before Rev. Flather might berate the unfortunate servant still more, Adam intervened. 'You sent this young man to find the constable before you knew the identity of the dead man, sir. I expect neither he nor the good constable had any reason at that time to consider the matter of unusual importance.'

He turned to the servant. 'You knew nothing of the circumstances beyond the discovery of a dead man. Is that so?' he asked.

The man nodded, grateful to be saved further scolding.

'Sir, you are right, of course,' the pastor said. 'There is no need for me to scold young Peter here. He did what I asked him at the time and knew nothing more of this matter. I am sorry, Peter. I should not have spoken to you thus. Off you go now.'

Flather turned to Adam again and stretched out his right hand. As Adam took it in friendship, the pastor thanked him for his help.

'I shall go to the constable myself, sir,' he said. 'Once he understands the importance of this event, I am certain he will respond with all due diligence. He is somewhat lacking in finer feelings, as are most of his kind. Lacking in honesty too, at times, but that is also common enough in this fallen world. There is no need to detain you longer. You must be in sore need of breaking your fast. If you return to the vicarage, I am sure my wife would be more than willing to provide you with suitable sustenance…'

'No need, sir,' Adam said, interrupting the flow of pleasantries. 'I am staying with my brother at Trundon Hall and he will be wondering at my slow return from a simple morning walk.'

'Trundon Hall? You are a Bascom then?'

'Adam Bascom, sir. The younger brother of the squire—though I find it hard to remember that my brother is squire now. Somehow I still think of my father in that role, though in truth it fitted him ill.'

'I know something of the last squire's manner of life, sir. But I will detain you no further. We both have urgent errands before us. I to fetch the constable and you to bring reassurance to your family and food to your needs. I hope that at a later date you will be good enough to call on me, Mr. Bascom, for I should like to enjoy your company in better circumstances. I had heard that Squire Bascom had a brother who was a medical man. Now we have met once, I hope it will not be for the last time.' And so, with mutual protestations of future contact, the two men parted.

As Adam was leaving the church, a man of perhaps five-and-forty entered. Since he wore fisherman's clothing and smelled of pitch, it was easy to deduce this was the parish constable. Yet when he encountered Adam in the doorway, he became at once truculent and threatening. 'I don't know your face,' he said. 'Who are you? What are you doing here?'

Mastering his anger, Adam gave his name. 'As to what I am doing,' he said, 'I am just leaving.'

As soon as he heard the name Bascom, the constable became as deferential as he had been aggressive before. 'Begging your pardon, sir,' he said. 'I am but a poor man and my rough, local manners sometimes betray me. I will not detain you, I am sure.'

At this, the Rev. Flather intervened to explain Adam was out for an early morning walk and found the body. Garnet, now meekness itself, asked Adam what he had found. Yet Adam was almost sure he would not have done so, had the pastor not forced his hand.

'Little enough, Constable,' Adam told him. 'At the pastor's request, I made a cursory examination of the body and found a fracture of the skull. It is possible this came from a heavy blow, yet I could see no weapon nor sign of a struggle. He may simply have fallen'

These few remarks seemed to make Garnet happy. 'There! You have hit upon it at once, sir,' he said. ''Twas an accident surely. The man fell and hit his head.'

'Perhaps so,' Adam said. 'Yet if that is the explanation, where is his horse? If he came by carriage, where is that?'

'Don't you worry about such things,' Garnet said. 'A horse will wander, sir, and a carriage like as not be stolen in these parts. You may leave all to me and to the magistrate. I thank you kindly for what you have done. There is no need to detain you further. I will relate the circumstances of the body's discovery to the magistrate.'

'The magistrate will, of course, wish to speak with me in detail. I will tell you where I may be found,' Adam said.

'No, no, good sir. I doubt much he will need to do that. 'Tis such an obvious case of a fall. The magistrate will see no need to ask you more questions or drag you back to Gressington, I warrant.' And with that, the man dismissed Adam for a second time and turned to engage the pastor in conversation. Baffled and angry, Adam went on his way.

AN UNLAMENTED DEATH

Chapter Three

The Puzzle Begins

Wednesday, 11 April 1792, Trundon Hall, Norfolk

'THIS DEATH IS MOST PUZZLING,' Adam's brother, Giles Bascom, said for maybe the fourth or fifth time. 'I cannot see how anyone can solve it.'

'By the application of reason, brother,' Adam said. His brother's wonderment was causing him to repeat himself as well.

Amelia, Giles' wife, had left them to attend to some household business with the housekeeper and the cook. Now the brothers sat alone over the remains of what had been a substantial breakfast. Adam was in no hurry to leave. One of the benefits of being an unmarried man was the freedom to come and go as you wished. Servants were expected to cope with their master's vagaries.

'But the Archdeacon himself…' Giles said. 'I knew our new archdeacon was not a popular man, but I cannot imagine anyone killing him. And why in Gressington, of all villages in the county?'

'You say new archdeacon?'

Giles laughed. 'I forget sometimes that you are such a heathen, Adam, like most of your profession.'

'Not heathen at all. Heathens worship primitive gods and follow strange superstitions. I try to be a man of science and reason—both strong defences against any belief in the supernatural, be that gods, ghosts or ghouls.'

'Heretic then,' Giles said. 'for so you must admit. Atheist. When did you last attend service in a Christian church, my dear brother?'

'I cannot recall,' Adam replied.

'Perhaps at my wedding?' Giles said. 'That was ten years ago. Dr. Nathaniel Ross, when he was still living, would would have disapproved of you, Adam. Of that I am sure.'

'And I of him then,' Adam said. 'Was he such a rigid and bigoted man? And why did you call him new?'

'I declare you are like a dog with an old bone,' Giles said, 'for once you have seized on a question you will not give it up for anything. I call him new because he has been—had been, I should say—archdeacon for less than two years past. And yes, he was a Tory of most unbending style: a true High-flyer. He revered the first King Charles as saint and martyr. He also wished to return to the manner of church services and government that Archbishop Laud tried to impose under that king's rule. If he could, he would have tied up all you atheists and your dissenting friends and committed you to the flames. After that, he would reimpose strict uniformity of worship and doctrine within the Church of England. Aye, and restore the full powers of the church courts to regulate everyone's lives and morals. For him, the Divine Right of Kings to rule was but a pale reflection of the Divine Right of Archdeacons—to be obeyed.'

'I did not realise that you are so learned in church matters, Giles. You are correct, the archdeacon and I would have disapproved of each other with equal force. I cannot abide a bigot. A religious bigot is by a long way the worst of that loathsome breed.'

'There is worse, brother. I never met the man, but sound witnesses have it that his manner was haughty in the extreme and his ambition unbounded. He had set his eyes on a bishop's mitre, perhaps even the See of Canterbury itself. The man made enemies on all sides, it seems, as naturally and thoughtlessly as a cow makes dung.'

'Nevertheless…' Adam was like a dog with a bone again. '…there was no evidence of violence, so far as I could see.'

Giles suddenly rose and pulled the bell to summon a servant. 'Ah, Jane' he said to the flustered young girl who came to answer his summons. 'Ask Mr. Jenkins to bring me the copy of The Norfolk Intelligencer that I believe I left on the table in the library.' Jane bobbed her head in response and left.

Noticing Adam's smile, Giles explained. 'Jane is quite new here and is still in some awe of the squire. It will not last, I assure you. Our servants know of our financial situation and why we cannot afford a full company to serve us. They indulge us in overworking them all and we indulge them in some lack of polish.'

Jane returned with the newspaper. Mr. Jenkins, the butler, must be overworked somewhere else in the house. She handed it over without a word, paused on her way to half-turn and bob a vague curtsey, then fled.

'Here it is,' Giles said after a moment. 'Let me read you a small section from a letter our good archdeacon sent to the editor of this admirable publication. He is, as you will gather, writing on the topic of the convulsions currently taking place in France.'

Assuming a voice reminiscent of a preacher of strictest Calvinism, Giles intoned the archdeacon's words. 'Let the mob believe the king has no power save the will of the people,' he read, 'and there will be an end of order, morality and civilisation. Popery has descended into rank superstition and false doctrines. Its priesthood is content to place the empty forms of religious practice before the demands of a righteous and severe God. If such wickedness as has arisen in France cross the channel, England will be destroyed.' His voice rose to a near-shout. 'Tolerance in moral and theological matters is unacceptable. It is tantamount to opening the door to republicans and atheists. Such people are hell-bent on seizing the property and power divinely vested in their betters. What do you think of that, Adam?'

'Arrant nonsense,' Adam said. 'The ravings of a lunatic.'

'Yet a highly-placed lunatic. I have little doubt that he would have attained to a bishopric, one way or another.'

'What puzzles me more…' Adam began.

'Everything puzzles you, brother, from the construction of the meanest flower to the way the Earth spins in the heavens.'

Refusing to be distracted, Adam forged ahead. '…is where the archdeacon's horse may be, or his carriage? He cannot have come to the village on foot. How did he get to Gressington churchyard? That is as much a puzzle as why.'

'If his horse wandered off, someone will find it soon enough' Giles said. 'No one around here could keep or sell the kind of beast the archdeacon would own. It would arouse instant suspicion. I told you, the man had the highest opinion of himself and what was due to his dignity. Horse or chaise or carriage, he would accept only the finest quality.'

'Will you let me know what transpires, Giles?' Adam said. 'Please. I must return home now, but I know my mind will not rest content with so many questions unanswered. Tell me whatever you learn and do so speedily.'

'You may be assured of my prompt attention in this matter. Now, be off. Your many patients will be agog for your return.'

'You are right, Giles,' Adam said. 'I must not keep both of them waiting. Farewell…and remember your promise. Ask Amelia to be sure to give Mary the medicine I left with her. She must have it every night, at least until the weather grows warmer. I have hopes that this bronchitis will improve with age, but do not view it lightly. I gave your wife the receipt for the medicine, so that she may have the apothecary prepare more when needed.'

'Brother, brother. You know well how Amelia fusses over our children. You have no need to remind her, or me, of the care we should take of them.'

'I know,' Adam said, as he rose to leave. 'I say these things to comfort myself at having to leave my little patient, not in fear that you and her mother may not be diligent in her care. Goodbye again. I will return at any time you need me, day or night.'

'Go! Go!' Giles said. 'You have wasted enough time with me this morning. No, go, sir. Not another word. I declare that if you talk as much with your patients as you do with me, they will either cure themselves to get peace or die for the same reason. Go!'

As it turned out, Adam had little time to attend his own business on his return home. Early the previous morning, a messenger had arrived from the coroner in Gressington, requiring his presence at the inquest on the archdeacon. It would be held the following day in The White Lion Inn in Holt, commencing at 10.00 a.m. Adam had more than half expected this. Inquests were not held into every case of death. However, where the dead person was important, and the cause of death unclear, a formal inquest was certain. Since Adam had both found the body, and carried out a preliminary examination afterwards, he would be a key witness.

Such a date offered little enough opportunity to make the journey to Holt. Once again, he would be away for at least one night. The roads were too uncertain and treacherous to consider travelling after dark. There was also the minor but possible threat of robbery on the way. He would return first to Trundon Hall, where his brother would give him a bed.

'I thought I would never feel glad to have so few patients,' Adam said to his housekeeper, Mrs. Brigstone. 'But under the circumstances it makes things somewhat easier. If anyone does call, or send a servant, please explain that it is my duty to attend on the coroner in this way. I will deal with medical matters as soon as I can return.'

William, Adam's groom, gardener and general factotum in all matters outside the house, had already harnessed Betty, his horse, and brought her around to the front of the house. He now stood holding the horse's head.

'I'm surprised Betty seems so quiet and well disposed, master,' he said. 'Like the rest of us, she enjoys her home and I expected her to be none too keen to be called out again so soon. Don't you go upsetting her then. Take it easy and I warrant that she will serve you well enough.'

'You and Betty grow so fond of one another that your wife will grow jealous,' Adam said, laughing. 'You need not fear, William. I will treat your love with all tenderness and bring her back to you just as soon as I am able.'

Keeping his promise, Adam let Betty take a gentle pace and reached the Hall just as the sun was setting. His brother knew about the inquest, as did everyone else in Trundon and Gressington, so Adam's speedy return to his house did not surprise him. After a late dinner, they spent the evening talking of family matters. There would be time enough to consider the archdeacon further at the inquest on the next day.

Chapter Four

The Inquest

Friday, 13 April 1792, Holt, Norfolk

ADAM WAS WELL USED TO TAKING HIS BREAKFAST early and keeping irregular hours. He was up, breakfasted and on his way to Holt before his brother and Amelia had left their chamber.

It was a glorious morning. The birds were in full voice and he fancied he may even have heard a cuckoo calling somewhere in the distance. He had known this countryside since his birth, and his heart was always gladdened when he returned there.

Betty was less pleased to be abroad. The stables at the Hall were larger than she was used to and the food probably better. Giles loved his horses and was wont to lavish more on their welfare than he should. Now her master expected her to drag up the steep hill into Holt from Letheringsett. At least he had the consideration to get down and walk beside her on the steepest section.

Though much the same size as Aylsham, Holt presented a somewhat grander view. Buildings of quite modern style lined the main street, in place of the jumble of wooden houses common elsewhere.

The White Lion was just such a property: substantial, brick-built and well sited on the edge of the market place. Its stables would be just as well made. Adam had good hopes that he would be able to reunite William and Betty with his promise of gentle treatment fulfilled.

Although the room now set aside for the coroner's inquest was large, it was already almost filled when he arrived. Fortunately, the usher had kept spaces free for witnesses on the bench nearest to the front. Adam hoped he might be seated next to the Vicar of Gressington, but that was not to be. That reverend gentleman was right at the other end of the short row of benches. The man next to Adam was elderly and had a somewhat florid and whiskery complexion. He was also most eager to strike up an acquaintance.

'Captain George Mimms, sir,' he said, twisting round with difficulty to offer Adam his hand. 'Once of His Majesty's Navy, then a merchant. Not a witness, like yourself. Merely an old man allowed to have this seat by reason of my infirmity…and a small donation to the funds of our good usher!'

'Adam Bascom, sir. A physician.'

If Adam hoped by his brusque reply to stifle further attempts at conversation, he was soon set right on the matter. Capt. Mimms had either failed to notice the snub, or chose to ignore it. 'Bascom…Bascom. Then you will be from Trundon Hall, sir? A relative, perhaps, for I have seen the new squire on one or two occasions and you and he bear a striking resemblance.'

'He is my brother,' Adam said. It was impossible not to reply without showing the most egregious rudeness.

'Indeed, indeed. And a physician. A most worthy profession, sir. To have such a profession is a great good fortune. Though it may be hard and wearisome to attain, it confers sufficient status to talk at ease with the gentry and the nobility. Yet is does not deprive you of an equal ease with the merchant, the tradesman, the farmer and the man who follows the plough. I, sir, have no profession at all. I was an idle and feckless youth, who ran away to sea before my twelfth birthday, consumed with stories of pirates and privateers. I faced the most cruel disappointment, for the sea is a harsh mistress and the captains of ships learn their skills at her hands. In the end I saw that I must work hard or perish. Thus I prospered and became the captain of ships belonging to others. Later I had my own ship, and finally I have shares in ten ships and own a trading house at Yarmouth besides. Nowadays, I am too old for such work and the hard years at sea have left me lame and short of breath. I have given my business to my sons to run and live in this pleasant little town. I have become a source of amusement to many, sir, but I hope of pleasure to a select few.'

At once, Adam regretted his rudeness of a few moments ago. Here was a man of sharp wit and long experience. He should have treated him with respect for his age and his ability to turn a poor start in life into significant wealth.

'Forgive me, sir,' Adam said. 'I have been deuced rude in my response to your politeness. I can only plead that I am more than a little apprehensive at what is to come. I have never attended an inquest before, and now must give my evidence before such a multitude of persons.'

Capt. Mimms smiled and patted Adam on the arm. 'Think nothing of it, my good sir. For I took no offence, seeing that none was intended. Nor should you feel the least nervousness at what is to come. Mr. Allsop, the coroner, is a most punctilious lawyer and will have nothing take place that is not proper to such a solemn event. It was at his instigation, I hear, that they moved proceedings from Gressington into Holt. The inn at Gressington has but a small barn available. The death of such a prominent personage as the Archdeacon of Norwich is bound to draw a good crowd of the curious.'

'Is that the measure of this crowd then, Capt. Mimms?' Adam said. 'A mere congregation of the curious?'

'Not all, young sir. I see many of our local clergy, attending out of respect to one of their number. Or do they perhaps wish to be seen to do so by that tall person standing up to your left to survey the crowd? That is Mr. Yerkins, the bishop's chaplain and his right hand man. Over and beyond Mr. Yerkins, I see Col. Mansard and Mr. Unscombe, both persons of quality and owners of substantial estates. Maybe they knew the archdeacon. There I see Mr. Loffard. He will, I imagine, be writing a report on proceedings which we will see in The Norfolk Intelligencer in a day or so. John Refford to my right is a merchant like myself...Ah, here is Mr. Allsop. The game is afoot!'

A dull game it was too, at the start. The members of the jury had already been sworn in and had viewed the corpse in the presence of the coroner, as the law required. Still Mr. Allsop proved to be as Capt. Mimms predicted. First he read out the rules the jury must follow. Then he listed the steps already taken: empowering a suitable jury and moving the proceedings to more commodious premises. Finally, he explained he would be calling several witnesses, before asking the jury to reach a verdict on the cause of death. There was much shifting of feet and muffled coughing from the assembled crowd. This provoked angry looks from the coroner and, twice, a sharp rapping of his gavel.

First, the Vicar of Gressington gave his evidence. He explained how he knew the identity of the dead man and confirmed the place where his body had been found.

That over, the coroner proved that, though he was a legal pedant, he was no fool. His questions to the vicar were precise and admirably directed and he drew out clear and concise answers. The vicar deposed that Dr. Bascom had come to his house early in the morning and informed him that he had found a man's body in the churchyard. He himself had at once sent a servant to fetch the parish constable and had accompanied Dr. Bascom back to where the body lay. They had both inspected the ground, but had found no evidence to suggest what might have happened.

The vicar then recounted how he had summoned the sexton, had the dead man set on a bier and taken to a more fitting place. Since Dr. Bascom was a physician, he had asked him to make a preliminary examination of the body. He feared the passage of time might obscure relevant items, he said, before the magistrate—or a person appointed by him—could conduct a fuller examination.

Now it was Adam's turn. He moved to the place pointed out to him and was duly sworn to tell the truth.

'Inform the jury of the precise circumstances of your being in the churchyard at Gressington so early in the morning,' the coroner said. Adam could not help sensing some accusation in that dry, precise voice.

'I had stayed the night at Trundon Hall as the guest of my brother, the squire,' Adam said. 'I have an interest in nature and natural philosophy—one that I am rarely at leisure enough to indulge. I therefore rose early and determined to walk along the river towards the sea. I hoped to find some interesting specimens of fauna or flora.'

Mr. Allsop interrupted him, perhaps fearing a full account of what he had seen. 'And you came to the churchyard at Gressington,' he said.

'I did, sir, and entered at once. I have found that the sheltered areas of churchyards are often the best places to find rare plants and insects. The body was lying just within the walls of the graveyard. I almost fell over it.'

'And you knew the man was dead?'

'I did. As a physician I have looked upon the dead more than most and recognise fatality at once. Still, I could see no obvious signs of the cause of death. No weapon was visible. There was no disarrangement of the deceased's clothing or marks of blood upon it that I could see. Has any weapon been found subsequently?'

That question drew a frown and a rebuke from the coroner. 'It is my duty to ask the necessary questions, Dr. Bascom, and yours to answer, not the other way around. Did you examine the ground about the body?'

'I did,' Adam said, his face red with anger and mortification. 'There were no signs of a struggle or a large number of people marking the grass. The dew was present in all places, save where my own feet had disturbed it. The ground was level and grassed over. The few stones that I could see were about the size of a man's fist or smaller. The only larger stones were in the form of two grave markers. I examined both for signs of blood, but found none.'

'I believe you made a brief examination of the deceased, once the body had been taken to the church.'

'I found rigor mortis well established,' Adam was determined now to stick to the point. 'From that, and the fact that the deceased's back felt dry to the touch, I estimated that death had occurred in the late afternoon or early evening of the previous day.'

'And did you find anything else; anything that might bear on the cause of death?'

'I found a depression on the back of the skull, consistent with the deceased having suffered a heavy blow there. The skull was fractured. There was a small cut in the area of the depression too, for my hand came away spotted with blood. The body was too stiff to allow of a more detailed examination without turning it fully over. I also confirmed that there were no obvious signs of other wounds. There was a silver cross around the man's neck and a gold ring on his finger, so I deduced that no robbery had taken place.'

'Dr. Bascom. Your deductions are not evidence, sir,' Mr. Allsop said. 'Kindly confine yourself to what you saw.'

Adam bowed his head, annoyed at himself and the coroner in equal measure. 'Then I have nothing more to add,' he said.

'You may stand down,' Mr. Allsop said, and the ordeal was over.

AN UNLAMENTED DEATH

Chapter Five

Captain Mimms

Later that morning

ADAM PAID LESS ATTENTION THAN HE SHOULD to the rest of the inquest proceedings, though they were, in all truth, brief enough. What was happening? Despite his anger towards the coroner and shame at his loss of countenance, Adam felt bewildered. These proceedings seemed only the barest bones of an inquest into the cause of death. Doubly so, given the standing of the person dead.

A certain Mr. Manton now gave evidence. He was a physician from the town of Wells, whom the coroner had called to examine the corpse. Manton confirmed Adam's findings in every respect. He made no mistakes, as Adam had done, by drawing attention to anything beyond the state of the corpse. Then ended by saying that the most likely cause of death was from a severe blow to the head. He never ventured any opinion about what might have caused it.

'He sounded well-rehearsed,' Capt. Mimms muttered, just loudly enough for Adam to hear. Adam nodded agreement.

29

After Mr. Manton, John Garnet, the constable, was called. He explained how the vicar's servant had called to inform him of what had been found. How he viewed the body on the bier, questioned Adam on the place and time of finding the body and examined the ground. He had, he said, noted several flints or stones, large enough in his opinion to have given a severe blow to the head of a heavy man who fell upon them. In answer to the coroner's questions, he also confirmed he had seen no signs of robbery, nor of any weapon in the vicinity.

The coroner's summing up was as near to a direction to the jury as it might be without breaching the letter of the law. There was, he told them, no evidence for any crime. The fact that the man had suffered a single blow to the skull was, in his view, consistent with him having fallen and hit his head. Their sole purpose now was to determine the cause of death. All the rest was the province of the magistrate, should he see fit to make further investigation.

With that, the jury retired. It took them almost ten minutes to return and deliver a verdict of accidental death. In many ways, how long they took was the most surprising aspect of the morning. The inquest over, the audience began to leave.

Adam would have left to start his journey home as well, had not Capt. Mimms detained him. The old man insisted that he should come to his house for refreshment before his journey and would not accept any excuse. To be honest, Adam was not sorry to have some source of diversion. His mind was still held by a whirlwind of passions and curiosity.

Now he strode ahead to quit a scene he hoped he would never look upon again and so outstripped his companion. Capt. Mimms seemed to know everyone and stopped every few paces to share a greeting. Thus it was that Adam passed outside on his own and stood by the roadway, unsure where Capt. Mimms' home might be.

'Dr. Bascom?' The speaker addressed Adam with the air of someone uncertain of himself and his reception. Yet he was neatly enough dressed in good, if workaday clothes.

'My name is Newbridge, sir,' he said. 'I am clerk to Mr. Josiah Playley, a lawyer of Norwich. My master sent me here to report back to him on the verdict. He is advising Mrs. Ross, the wife of the late archdeacon. She is, as you can imagine, much distressed by her husband's death. It seems she has therefore chosen to spend a little time with her daughter's family near Cambridge. However, before she went, she was most insistent that Mr. Playley should send you a message on her behalf. Knowing you must be here today, he entrusted this second errand to me also.'

'I see. And the nature of the message?' Adam could make no sense of this. He did not know the lady. If she needed medical advice or assistance in her loss, there were a great many doctors in Norwich. Most were also older, more eminent and more experienced than himself.

'Mrs. Ross desires that, on her return from Cambridge, she might ask you to wait upon her at your earliest convenience. She was most insistent, sir, and Mr. Playley asked me to add his own desire that you might comply with her request. She would not explain to him further. He also told me to tell you that her mind seems much troubled by some circumstance that she refuses to divulge. He hopes that she might be willing to speak of it to you and thus find some relief.'

Adam was amazed, but a refusal would be neither polite nor an answer to his inflamed curiosity. 'My compliments to your master and please tell him that I will be happy to agree to Mrs. Ross's request. Only let me know when she has returned and I will make the journey as soon as I am able.'

The clerk moved away, relieved to have discharged his duty and be returning with a favourable answer. In his place, a tall gentleman of middle years moved forward.

'Henry Harmsworthy, sir,' the man said. 'His Majesty's Justice of the Peace. Constable Garnet dropped the problem body you found onto my plate, in a matter of speaking. It is fortunate that it has proved not to be as troublesome a dish as I first thought.'

'I am glad to hear that, sir,' Adam replied. 'You will, of course, wish to speak with me in detail. I am at your service in that respect whenever you wish it.'

'You mistake me, Dr. Bascom. The jury have found the death accidental. There is no more need for me to investigate or for you to waste your valuable time in coming to speak with me.'

'But there are questions still unanswered,' Adam said in bewilderment. 'The missing horse, the reason for the archdeacon being in Gressington...'

'The archdeacon's horse and his curricle are in my stables, Dr. Bascom, where he left them. He suffered an accident to the wheel on our foul roads and could not continue until our local blacksmith might effect repairs. He was most eager to reach his destination that day and so I arranged for him to be carried in one of my vehicles.'

'But why?'

'I did not enquire,' Harmsworthy said, 'and he did not tell me. I am not so impolitely curious as to demand answers where none are necessary—as it seems some persons are, sir.' And, with that sharp rebuke, he walked on.

Scarcely had Mr. Harmsworthy departed than Capt. Mimms came up to Adam. The old sailor at once touched Adam on the arm and encouraged him to move away from the spot by the door. 'It is not far to my house, sir. I see you are much discomforted by something. You will gain nothing by waiting here. Indeed, you have now an even greater need for rest and refreshment than I noticed earlier. I will send my groom to fetch your horse. It will be ready and waiting when the time comes for you to depart. Do not judge this town and people too harshly, my friend. It seems you have seen the worst of several of our community today. Now let me show you something of the best.'

Along the way, Capt. Mimms was careful to talk of nothing save pleasantries. He also pointed out various fine brick houses that were the result of rebuilding after a great fire on May 1st, 1708. Fearing another conflagration, the townspeople had banned all wooden structures. The mediaeval township had been wooden. Today's market town was nothing but brick and stone. The result was a neat and fashionable place with almost no buildings more than seventy or so years old.

Capt. Mimms' house proved to be a fine and solid gentleman's residence. The builder had erected five bays and three stories and placed it back a little from the highway. Like its neighbours, it was constructed of red brick, with stone adornments and fine sash windows. The old mariner had done well for himself. Many a gentleman from an old-established family would be glad to live in such a property.

His servants too appeared well-chosen and used to their master's vagaries. Although he had brought home an unexpected guest and called immediately for food they showed no discomfort.

Only when Adam and his host were seated in a comfortable parlour, each with a glass of excellent punch, did Capt. Mimms return to the events of the morning.

'I observed you speaking with Mr. Harmsworthy the magistrate,' he said. 'If I may speak plainly, I do not much like the man. He is proud and somewhat full of windy discourse. Yet I have heard others speak of his consideration and care for his family. His words seemed to leave you upset, I thought.'

'He told me to mind my own business, sir,' Adam said, 'and came damnably close to rudeness in doing so.'

Capt. Mimms banged his hand on the arm of his chair, his voice rising in anger. 'The proceedings were a disgrace, my young friend. I told you that Allsop was a pedant for the law, but the way he treated you was abominable. I never so much admired any man as when you refused to be put out of countenance by his rudeness. The questions that you posed were pertinent to any inquest, if properly conducted. Yet he used the letter of the law as a weapon to quiet you. That verdict was decided upon in advance, I tell you. Allsop was under instruction to make sure that it was duly delivered by the jury, staying as near within the law as he could manage. It was the fact that you came close to upsetting his plans that made him so annoyed.'

'Why?' Adam said. 'The archdeacon was an important man in the church. Did his death not warrant the fullest possible investigation?'

'Indeed it did, sir,' Capt. Mimms said. 'Yet someone with authority and power was able to make things otherwise. It was not our Mr. Harmsworthy, you can be sure. He was under orders like the rest. Indeed, I would venture that someone noted your curiosity and told him to quiet you forthwith. I wonder...'

For several moments the old man was silent. Adam was moved by the way he offered his support, without suggesting Adam might need it. He was soon to be amazed at the man's sharpness of eye and wit.

'I believe that I pointed the bishop's chaplain out to you, Dr. Bascom,' Capt. Mimms said. Adam nodded in agreement.

'There was a gentleman close by his side, I observed. A well-dressed man of some breeding and substance. Yet he is not from these parts, for I know every person of quality this side of Norwich by sight, and not a few from much further afield. Nor was he a churchman, by the fashionable cut of his clothes. No...he came from London in my view.'

'Then he must have come in uncommon haste,' Adam said. 'This inquest has been held but one day beyond the time specified by law. That might easily be explained by the need to move it to a neighbouring town where more people could be accommodated.'

'Yet was that the sole reason?' Capt. Mimms said. 'The room at The White Lion was full enough, I give you, but not packed out. What if that was but a convenient excuse to allow someone to arrive from London to observe—even to direct—the proceedings?'

'Perhaps we are allowing our imaginings too much freedom, sir,' Adam said. 'I own that I felt the inquest was conducted in a superficial manner. I was also annoyed that my curiosity on certain matters was so brusquely dismissed. Still, I have never attended a coroner's hearing before and may well be expecting what would not be usual.'

'No, sir,' Capt. Mimms said. 'I have attended more than one such— old men have time on their hands. Many say I have also more curiosity about what goes on around me than is perhaps becoming. I tell you it was rigged…rigged most firmly. By why—and by whom—I can scarce even guess.'

'Nor I,' Adam said, but his host continued as if he had not spoken.

'Now, my friend, set your mind at rest. George Mimms is not to be trifled with in this way. He is not a fool, even if some think it so. They see only an old man and do not consider what it took to rise from cabin boy to captain, then a ship-owner and finally a successful merchant. I shall find the truth. Like you, I am filled with curiosity about this event. I will not rest easy until I have answers in place of questions.' He paused and grinned at Adam. 'Henry Harmsworthy, J.P. might have warned you off, sir, but nothing has been said to me on that score. Ah, here is food. Eat, my friend, eat, for you have a weary journey ahead. Do not let your mind be troubled, for I shall have my answers—and you shall know them too. Return to your surgery and your practice and leave all to me. Only, I pray you, be so good in return to apprise me of anything else that may come to your ears. For I hope to see you in my house again, sir, and that I may count you a friend, as you may indeed count me.'

'A friend indeed,' Adam said, 'and one much in your debt for both food and company. You have restored my spirits most wonderfully. You have my promise that I will keep you abreast of whatever further information comes my way. Besides, I will certainly visit you again, when it is convenient to us both.'

With that, they went to an excellent table, to which they both did ample justice. Thus it was that when Adam set out on his way home, he found he had eaten far more than was comfortable for a man on horseback.

Chapter Six

Peter Lassimer, Apothecary

Thursday, 20 April 1792, Aylsham, Norfolk

ADAM HAD SPENT THE PAST FEW DAYS catching up with the demands of his practice. He had few patients at present. Nor would he ever have more unless he seized every opportunity to place his name before any who might become patients in due course.

Aylsham already had one physician, a Dr. Pennycoats. His established practice should have been a formidable block to Adam's progress. Fortunately for him, if not for the little town, Pennycoats was both an indolent man and much given to good living. When Adam first placed his shingle outside his modest house, he had visited the man, expecting to meet firm opposition. Instead, he had found the doctor still in his bed past ten o'clock in the morning. He was recovering, his manservant said, from a good dinner taken at the local lodge of freemasons the evening before.

Since then, Dr. Pennycoats had taken every opportunity to send patients Adam's way rather than keep them from him. The man, it seemed, had a substantial private income. Most of his limited attention was spent on compiling a book on the chemical composition of different types of rocks. At least, he said he was writing such a work, for not a single page had ever reached a printer's hands.

Given their doctor's peculiar attitude to his profession, it was no surprise that most people of the town sought medical advice from the apothecary. The wealthier folk and the gentry turned to doctors living elsewhere.

Today's apothecary was expected to have medical knowledge beyond the mixing and dispensing of prescriptions. Still, most still sold a range of nostrums, spices and teas as well as more potent herbal brews. In London, the Worshipful Company of Apothecaries controlled the profession. Here, far to the north, there was less regulation over who might set themselves up in that business. Nevertheless, the law of the land was at last bearing down on the worst quacks and charlatans.

Now, hearing that Aylsham's old apothecary had decided to retire and sell his business to a successor from elsewhere Adam felt some trepidation. He therefore determined to visit the shop in the High Street to take the measure of the new apothecary in person.

Above the window was a painted shop board: 'Edward Gerstone, Apothecary and Herbalist'. In the window stood the typical range of bottles of coloured water and labelled china herb jars. Neither gave him any enlightenment. He would rely on this man to mix medicines to his prescription, yet must also regard him as something of a competitor too. Good relations might greatly assist his business. An adversarial turn of events would promise many barriers to progress. Yet as he entered the shop, he encountered the greatest surprise imaginable. For the voice which came to him from the dispensing room, hidden behind the counter, was instantly recognisable.

'Lassimer? Lassimer?' he said. 'Can it be you?'

The reply was a loud burst of laughter. 'Dr. Bascom, I believe. I had expected you before this. You are come to sniff around and steal my patients, I warrant.' The words might sound harsh, but the voice that spoke them was filled with amusement.

'Had I known whom I should find, I would have been here on your first morning,' Adam said. He was delighted to see the apothecary emerge into the shop and recognise the smiling face of Peter Lassimer.

'My dear friend. I thought you must be a grave physician by now, filling your patients with awe at your magisterial manner. But wait... above the door is the name of a Mr. Gerstone."

'Mr. Gerstone is my master in the Worshipful Company of Apothecaries,' Lassimer replied. 'He is also the principal owner of this business, until I obtain freedom of the Company and can buy him out. You find me a humble journeyman apothecary, treating the good people of this town with foul brews and rank potions.'

'Lassimer, my old friend. While I should be disapproving of your levity towards the materia medica, you know I would not have you change for an instant. I wager you are still casting a lecherous eye over every serving maid whose mistress is fool enough to send her here. But were you not well on your way to a doctor's qualifications when I left Glasgow?'

The apothecary stepped quickly around the counter and closed the door to the shop, pulling down the blind. Then he advanced upon Adam and grasped him in an embrace that would have done justice to any bear.

'There,' he said. 'I have closed my shop and we may retire to my parlour to talk properly. I want to know all about your adventures in the United Provinces. As for my own story, it will prove familiar enough. Still, I own that what once seemed the worst of fortunes has proved to be nothing of the kind.'

The two men were soon seated in a comfortable parlour, each holding a glass of punch, which had been served by a well-dressed and attentive maidservant.

'You are not married, Lassimer, I think,' Adam said, after tasting the punch and nodding his head in pleasure. 'The looks that passed between you and your maid would have quickly drawn the ire of any wife.'

'Married?' Lassimer said. 'Nay, sir, that is a yoke to which I will long be loathe to bend my neck. For who would settle for a single wine when he might taste of as many of those that are on offer as his stomach—and his fortune—may bear. Unless, of course, he spurns the native beauties of his own land to seek out exotic beauties from over the seas.'

'I am not sure that I would allow any exotic beauty to make your acquaintance, sir,' Adam said. 'Not only would you turn her head with outrageous flattery, but would soon win her away from a dull dog like me.'

'You may rest easy, my friend,' Lassimer said. 'You are no dull dog. But are you not wed?'

'Indeed not. I am too poor, my friend. Besides, like you, I value my freedom to do as I wish, though perhaps not in quite the same way.'

'Yet I am sure you do not lack female company, Bascom. At Glasgow, as I recall, you had your pleasure of many a Scottish lass. Indeed, there was sometimes quite a queue.'

'Do not mock me, old friend. You make me sound a veritable terror to the fair sex.'

'As you were. I speak only the truth.'

'Nay,' Adam said. 'Not even then and certainly not now. Am I not a grave physician, devoted only to my books and patients?'

'I pray that is not so,' Lassimer said, laughing. 'But if you do lack for suitable diversions, I will be happy to supply you with the names of several lusty widows of my acquaintance. One man alone can do only so much. I would welcome assistance to lessen the demands placed upon me.'

'Lassimer,!' Adam said. 'You are as given to boasting of your exploits now as you ever were. I can find all the ladies I need by my own efforts, thank you.'

If that was not strictly true, it would suffice. He did not doubt Lassimer would arouse a fury of speculation and gossip if he did as he promised. What husband would then trust Adam to attend on his wife? What father would trust him to treat his sick daughter? 'Enough of such nonsense, sir. I never expected to find you an apothecary, and in Norfolk too. Still, I am in no doubt that you are an excellent practitioner of your art, and much valued by your customers.'

'Yet are you not well upon your way to fame and fortune as a physician of note,' Lassimer said, 'while I will languish in this small town for the rest of my days?'

'Fame I care about little. Fortune would be enough. But now, sir. You promised me an answer to my question on how you came to be here. You say you met misfortune. Yet here you are, frightening the grave virgins of this county and in possession of what I see to be a fine house and shop.'

'My tale is soon related,' Lassimer said, his levity gone for the moment. 'I was set upon my way to obtaining my degree at the university. I proceeded more slowly than yourself, for I lack both your fine brain and the education you had at Cambridge, but well enough. Then, on a sudden, such a storm engulfed my father's business as drew away all his money, so that I might no longer pay my way. Indeed, in the end it took his life.'

'That is ill news indeed,' Adam said. 'I am sorry such a heavy fate fell upon you, who deserved none of it. It seems yet more proof that

Divine Providence is naught more than mankind whistling to keep up his spirits.'

'My father had always been most liberal in extending credit, as you know, Bascom,' Lassimer said. 'Especially to the gentry and merchants of Shrewsbury. That liberality ruined him. Two young blades, both of noble parentage, patronised his tailoring business to fit them for the fashionable life each believed he deserved. Both were profligate, idle and licentious, as is too often the way of the sons of the gentry. Now each proved that he was as poor a player at the gaming tables as the veriest country bumpkin. They gambled away their allowances. Then they fell into the hands of money lenders. Soon they learned also that gentlemen of that sort were unwilling to wait for the settling of debts.'

'But your father was a prosperous man,' Adam said, 'in good standing in that city. Could the debts of two such men cause him to fail?'

'By themselves, no,' Lassimer said. 'He saw that he would never recover what each owed him. They denied not just the debt, but ever having patronised his shop. Worse was to come. Their fathers were eager to limit what they must pay to save their offspring from the debtor's prison and chose to believe them. Then came the worst blow of all. His chief clerk had, it seems, grown tired of his wife of twenty years and taken up with the young wife of his neighbour. The two of them were in bed together, when they thought the husband safely gone for the night to stay with his brother. It was not so. The woman's husband suspected her of adultery. Now he sprang his trap and drove them out into the night, inflicting some severe wounds on the man who had cuckolded him. The two lovers were forced to flee. Well aware that he would find it hard to find well-paid work elsewhere, the wretched man emptied the safe of the money my father had placed there ready to pay his own creditors.'

'What depravity,' Adam said. 'Was the thief apprehended?'

'Alas, no, for none knew which way the two might have gone from the town. My father was ruined. He sold his business and managed to pay all his creditors from the proceeds. Only just enough remained to pay for me to take up an apprenticeship with an apothecary in Leicester. My father insisted I move as far away as I could. He knew that the disaster would forever be attached to the name of Lassimer, should I stay in Shrewsbury.

'When I finished my apprenticeship early, thanks to my medical studies, here I came. The arrangement suits both Mr. Gerstone and myself. No sooner had he purchased this business than his own health failed. He cannot now make the calls necessary to sustain a country practice. Though I am still a journeyman, we have agreed I shall buy him out by stages and become his successor. He now lives in a fine house on the edge of the town, where he hopes to end his days in quiet retirement.'

'When will that be?' Adam asked.

'I must serve another two years at my present level, under the professional—but very occasional—supervision of Mr. Gerstone. Then I may seek to be entered a Freeman of the Company.'

'And your father?' Adam said, fearing what he suspected must come.

'My mother died some years ago, as you know, and I have neither brother nor sister. I pleaded with my father to let me stay at his side, but he would have none of it. Though my heart demanded I set all else aside to support him as best I could, my head told me that he was right. Had I stayed, I would always have been "that man whose father lost his fortune through his own trusting and foolish actions". My future would be blighted by such words and my father could not bear that. So, in the end, I gave in, believing I could make my fortune, then return to help him reclaim his. It was not to be. He died within six months.'

'Some of our vaunted authorities claim mind and body are quite separate,' Adam said. 'Yet both my studies of the most up-to-date natural philosophers, and my own experience, such as it is, tell me they are wrong. We are a unity: a thinking animal, using our brains to reason as we use our legs to walk or our gut to digest our food. Many a sickness of the mind has its causes in some bodily malfunction or imbalance. Grief and loneliness are as swift to end life as the smallpox or any fever.'

'Enough of gloom,' Lassimer said. 'The past is past and cannot be changed. I have found happiness and good fortune in my new profession. I will not allow dark musings to take them from me. Does your practice show promise, Bascom? You may be very sure I shall send all my most difficult cases to you. Thus I will win a fine reputation as a healer by restricting myself to simple maladies. You meanwhile will struggle with the most intractable diseases.'

Chapter Seven

Gossip and Punch

Monday, 30 April 1792, Aylsham, Norfolk

MUCH CHEERED BY FINDING THIS UNEXPECTED FRIEND and ally in the town, Adam now gave all his attention to his practice. He was pleased to discover several new patients had sent in their requests to consult him. Had they heard good reports of his skill? Or were they eager to have someone visit them who might be persuaded to pass on information about the archdeacon's death? He neither knew nor cared. A patient was a patient. Without them, he would sink into penury.

Even routine business was not to be spurned. Adam arranged several visits to the better class of people in the neighbourhood to inoculate them and their households against the scourge of smallpox. Even in his short period so far as a country doctor, Adam had every cause to bless the name of Lady Mary Wortley Montagu. Finding the procedure used by the Ottoman Turks with signal success, she had not only had her own daughter inoculated, but interested others. Amongst these were the King's doctor, and soon the practice was introduced into the Royal Family. It was then but a small step for the gentry to follow suit. Although it was not yet itself free from risk, the benefits far outweighed the drawbacks.

Many of the older physicians in the county were unwilling to learn the technique. Some were so set in their ways as to deny its efficacy altogether. As a result, inoculation was too often open to quacks and half-trained practitioners. Fearing such people, the gentry were eager to find a better alternative. As the only doctor in this part of the county willing and able to provide this service, Adam had a near monopoly of their business and could charge handsomely. He was, however, humble enough—and wise enough in the ways of business— to realise that others would soon come to challenge him. He therefore offered handsome reductions in his fees to any who would have their whole household, including servants, inoculated in a single visit.

It was more than a week before he could visit Peter Lassimer again. As he expected, he was greeted with great delight by the young apothecary and they sat in the compounding room where they could talk at leisure. Peter Lassimer was an able and hard-working man, whose heart was as large as his smile. While some of the stricter sort might frown on his delight in pretty women, few of them seemed to complain. Lassimer might be faithless and have an eye that wandered far and wide, but he made no secret of this to anyone. Nor did he ever used false vows or declarations to smooth his path into a lady's bedchamber. He neither gave nor demanded exclusivity in his affections. His much-admired prowess in the amatory arts, gained from a mass of experience, ensured a steady stream of female customers.

Lassimer did have one vice. He loved gossip. About his love affairs he maintained the strictest discretion. No lady likes to find her matters of the heart spread around the town. For the rest, he was most assiduous in collecting information. Many in the town had found some reason to buy remedies, herbs or spices during the past week, so that they might glean some information about the mysterious death of Dr. Ross. Lassimer's supplies of fresh gossip were now diminishing and he looked eagerly to Adam for ways to refresh them.

'So…you have at last found time to visit your old friend,' Lassimer said. 'I thought you must have fled overseas to escape your reputation as the doctor who finds dead bodies, as well as producing them.'

'Enough!' Adam replied, laughing. 'I must see to my business as much as you. Nor do I have the benefit of most of my customers coming to my place of work, as you do. In these country areas, those few who can afford a physician expect him to go to them. It matters not how wearisome the journey, nor how foul the roads may be.'

'I hear you also spend your time infecting others with the pox.'

'That, sir, would be you, though I know you are most careful inn such matters. I seek only to help them avoid the smallpox, as well you know. My services are much in demand in that regard. Its effects are too often mortal, as well as scarring those who survive. I think we should not joke about such matters. Until recent times, there was little any of us medical men could do when the disease struck.'

Lassimer tried to look penitent, but his grin was never long away. 'I also hear, my friend, that you have a number of new patients.'

'The one who said that notoriety is no bar to success spoke truly,' Adam replied. 'Since chance brought me to play a small part in the discovery of the archdeacon, I have found people see consulting me as the best way to obtain information. Would you not agree that is a most disreputable mode of behaviour?'

'In no way, sir, for I hope to employ it myself,' Lassimer said. His total honesty about his motives made it impossible not to smile.

'Then you must be disappointed, I fear. I have little more to relate, save that the inquest was a most odd affair. It seemed more concerned with preventing any enquiry into the man's death than promoting one.'

'You call that a little matter? Come, sit down in my parlour, take a glass of punch, and tell me all, leaving out not the smallest detail. I will close my shop for this. Anne! Bring us two glasses of punch at once.' The servant clearly knew her master's habits, for she had entered the room almost as he called, bearing a jug of punch and two glasses. Lassimer looked at her fondly.

'Is Anne not a paragon amongst servants, Adam, as well as being the handsomest wench in the county?'

'You will make the girl blush, Lassimer,' Adam said, though he observed rather a look of pleasure on the young lady's face than any embarrassment.

'A becoming blush would only add the final crowning touch to your beauty, would it not, my dear? Yet I must with reluctance end my contemplation of your charms, for my old friend here has grave news to relate. Be off to your duties!' As she turn away, he landed a resounding smack upon her rump, which brought forth a squeal. Whether of indignation or delight Adam could not tell.

'One of these days your familiar ways will land you in serious trouble,' Adam said, trying, with scant success, to look severe.

'Nay, my friend' Lassimer said. 'I may be lecherous and pay more attention to the wenches than most, but I am no fool. I steal no man's wife. I seduce no lady of virtue, whatever her age or status. I will not force myself upon any, or pay those who make a business of pleasing men. There are enough and to spare who will join with me in love's pleasures of their own free will. Some are, perhaps, of lower station, but not all. Several widows of good fortune and breeding have cause to thank me for returning a spring to their steps and a smile to their faces. And not all of those who have found no husband wish to remain virgins too. I own that I play the devilish flirt with my pretty Anne, but I would stop in an instant if she asked me. I have never, I assure you,

'My affection for you, Lassimer, springs from many sources,' Adam said, 'but none more deep than your invincible optimism. You are right. I must not give in to the melancholy. But now, I must leave you to tend your business and go to mine. The day is passing, and there are many things that I must do before it is over.'

'One more question before you go,' Lassimer said. 'Are you doing this for yourself or for the man who died?'

It seemed a long time before Adam replied. 'Why do you ask?' he said.

'The way you were treated during and after that inquest was enough to anger any man,' Lassimer replied. 'You have every right to feel annoyed with the way the process was handled. Since it appears the authorities are concealing some aspects of this event deliberately, you may also, with reason, feel such behaviour is not acceptable and not in accordance with the demands of the law. Yet the fact still remains that you have no standing in this affair. You are not a relative of the deceased. No one who is has asked you to act on their behalf. I do not say this to criticise, Bascom. My purpose is rather to prepare you to consider what others undoubtedly will say if your interest comes to their notice. You have been warned to mind your own business once. A future warning may come with more force behind it.'

'If I am to be honest,' Adam said, 'I must own to the truth in what you say. My pride has been hurt. I also feel someone is trying to take me for a fool. Neither is a rational reason for fretting about this puzzle, but they are powerful enough all the same to deny me the simple alternative of ignoring it. Yet I will think hard about your words, old friend. I am not a student any more to throw myself heart and soul into any complex problem that catches my fancy. But something in this touches me as a doctor too. A man has died. How and why he did so remains unclear. That, as much as the wounds to my belief in my own worth, does not let me rest.'

With that they parted, their earlier light-hearted pleasure at meeting quite overshadowed by mutual concern.

Chapter Eight

Mr. Jempson Falls Amongst Thieves

Tuesday, 8 May 1792, on the road from Edgefield to Aylsham, Norfolk

PHYSICIANS WHO HAD GRADUATED FROM UNIVERSITY occupied the top level of the medical profession. Even a newly-qualified one, like Adam Bascom, could expect significant fees for his services. Eminent physicians with practices in the larger cities often had greater incomes than most of the gentry. Adam had a country practice and was not yet well known amongst the better-off families in the area. It would be many years before he could gain a reputation that would allow him to expect his patients to come to him. For now, he spent much of his time travelling to the houses of the gentry, prosperous farmers, merchants and shipowners, who made up his scanty list of clients.

This dull day at the beginning of May, he was riding Betty home, in company with a farmer and his wife and an elderly parson. Since there had of late been unrest amongst the poor and the agricultural labourers, it was best to travel in groups.

The little party had exchanged their names and the reasons for their travel. The farmer and his wife, Henry and Katherine Ushant, had been to the market. The clergyman, the Rev. George Domble, had been visiting some of the most outlying areas of his large and scattered parish.

Adam had been to conduct an examination of the conditions at the workhouse in Holt. Capt. Mimms had secured this commission for him. Once he told his fellow Overseers of the Poor of Adam's qualifications—from three universities—their agreement was certain. Adam was grateful to the old man. Yet he could not help a certain embarrassment when he considered how far his meagre experience had been overrated.

The farmer and his wife sat on the front seat of a cart pulled by a single horse, while Adam and the parson both rode. It was thus natural for the two of them to move ahead and fall into conversation. Mr. Domble was a kindly man and much concerned for those whom fate forced to seek refuge in the workhouse.

'How did you find it?' he said. 'The poor are terrified of ending their lives there. They consider it to be little better than a prison, and the days of those within unimaginably harsh.'

'It is not meant to be an easy place,' Adam said, 'and I would not like to live there. Yet I found the Superintendent to be a fair man, who carries out his duties to the best of his ability. The building itself is scarce a dozen years old. There is ample land around it where the inmates may grow vegetables, keep chickens for meat and eggs and even a few cows to provide milk. Most who live there are active and well nourished. Even the oldest benefit from a suitable, if plain, diet—which is more than can be said for many of those outside its walls. What I found hardest to bear was the large number of young women there with their babies. These poor souls are ejected from their homes and condemned to the workhouse by their own families. I suspect many are more victims than bent on scandalous living, seduced then abandoned by the father of the child.'

'You may well be right,' the parson said, 'for Satan has ever found lust and greed two of the easiest ways to lead mankind astray. It is also correct that there are many in the countryside at large who go hungry in these times. Resentful too. The discoveries of ingenious engineers have put many out of work. That is inevitable when we build machines which can do the work of many. Others have lost their land through the process of enclosure. All look across the channel to the dreadful events now happening in France. Perhaps they wonder whether there should not be a revolution here too.'

Adam was surprised. 'Is it that bad then? Would they destroy our constitution and social order?'

'I think they would—and the church along with it. Many now see the Church of England as a means for those at the top of society to maintain their privileges. They believe the people who produce this nation's wealth are thus held in subjection. And we clergy help them, sir, to hold such views. Many a parson is diligent in carousing and hunting with the local gentry, while paying scant regard to the needs of his parishioners—especially the poor. Such people pay curates to take the bulk of the services and do such visiting as they are able. They themselves enjoy servants, fine rectories, their books and the society of their wealthy neighbours. Did you hear of the recent sad death of out archdeacon? That took place not far from here.'

Adam agreed that he had indeed heard of it, though he also took care to conceal his close knowledge of the events. He had told his story far too often already, and did not want to be drawn into it again. 'Did I not hear that the jury had ruled it an accident?'

'Yes,' Mr. Domble replied. 'Yet I cannot quite put the matter from my mind. I have heard the late archdeacon preach and he was most unbending in his demands. He wished for a return to a rigid, hierarchical society, overseen by a unified church. He would have the king at the top of the heap. The nobles and gentry should come next below him. Then the middle classes below them and the working people and poor firmly at the bottom. God, he said, had put each in his proper place in society, and it was blasphemous to attempt to change this. He was also most strong in his denunciation of dissenters and noncon-formists.'

'But surely those are just the views of one man,' Adam said. 'There are, I believe, plenty of people in the Church of England who would not share them.'

'That is true, Dr. Bascom. But there are many dissenters and non-conformists in this county. They have little reason to feel any love for the established church. We have tried to force them back into our fold, where we should have sought to persuade them. I have met many who attend the chapels and conventicles, and I have always found them to be quiet, godly people. They seek to find the Lord in their own way, as we do. Yet still I regret that we are no longer all members of the one church.'

'Why is that?' Adam asked.

'The church used to be the centre of each community,' the parson said. 'All came together there, from the highest to the lowest. Each group could see the other, every Sunday. The rich could not quite iso-late themselves from the people around them. The poor would un-derstand that, for the rich to enter the Kingdom of God, they must care for those less fortunate than themselves. Now we are but one sect amongst many, sir. Those who attended the chapels feel they have little or nothing in common with those who go to the parish church. The rich, seated in their grand pews, may hear that Christ died to save all mankind. Yet they act as if most people except them are beyond salvation.'

'But how would this bear on the death of the archdeacon?' Adam said.

'As I said, sir, there are some disaffected people who see how the French have brought the church and the aristocracy down. They would do the same here if they could. The archdeacon was well known to be a fervent Tory. If any people of this revolutionary viewpoint had recognised him, they might have felt justified in bringing about his death.'

'If some revolutionaries had done this, would they not have robbed the man, if only to give the proceeds to the poor?,' Adam said. 'His body was not touched…or so I heard,' he added hurriedly, for he had almost given himself away.

'Maybe…maybe. But if the reason for his death was hatred of what he stood for, why give anyone the opportunity to dismiss it as a simple robbery?'

Adam was amazed at the idea and they rode on in silence, while he tried to come to terms with the picture thus painted. Could it be true? He knew some were bent on overturning society and depriving the gentry and the rich of their easy sense of entitlement. Yet would even these have gone so far as to lure a prominent churchman to a lonely place where they might strike him down? It sounded far-fetched. Yet, as Mr. Domble had admitted, once considered it was impossible to dismiss. The government would wish to use every way available to prevent those who had done the deed from using it to stir up even greater unrest. That would give a powerful logic to the way in which all questions about what had happened were suppressed from the start. If it were just an accident, it was of no importance. An assassination would be reported in every newspaper in the land. From there, it would breed speculation, argument and still more dissension.

Adam was so intent on this inward speculation about the archdeacon that he stopped paying attention to anything else. He must have heard the cry that startled Parson Domble from his reverie, but he could not be certain. What definitely made him spring to the alert was the exclamation from the elderly clergyman. 'Good gracious! Ahead there! See!'

The road had, little by little, climbed upwards. Now they were just coming over the rise and looking down into a shallow valley beyond. And ahead and to their left, maybe one hundred yards distant, three men were struggling by the side of the road. One was a tall man, wearing sombre but well-made clothing; the other two were dressed in rags. With but a single glance, Adam knew that a robbery was taking place. One of the ruffians had his hands around the tall man's throat, while the other was searching through his pockets.

Their little party surged forward. The parson urged his horse into a stumbling trot. The farmer and his wife caused their cart to sway and rattle loudly, as their elderly horse tried to keep up. Flapping the reins and banging his heels into his horse, Adam persuaded Betty into a clumsy canter. Thus he rushed ahead towards the three men, still struggling, though now alerted to the rescue party. As he rode, he managed to jerk open one of his saddlebags and pull out a small pistol. He was often upon the roads and it did not do in these turbulent times to travel without some kind of protection. He always put two loaded pistols into his saddlebag, though this was the first time he had had cause to put either to use.

For a dreadful moment, he thought the ruffians might put up a fight. Then, whether intimidated by superior numbers or by the sight of a madman bearing down upon them, yelling and waving a pistol, they took to their heels.

Foolishly, Adam fired at the fleeing men, though he had little hope of hitting anything. In truth, what he did was more to relieve his own feelings than to hasten them on their way. Then, the next moment, all his attention was on bringing his horse to a stand where the victim now lay fallen in the road. Though the mare had been loathe to hasten, once into her stride she was reluctant to come to a stop.

So it was that Adam came up to the wounded man and rather fell as much as dismounted beside him. 'Peace, sir, peace. You are safe now. Are you much hurt? I am a doctor and may be able to relieve your pain a little.'

At first, the man on the ground was unable to speak, for the one ruffian had so gripped his throat that he had come near to choking the life from him. Only when surrounded by Adam, Reverend Domble and both the Ushants was he able to say anything. 'Dear friends, Providence sent you, like Good Samaritans, to save me when I had fallen amongst thieves. I gave them the few shillings that I had, and gave them freely, for I could see their need was great, but they were not satisfied. Believing I must be a gentleman, they cried out that I must have more. One seized me by the throat to choke the truth from me. The other rifled through my pockets in the hope of riches.'

'And found none,' Adam said.

'Not at all,' the other said. 'They found the greatest riches of all, though they perhaps did not think so. There, on the ground.' He pointed to a small book. Mr. Domble picked it up at once and looked at the title page.

'The New Testament,' he said. 'You are right enough. Are you a man of the cloth then, as I am?'

'Nay, friend. I am a merchant and now a ship-owner. Yet the Good Book has been my constant companion and helper these many years, ever since I joined the Society of Friends.'

'A Quaker,' Mr. Domble said, though he smiled when he said it. 'A dissenter. Yet, I believe, a good and honest man for all that. I am George Domble, Rector of Aylmerton. My companions are Dr. Adam Bascom, whom you have already met in the guise of a charging dragoon. And Farmer Ushant and his wife.'

'Joseph Jempson, friends. A merchant of Norwich, though shortly to take up residence in Aylsham.'

'Then we will be neighbours,' Adam said, 'for that is where I have my practice. Was that your destination when you were set upon?'

'It was,' Jempson said. 'At least for the night. I have not yet moved my household from the city. I went today to Blakeney to render payment to a fellow merchant living there. I have just bought from him shares in a fine ship plying between Yarmouth and the Baltic ports. Had those sad men come upon me on my outward journey, they would have found themselves in possession of notes amounting to what would have seemed to them a fortune indeed.'

'To venture abroad, alone and in possession of a great deal of money, was not wisdom,' Adam said. What could this man have been thinking to do such a thing?

'I suspect that thou, like most of thy medical colleagues, are a sceptic,' Jempson said. 'I do not blame thee for scolding me so, for by the standards of this world it was indeed a most foolhardy action. However, I was not alone, having with me for company a young couple newly married and received with joy amongst our congregation. Few enough join our Society these days, unless they are born to it; fewer still who have chosen to do so with such careful thought. The young woman was indeed born into a Quaker family, as thou wouldst have it. Her husband was not. Indeed, Parson, he was until recently a member of thine own church.'

'Ah,' Mr. Domble said. 'I suppose I ought to be censorious of his action, but I cannot bring myself to that state. Many leave religion behind out of nothing but idleness and apathy, for our churches do little to prevent it. Some, like those in France at the moment, vent their anger upon their priests, who have put wealth and ambition before Christian principles. When a man decides to follow what he believes to be his path to the Lord, who am I to say he is wrong?'

'Thy words do thee credit, friend,' Mr. Jempson said. 'I would that the young man's father had been of your mind. Instead, he railed against his son in a most unseemly manner for any Christian.'

'Gentlemen,' Adam said softly. 'You should postpone such a conversation to another time. At present, Mr. Jempson is in sore need of rest and medical attention.'

Neither Adam nor the other two had noticed Mr. Ushant slip quietly away. Now, however, he stood by in silence, holding the reins of what must be Mr. Jempson's mount. 'I have your horse, sir. She'd not gone far and those wicked men were too frighted by our dashing hero to think to steal her or what she carries.'

'Dashing hero is right,' Jempson said. 'Thou hast saved my life, I believe, Dr. Bascom and I thank thee most heartily. Now, let me delay thee all no further.'

'Nonsense,' Adam said, more roughly indeed than he had intended, being much embarrassed by the praise laid on him. 'Come, my friends. Let us set Mr. Jempson to lie in the bed of your cart, if that is convenient to you, Mr. Ushant.'

'By no means, doctor,' Jempson interrupted. 'I am sure I can ride. But let me raise myself from this hard ground...'

When he did so, his groans showed that he was hurt more that he had admitted.

'Be led by the doctor,' Parson Domble said. 'It is still a good way to Aylsham. He will lead your horse and Mr. and Mrs. Ushant will find space for you beside them, if you will not consent to lie. I must leave you by and by to turn northwards towards my home, but Mr. Ushant's farm is on your route a little further on.'

'I will take Mr. Jempson to my house,' Adam said. 'I have not yet examined him for further hurts and it is not seemly to do so by the roadside, where any might pass. Now, sir,' he added, turning to Jempson, 'be but patient to ride in the cart until the farm is reached. Then you may try your hand at riding again, for it will be scarce two miles to my house and I will be there to support you.'

After a little more protesting—for he could see the good sense of what was being suggested —Mr. Jempson agreed and they set out again. Two or three miles further on, Parson Domble left them, first having secured promises the others would call upon him whenever they might again be in the area. Another two miles and Mr. Jempson left his seat on the bench of the cart. He had been wedged somewhat tightly between the burly farmer and his well-padded wife. Now he climbed painfully onto his own horse.

Once again, hearty farewells were said and Adam and Jempson moved slowly on. Adam still led Jempson's horse so that he could hold fast to the creature's mane to steady himself.

Thus it was that they reached Adam's house. William the groom took both horses, though not without a muttered reproach. Betty had been brought home flecked with foam after the excitement of the chase. Mrs. Brigstone, Adam's housekeeper, had been looking from a window an hour and more, anticipating her master's return. Hannah, the parlourmaid, was therefore sent at once to bring food and drink, while Mrs. Brigstone bustled around Mr. Jempson. She found him a comfortable chair and then hurried to the kitchen for water to bathe his wounds and wash the dust from his face and hands.

Since they were now alone, Adam examined his patient. As he expected, he found him badly bruised, but not seriously hurt. He gave him five drops of laudanum from his medicine chest to ease the pain. Then he sent him to his bed with a cup of warmed wine in which he had dissolved a little sugar with tincture of valerian and hops. The man needed sleep more than food. In contrast, Adam's own stomach was growling in the most insistent way.

When, half an hour later, Mrs. Brigstone brought him a most welcome supper, Adam was content. Nor could he restrain himself from describing how he and Betty had put the footpads to flight.

If he expected praise, he found himself disappointed. Mrs. Brigstone knew her master too well to indulge him in this self-congratulation. When he ended his tale, she looked at him a moment, then gave her verdict. 'I am not surprised they ran off. They must have thought a madman was on the loose with a pistol. What sane person would risk staying?'

Then she called out to Hannah to help her clear away the dishes and douse the candles. At the doorway, she paused for a moment. 'It is time for your bed, master. Even heroes need their rest. You have done a brave deed. I only hope the other gentleman is as grateful as he should be for it.'

And she was gone.

AN UNLAMENTED DEATH

Chapter Nine

Messages from Mrs. Ross

Wednesday, 9 May 1792, Aylsham, Norfolk

ADAM AROSE EARLY THE NEXT MORNING, expecting to find Mr. Jempson still abed and possibly in need of his help to leave his bed. He was therefore surprised, on entering the small parlour, to see his guest already at the table, where Hannah had laid a plentiful breakfast.

The merchant rose as he entered, but slowly and with several sharp intakes of breath. He had the look of one who suffered pain and sought, if he could, to cope stoically with the extent of his hurt.

'I thought you would stay in bed, sir,' Adam said. 'You were sore hurt and it would be much to your benefit to rest as much as you can. I may, perhaps, be able to ease your pain somewhat, but healing is more a matter of time and patience than any skill I may have.'

'I do not deny that my old body aches a great deal, friend,' Mr. Jempson said. 'Nor that it besought me to let it lie in idleness longer. Yet I have trespassed enough on thy great kindness and should be about my business with the small community of Friends in this town.

I will manage well enough. I know of one who will stable my horse until I come again. I am also sure I will find some who will provide a carriage to get me back in safety to Norwich. Our religion is not kept for Sundays. When we see a brother or sister in need, our duty stands plain before us. Whatever help we can give we give freely, as our testimonies exhort us.'

'I am ashamed to say that I have little knowledge of your religion, Mr. Jempson. Only what is commonly spread abroad: that all live and speak plainly and observe no ranks or hierarchies,' Adam said. 'In our imperfect world, many must find that an affront.'

'Indeed so. In the past, our little movement has been persecuted most cruelly. Thus we have perforce learned well to avoid controversy and keep ourselves to ourselves for the most part. There are even some who would prevent marriage outside the Society, believing it essential to maintain the vision of our founders. I am not such a one, but I do not deny their honesty in their fears.'

Adam nodded. In his own profession, there were those who so feared change that they would halt all progress and discovery. Happily, it was not possible. 'You said you are a merchant, I believe?'

'I am. We, like all those who stand apart from the Church of England, find the universities closed and the professions barred to us,' Jempson replied. 'We provide our own schools, so that our children may learn to read and reckon. We offer apprenticeships, so that useful knowledge can be passed on. Sometimes our members attend the Dissenting Academies in search of the higher levels of learning. Mostly, we focus our energies where the law allows us to earn our bread. I trade in grain, malt and, now, timber. Others excel in all the harmless trades. Some are iron-masters or brewers. Others engage in manufacturing and the production of food and medicines. There are even those who now devote most of their wealth to banking.

'We believe in the truth and in integrity in all aspects of life,' he went on. 'What we promise, we undertake, needing no oaths to bind us. The price we ask is the one the customer must give, since haggling is possible only if the first price men state is not the true one. As I told thee, I have just purchased a half share in a fine ship. The man from whom I bought it is one of our community. He asked a fair price, which, since it was one I could afford, I paid without artifice or attempts to drive him lower. Is that not the right way to do business, friend? For we were both happy with the outcome and will remain as good friends in the future as ever we were in the past.'

'An admirable way,' Adam agreed. 'So, in that same spirit of plain speaking, let me tell you this. You must spare yourself as much as you can in your journey to your home. Nor must you by any means over-exert yourself for some weeks to come. I mean what I say, sir. You are no longer a young man. Even the old may heal, though somewhat more slowly than those still blessed with the resilience of youth. I will send you on your way with enough medicine for your journey. Also some receipts you must take to a reputable apothecary or chemist to have prepared for you.'

'For this, as for all else thou hast done for me, thou hast my deepest thanks,' Jempson said. 'I will not insult the hospitality of thy house by offering to pay for my bed and board. Yet I charge thee to tell me honestly the extent of your fee and the cost of the medicines thou hast given me.'

'There is no fee,' Adam said. 'I did not offer my help in any mercenary spirit, nor were you in any position to choose whether or not to accept. As for the medicines, five shillings will cover the cost in full.'

'Thou art a fine physician, friend, and, what is still more valuable, a good man. If I cannot offer thee of my goods, thou shalt have most freely of my esteem and friendship. Now I must depart indeed, for thou hast thine own business to look to, I am sure, as I have mine.'

Adam called to Hannah to tell William get Mr. Jempson's horse ready, while he prepared the medicines he promised and wrote out the receipts. It did not take long. When William stood at the door, Adam told him to go with Mr. Jempson, both to help him along his way and to lead his horse to its temporary home. Adam and Jempson now shook hands warmly and Mrs. Brigstone was called to add her own farewells and good wishes for a speedy recovery.

Mr. Jempson smiled down at her and praised both her house-keeping and her kindness to a stranger, which made her blush some-what. 'My dear friends. Farewell again. When I am come to live in this town, I hope you will make as free of my poor dwelling as you have made me of yours.'

And with that, he took William's arm to support himself and departed.

If Adam had thought that he might be free in the following days to mull over what he had learned about the archdeacon's death, he was disappointed. The number of patients swelled. Mr. Jempson had been prompt in sending some of his friends in the local Quaker community Adam's way. He was thus busier than he had been since coming to Aylsham. The days had slipped past without leisure to solve any but medical puzzles. Then one morning he received two letters. They rekindled the whole affair of the archdeacon's death.

What was most baffling was that they concerned the same person: Mrs. Ross, the archdeacon's widow.

The first came from Mr. Josiah Playley, the Norwich lawyer. It was his clerk who had stopped Adam after the inquest with a request that he should wait on Mrs. Ross as soon as it should be convenient. Shorn of the flowery legal language, this letter's message was simple. Mrs. Ross had decided to remain with her relatives near Cambridge for the foreseeable future. Thus she did not need to trouble him to seek her out. She apologised for bothering him. Mr. Playley offered no further explanation.

The second, which arrived by the same post, was from Mrs. Ross herself. She must have written in some haste, for she had not wasted words. 'Dear Sir. I do not doubt but that you will soon receive a message from Mr. Playley telling you that I no longer wish to speak with you. Please, I beg you, ignore what he says. My desire in this regard is unchanged. Indeed, it is stronger than ever. As soon as I am able to arrange my escape from the loving but misguided confinement that holds me here, I will contact you at once. Pray then come to me with all dispatch, for I am much distressed and believe you alone can ease my mind.'

Having puzzled over what this might mean, and found no answer, Adam took his bafflement to Peter Lassimer's shop. He needed another mind to vex.

'It is a simple matter surely,' Lassimer said. 'Someone in her family does not wish her to speak with you. She describes her confinement as loving.'

'Yet who and why?' Adam asked.

'As for who, I cannot say,' Lassimer responded. 'Nor can I tell you why, though the alternatives seem quite limited. Perhaps someone is seeking to suppress inquiry, as they did at the inquest. Perhaps the matter on which she desires to consult you is like to embarrass her family.

'Of course,' he added a moment later, 'it may be the lady has lost her wits through grief. If you find her, she is like to burden you with some fancies of a distempered brain. Maybe her family has arranged for her confinement in some suitable place until the fit passes.'

Adam laughed. 'If anyone's brain is distempered here, I vow it is yours, my friend, for your imagination has quite carried you away.

Nothing in the lady's letter suggested a sickness of the mind. That she feels grief I don't doubt, but many a woman loses her husband. If all ran mad as a result, there would not be enough madhouses in the realm to hold them.'

'Mock if you will,' said Lassimer, 'but do not blame me if you find yourself seeking to find sense in the ravings of a madwoman.'

'You have missed the most important aspect of this letter,' Adam said. 'Mrs. Ross has every reason to be most deeply interested in all matters surrounding her husband's death. Suppose she wants me to investigate further on her behalf. Would I not then have abundant standing from which to try to solve my puzzles?'

'Oh dear,' Lassimer said. 'Now who is getting carried away. Why on earth should she turn to a country doctor for such help? Would she not be better served by paying to employ a Principal Officer from the Bow Street court? Someone who knows what he is doing? Bascom, Bascom, be reasonable.'

'Now who is mocking whom?' Adam said, though he could not prevent himself from laughing at the same time. 'Yet maybe you are right. Perhaps my wishes are getting away from me.'

'You should consult a reputable apothecary, sir,' Lassimer said, laughing as much as Adam. 'I am sure he could sell you a remedy suitable for cooling such inflammations of the brain.'

'Enough!' Adam cried. 'I will not buy any of your witches' potions, however you describe them. I think we are both quite departed from reason and sanity—and we do no have grief as an excuse. Now goodbye, old friend. It is time to leave before worse descends upon me. Thank you for your counsel, such as it was. But thank you still more for making me laugh. Be sure I will tell you of the outcome when the lady and I can meet. Then we will see which of our fantasies is nearer to the truth.'

Chapter Ten

Trapped!

Wednesday, 23 May, 1792, Trundon Hall, Norfolk

ADAM NEEDED NO SPECIAL OCCASION to visit his brother at Trundon Hall. The two had always been close. Besides, Adam was fond of his sister-in-law and a devoted uncle to their children. A letter had arrived from Giles with a message from Amelia. She still felt uneasy about her daughter, Mary, who was not yet recovered in full from the bronchitis that plagued her. There was, they hoped, no cause for instant alarm, but every reason for Adam to go to see her as soon as it might be possible.

In the event, by the time he arrived, braving a sudden return of weather more suitable for November than May, the girl was much recovered. Amelia's worry had proved mostly due to a mother's protectiveness. Still, Adam determined to take no chances. He examined his niece most carefully, observing her eyes, tongue, skin colour and the strength of her pulse. Then he prescribed plenty of strong beef tea to build up her strength and handed over a prescription for an ointment.

This was to be applied to her chest at bedtime to ease her breathing during the night.

'It would also do no harm to give Mary a glass or two of port wine most days,' he told her mother. 'Girls of her age grow quickly and must soon develop into women. Such rapid alterations make heavy demands on their strength. Nor should her mind be neglected. As I have said to you before, those who treat mind and body as separate make a grave error. Each affects the other in ways we do not yet comprehend well enough. Encourage her to stimulate her mental faculties with suitable diversions. I know she likes to draw and paint. The pretty landscapes most young women produce are charming, but it would be far better to study nature. I suggest she strives to make the most accurate drawings she can of flowers or insects. That kind of art challenges the intelligence as well as the hand.'

'Mary is like her uncle in that respect,' Amelia said. 'The works of nature fascinate her. I often find her in the gardens, staring at a butterfly or a flower.'

'Then I think it would be wise also to encourage her to walk further afield in the park and around the fields,' Adam said. He was quite carried away with his own enthusiasm. 'Proper exercise does much to ward off disease and encourage healthy growth. We are, at the most fundamental levels, merely animals.'

'There are clergy who would count that a blasphemy, brother,' Amelia said, laughing despite herself. 'Would God really concern Himself with saving mere animals?'

'That I cannot say,' Adam said, laughing himself now. 'Just as I am unable to say whether any God exists to take an interest in our salvation. But all this is of little matter. I know you are the best of mothers and need no advice from me on your duty to your family. If I seem to interfere, it is from love only.'

Amelia made as if to push him from the room, exclaiming that she had work to do if he did not, but she reached up quickly to kiss him on the cheek as she did so.

Much later, as they relaxed alone together and shared a bottle of port, Adam's brother, Giles, had an announcement. Assuming an ostentatious air of calm disinterest, he said that the Lord Lieutenant of the County would soon appoint him one of the justices of the peace. 'It goes with being the squire of Trundon. I dare say though that I will deal with petty theft and enforce the game laws as well as any. The worst part will be to learn enough of the law to be credible. I do not have your talent for studying, brother.'

He waved Adam's congratulations aside with a grin he could not quite conceal. 'Anyway, they decided that I had been given enough time after our poor father's death to get the estate into some sort of order again. Now I should step up to my local duties. Mr. Harmsworthy, who was so rude to you that time, has quit the position and that leaves a gap on the local bench. Indeed, he has been absent for most of the time since the inquest on the archdeacon. He left, it is said, last week, when there was that strange affair at Gressington.'

Adam sat upright in an instant. Giles, seeing this, groaned and looked dejected. 'The deuce of a fool I am! I forgot to tell you. I was so eager to share my own news that I quite overlooked your adventures. Please forgive me for my selfishness, brother. Amelia and I have been preoccupied with Mary's health.'

'What happened?' Adam said, sure that his eagerness must make him appear as a hound catching the scent of its quarry. 'Please, Giles, leave no details out, I beg of you. What exactly took place at Gressington? Who was involved? Why did the magistrate's absence cause a problem?'

'I will do my best,' his brother said, 'though much that was done then made little enough sense and still puzzles me now.'

It had begun, Giles explained, ten days before. The company of men of the local militia stationed at Gressington were sent to Lynn with scarcely a day's notice. That left the coast unguarded. A day later, the rumour circulated that the two Revenue riding officers had also been called away. It seemed they were to assist their colleagues at Lynn. The story went about that there was to be a seizure of a large shipment of contraband goods the smugglers planned to land between there and Hunstanton.

So the rumours went on. The authorities were planning to make a descent on the privateers. Some were known to be taking shelter amongst the reefs and sandbanks off the Lincolnshire coast. They would bring their prisoners to Lynn and send them to London under heavy guard. French spies were newly arrived at Lynn, posing as merchants from Norway, and were to be taken before they could leave the area. Each disclosure was more dramatic and far-fetched than the last. Yet all centred on a single element: some event of great moment was about to take place in the environs of Lynn and all eyes were fixed upon it.

In truth, whoever planned this series of revelations—for planned they were and not one of them true—acted with the subtlest cunning. Everyone along the north coast of the county was watching Lynn. And so, while all were distracted, the government were able to make their own preparations in the greatest secrecy.

Quietly and without fuss, the best part of two full companies of dragoons were encamped near Holt. When word of their presence slipped out, it was put about that they were on route to Fakenham and beyond.

Meanwhile, two fast Customs cutters were sent to lie off Winterton Ness. These were, it was later said, disguised as privateers. The troubles in France had greatly increased the number of such vessels, while the merchant ships that passed each day north and south made tempting prizes.

Finally, as many as a dozen Revenue officers arrived in secret, though none knew how that was done. In such a lonely area, strange faces are apt to draw swift notice. Yet no one suspected their presence, so thoroughly had the operation been prepared. Some, it was said afterwards, had posed as travelling merchants. Others had slipped quietly into the area, then lay low as pretended guests of farmers. Others lodged with those members of the gentry most trusted by the men in London.

'This was no local initiative,' Giles said. 'The highest people in the land were surely aware of what was to take place. They must have approved the action and the cost too, for it was clear after that no expense had been spared to bring it off successfully.'

Then there was a pause.

The rumours about distant raids and seizures at Lynn, Hunstanton and The Burnhams reached a climax. Now the gang of smugglers using the part of the coast near to Gressington believed the time was propitious to land a substantial cargo. All eyes were on Lynn. None would be looking at Gressington.

So the authorities set their trap. When it was sprung, the whole band was taken, including those local men who were helping land the contraband and bring it off the beach. No lives were lost amongst the smugglers, though some of them fought hard for their liberty. As far as Giles knew, the final tally was half a dozen injured. Amongst the soldiers, sailors and Riding Officers who had seized them, two men were slightly hurt.

'There was but one fatality amongst the government men, and the circumstances of that will interest you,' Giles said. 'The Revenue cutters seized both the gang's principal ship and the smaller boats. Shots were fired in both actions. Amongst those taken in these exchanges was none other than Mr. Garnet, the Gressington constable. It seems he proved a troublesome catch, firing a brace of pistols in the darkness, then proving to have a knife about him. With this he struck at those who jumped into his boat to take it. Two men were sore wounded before he could be overpowered. One died before the boat was brought ashore within reach of the dragoons waiting there. Now Mr. Garnet lies in the gaol in Norwich and will surely have his neck stretched by the hangman's rope after the next Assizes.'

By now Adam's mind was turning so furiously that he feared his head might explode. Instead, he blurted out the most insistent question tumbling around there. 'Mr. Allsop, the coroner. How have they disposed of him?'

'What a strange mind you have to be sure,' his brother said. 'No one has disposed of him, so far as I know. Yet I do seem to recall reading in the Norfolk Intelligencer that he has been appointed a judge of the Court of Admiralty. He will be giving up both his legal practice and his role as a coroner.'

Adam slept little that night. Instead, he spent the hours pondering and weighing all that he had learned. Indeed, at breakfast his mind was still full of it. He wished for nothing save leisure and solitude to bring some order to his thoughts. Instead, he had to endure a long and loving leave-taking, then a tedious journey home on an unseasonably damp and cold day. For company along the road he must even endure two merchants. These talked first of the weather to come and their fears of a poor harvest. Then they moved on to the dismal state of barley prices and the pitiful returns offered by rapacious maltsters and brewers. Their wives, learning that Adam was a physician, questioned him on the best treatments for the vast array of ailments they, their families and friends seemed to suffer. They also, most generously, contributed their own homespun remedies. Some, it seemed, had been handed down from their most remote forebears. Adam suspected they would all generate results worse than the sicknesses they purported to cure.

Finding Adam distracted and unwilling to add any comments of his own, a more polite pair of women might have stayed silent for a while. Not so these two. Their response to his tepid interest was to demand that he answer their every observation. When he still proved silent, they plagued him with yet more remedies to allay whatever anxieties rendered him melancholy. He did not believe the day could turn worse. Then a thin rain set in an hour and a half from home, drenching him to the skin and spattering them all with mud and ordure from the foul road.

AN UNLAMENTED DEATH

Chapter Eleven

Mr. Lassimer's Solution

Saturday, 26 May 1792, Aylsham, Norfolk

IT WAS LATE IN THE day and Adam was wet, tired and mud-spattered. For the last few miles Betty, his horse, appeared at least as dejected as he was. The two of them plodded along, heads down, intent only on finding warmth, food and some escape from the endless drizzle.

As soon as they reached home, William took Betty to food and a warm stable, while Mrs. Brigstone bustled about Adam. She hurried him within and sent him to find dry clothes, then told him to sit and warm himself by the fire. Back in her kitchen, he could hear her harrying the maid Hannah to help prepare their master a good meal to cheer him. Adam did not know what he would do without her motherly concern, let alone her fine cooking. At length, the warmth from the grate seeped into his frozen legs and feet so that he began to feel drowsy. When his housekeeper came at last to summon him to table, she had to wake him first.

Still, good food and a soft bed did wonders and when he awoke the next morning he was much revived, at least in physical terms. As he lay in bed, however, luxuriating in the warmth and comfort, his mind was still troubled.

This whole matter was becoming too serious, he told himself. Was the death of the archdeacon truly a problem he should concern himself with? There had been an inquest where it was determined that he died by accident. Whatever Adam felt about the scanty nature of the proceedings, it appeared that the man's family and church were both content. Why should he be correct in seeing something suspicious, where others found nothing amiss?'

Still, he could not but wonder at the news his brother had imparted. If the authorities had taken such trouble to seize the smugglers —and the constable —at Gressington, why show no interest in why the archdeacon had been found dead there? The man had no business to be there, Adam thought. Yet he could not know that for certain and the archdeacon might have had good reasons. Adam was privy to very few aspects of the man's life. Might simple answers be already known to those who knew the man better?

Perhaps he should forget the whole affair, he thought. That confounded curiosity of his must not be allowed to lead him astray. The archdeacon's death was no business of his. Indeed, he had become involved by the merest chance. It was time to forget it and move on. He had given scant enough regard to his business of late. Yet in truth, Adam still felt torn. He had little doubt others would judge it sensible to mind his own business, but he also felt a nagging sense of worry. Even Lassimer had asked him whether any further interest from him in the archdeacon's death was justified. What was it that would not let his mind rest easy?

Was it just curiosity about an annoying puzzle? Was it a wish to show that his concerns about the gaps and inconsistencies in the 'official' version of events were justified? Neither seemed enough to account for the persistent sense of unease that surrounded every thought he had about that morning in Gressington churchyard. The whole matter offended his sense of justice. A man had died. Was life so cheap that the simplest, most convenient explanation should be deemed sufficient? Was his death to be considered less important than making plans to catch a group of smugglers? Should he accept such a cynical viewpoint, simply because it might save him from further effort? He did not think he could —and that surprised him most of all.

Hoping these reflections might make him a little clearer in his mind and rid him of the memory of yesterday's journey, he rose. Mrs. Brigstone had already brought him warm water. His ruminations had allowed it to cool somewhat, but he thought it a poor reward for her care to make her bring fresh. Instead, he washed and shaved, albeit in a somewhat perfunctory manner, then quickly dressed in a suitable morning gown. As he did so, he formed several resolutions. First, he would apply himself to the needs of his patients and practice. In that way, he believed, he could set a distance between his curiosity in the matter of the archdeacon and regain a better perspective. Then he would talk the whole thing over with his friend Lassimer. Finally, he would do what he should have done from the start. He would apply reason. Too many passions had been clouding his judgement. If reason told him to continue, he would. If not, he would set it aside, once and for all.

Thus fortified, he went downstairs and applied himself fully to the delicious breakfast awaiting him. Whatever other problems it brought him, the archdeacon's death would not be allowed to interfere with his appetite.

Later that same morning Adam attended the parish church as his patients would expect. He had little time for what the parson taught there, but it would be poor business to flaunt his unbelief. He could at least take enjoyment in the fine words Archbishop Cranmer had set down for the order of service. As usual, the sermon was tedious and sadly deficient in logic. The local vicar was neither a man of great learning, nor much interested in increasing the faith of his flock. As all knew, his passion in life was fishing. He was, it was said, preparing what he hoped would be the definitive work on all aspects of the art. Since he read the services as laid down, conducted baptisms and weddings and buried the dead, his parishioners forgave him any lack of religious zeal. Indeed, few would have him otherwise. Religion was for Sundays. The good people of Aylsham had other things to occupy them for the rest of the week.

So, with the service over at last, Adam made his way through the chill, wet streets to Mr. Lassimer's apothecary's shop.

Spring seemed to have deserted the countryside for the present. Most people stayed at home when they could. Only when shopping, or some other necessity, forced them outside did they face the bitter showers. Sunday was a good excuse to stay within. Adam would have been no different had not his need for counsel urged him forward.

When he at last reached Mr. Lassimer's shop, he felt as chilled as if he had crossed miles of winter heathland, though he had walked barely two hundred yards on a spring day. Since it was Sunday, of course, the shop was closed. For a moment, he thought he should not intrude on his friend's leisure. Then he shook his head and banged on the door. He needed help and he knew it would not be begrudged.

Adam found Lassimer making good use of the time in his compounding room. Such terrible weather always brought on on a rush of head colds and problems with the lungs. His stock of remedies therefore needed to be replenished in advance. Bad weather might be dangerous for most people, but it was very good for apothecaries' profits.

Letting Adam into his shop, Lassimer left off his work at once and called for Anne to warm a jug of good mulled ale for them both. 'You are chilled to the bone, I don't doubt,' he said. 'Indeed, I feel cold enough from looking at you. A draught of mulled ale will restore us both. You have news? It must be so, and news of some moment, or you would not have left your fireside in weather such as this.'

'I do indeed have news,' Adam said, 'but I will wait for your pretty servant to bring our ale before I speak further. Once I begin, I cannot risk such distraction as she offers.'

Lassimer clapped his hands with mirth at that. 'That's better. It may be Sunday, but there is no call here to be solemn as a Presbyterian elder. Is not Hannah Neston your maidservant? I declare she is one of the daintiest creatures in the county. She came in here the other day on an errand and I marvelled that she could work for such as you. I warrant you pay her no greater regard than you might a dog or a cat.'

'I am well aware of her charms, my friend,' Adam said. 'Yet she is under my protection and deserves respect as well. If I wish her to treat me as master, I cannot treat her as other than a servant. But look, here is Anne with our drinks. Thank you, my dear. I do not know how you suffer to serve my most provoking colleague here, but I am glad that you do.'

'I am never provoking am I, Anne?' Lassimer said. 'I am always the kindest and most considerate of masters.'

Anne was much too wise in the ways of menfolk to be tempted into any reply. She put down the ale, bobbed a graceful curtsey and bestowed upon each of them a smile of pure innocence as she left the room.

'Alas,' Lassimer said, 'I grow too fond of her. Still, a bout or two with a choice widow should set me right again.'

'Do you wish to hear my news,' Adam said, 'or do you prefer to spend the time boasting of your conquests?'

'Begin!' Lassimer replied at once.

Lassimer's response to the news Adam related was everything he could have hoped for. His friend gasped several times. Twice he cried out 'Damn me!' And, at the conclusion, he gulped down a mighty draught of ale before throwing himself back in his chair and crying, 'Enough! My head will burst with all your questions and speculations.'

'So what do you make of it?' Adam asked.

'Make of it? Why, Bascom, the answer to the mystery of the man's death is plain enough. Your archdeacon blundered into a smuggling gang that night. So they dealt with him, lest he alert the authorities to their actions. The blackguards must then have taken fright and fled the scene. I dare say the authorities already had a plan to set a trap for the rogues. Now the archdeacon's death made fair to wreck it. Because of that, the smugglers would expect too great an interest to be given to Gressington. Only when the fuss had died down would they risk returning to their business.'

'No accident, then,' Adam said.

'By no means, though that crooked constable tried to declare it so. He doubtless hoped to avoid anyone asking questions about who else might be abroad that night.'

'Yet why did the authorities not frustrate this intention?'

'Because it was a godsend to them. The authorities wanted no enquiries either. Every stranger sniffing around that village would delay their trap longer. In such places, all who have a right to be there are known. A strange face stands out at once, like a blackamore amongst Englishmen.'

'They simply wanted no fuss?'

'None whatsoever' Lassimer said. 'The inquest made the verdict of accidental death official and everyone assumed the story had reached its end. Then, after some weeks had passed, they judged that the smugglers must feel safe again and would be keen to get back to work. In case they still hesitated, the authorities tried to reassure them further. This they did by spreading tales of the supposed raids at Lynn. The smugglers took the bait and the dragoons and Revenue men sprang the trap. Simple. It explains all. We know now why the constable exclaimed at once that the death must be an accident. We know why the coroner made certain that his jury returned the required verdict of accidental death. We even know why the magistrate acted as he did. Each one, in his way, has received his due reward.'

Adam rubbed his chin. His manner of shaving that morning had left enough stubble to make him feel uncomfortable. 'It is not what this explains that bothers me,' he said after a moment. 'It is what it does not.'

He warmed to his subject, leaning forward and leaving his second pot of ale untouched. 'Perhaps I should be be satisfied that the matter of the archdeacon's death is as nearly solved as it will ever be. I am not. Maybe the man did suffer the misfortune to encounter desperate men. Maybe they were ready to kill to secure their freedom, as the constable later did. Even so, why did they not stay to rob their victim?'

'There may be any number of explanations,' Lassimer replied. 'They could have been disturbed. They could have set a greater value on a rapid escape than the goods the victim had about him. They might even have intended only to stun him or render him incapable of raising the alarm before they could get away. It is possible that his killers were horrified to find the man dead, and panicked.'

'All plausible enough,' Adam said.

'So why does your curiosity remained unappeased?' Lassimer asked.

'Because it scarcely matters if there are rational explanations for what took place in the churchyard. None have been advanced for why the Venerable Nathaniel Ross was there at all. Senior clerics do not, so far as I know, make a habit of wandering around remote churchyards after dark. There was no cause for the man to be in Gressington on that day at all. Until I know the answer to that mystery, no explanation of the results will quiet my feeling that Dr. Ross's death remains unexplained.'

Lassimer laughed. 'Bascom, my dear friend,' he said. 'It is your curse and your blessing to see hidden problems where others see none. In medical matters, this habit makes you the most thorough and conscientious of diagnosticians. In the rest of life, it condemns you to worry and fret over every loose end and unexplained trifle. Providence, in its infinite folly, failed to lay down that all things must be capable of explanation enough to satisfy Dr. Bascom. Sit back, forget Gressington, and drink up your ale. I assure you that Anne will not be pleased to find we have left any. She may have the face and figure of an angel, but she can put on the dark visage of Satan himself, if she feels her work is held at nought.'

Chapter Twelve

Sailors' Stories

Tuesday, 12 June 1792, Aylsham, Norfolk

IN THE DAYS THAT FOLLOWED, Adam made good his plan to use some of the fees from his new-found patients to buy himself a better saddle. After his recent escapades, William had come to him with a long face. Not only had the master failed to treat Betty with proper respect, all this riding had left her with sores where his old saddle rubbed. Adam hid his smile and agreed to make amends. Betty was not the only one to suffer from soreness after a long ride. When he could, Adam would buy a curricle to ride about in, as befitted a prosperous doctor. For the present, a new saddle must suffice. His reward for this purchase was a happy groom and that air of contentment about his house which befits a sound relationship twixt master and servants.

Nor did Adam neglect other business matters. He made visits to several patients, old and new, being careful to be home by nightfall. He reckoned up his accounts and rendered the resultant bills, though he expected few to be settled with promptness. Indeed, the richer and more distinguished the patient, the more he or she seemed to believe that prompt payment signified a common nature. Still, he had no doubt all would pay in time, once the delay was judged suitable to their status in society. He dealt with correspondence and creditors. He even found the time to write fresh advertisements. These he would place in local newspapers to solicit more business. Thus a week and more passed, until, one dismal afternoon in a month already marked more by rain and cold winds than spring blossom, Capt. Mimms called at his surgery.

Adam had no patients to see that day after dining, so had taken the rare opportunity to sit and read in his parlour. He struggled to stay abreast of developments in his profession. As a busy young doctor, he found it impossible to attend lectures given in Norwich by eminent physicians and scientists. Instead, he patronised the booksellers or the Norfolk and Norwich Subscription Library. He also drew information from letters sent by many of his colleagues in England and the Low Countries.

One such letter had arrived that morning. It contained an account of how infusions containing the common foxglove helped in cases of congestion of the heart. Adam was deep in its contents when Molly, the kitchenmaid, knocked at the parlour door. Adam had not heard the caller nor noticed Molly going to answer. With Mrs. Brigstone and Hannah occupied elsewhere, Molly was forced to undertake the duty, though it was much against her will. Since arriving in the household, she had rarely ventured to leave the safety of the kitchen.

Since he was preoccupied, Adam spoke somewhat more roughly than he had intended. He sought always to be as kind and polite to servants as any master, but Molly was new and her timid ways grated on him. Now the silly ninny stood shaking before him, seemingly unable to deliver her message. 'Speak up,' he said, more kindly now. 'What is it you must tell me?'

'A visitor, sir,' she said, her voice a high-pitched whisper. Adam put down his letter and gave his whole attention to coaxing the matter from her.

'Very good, Molly. A visitor. Does this person have a name? Has he or she vouchsafed the nature of their business with me? Take your time and tell me what message you bring.'

The girl swallowed hard, then gave her message in a single breath. 'Capt. Mimms sends you his compliments and apologises for coming without warning and has been to Yarmouth and is now going home and desires to speak with you if you are not engaged or seeing a patient…sir'.

She gasped in air and seemed ready to faint away.

'Capt. Mimms? Capt. Mimms?' Adam cried, leaping up from his chair so violently that the girl shrank back against the wall, putting out her hand to ward off whatever attack on her person he might intend. 'Capt. Mimms, you say? Why did you not tell me instantly, instead of quivering like the veriest mouse? I am not an ogre who eats kitchenmaids, Molly, though I am sorely tempted when I find one as faint of heart as you. Stand up, gather yourself and show Capt. Mimms in here as befits a sensible girl. Then be off to the kitchen and ask Mrs. Brigstone to give you a jug of punch and glasses and bring them back here quickly.'

As the poor child hurried off, not at all certain that he did not have it in mind to make an end of her, Adam put his letter to one side. As he stood to welcome his guest, he still mumbled curses on girls fresh from the farm, especially those who had neither wit nor stomach enough to serve a civilised household. She would be better off feeding the hens, or milking the cows or, best of all, tending to sheep as silly as her.

At that moment, the door opened and Capt. Mimms came in, all smiles and apologies for disturbing the peace of the afternoon. Behind him, Molly's white face showed only briefly, before she fled to the kitchen.

'A thousand apologies, dear sir,' Capt. Mimms began. 'It is, I know, most deuced rude of me to call unannounced in this way. I am on my way home from some days spent about my business in Norwich and Yarmouth. My sons are good lads and tend to matters as I taught them. Yet I venture to believe an occasional visit from their father is still of use to them.'

'I do not doubt it, sir,' Adam said. 'Besides, you need find no excuse to come to my home. I am most delighted to see you. Be sure that you will always have a hearty welcome here, should you call in the middle of the night. Where is that wretched girl? I sent her for punch, for I am sure you must be in need of refreshment after your journey.'

'The wretched girl, master, is blubbering in the kitchen in a fine state from your treatment.' It was Mrs. Brigstone who now came, carrying the tray herself. She set it down, then turned to the two men. Her expression commanded silence from both.

'As you know full well, sir, Molly is new and most unsure of herself. Where is the good of me seeking to encourage her to settle, if you bark at her and send her away in tears? Your pardon, Capt. Mimms. You are most welcome here. I am Susan Brigstone, the Housekeeper.'

'Mrs. Brigstone,' Capt. Mimms said, while Adam stood torn between embarrassment and shame. 'The maid answered the door with every politeness, invited me within and took my message in the most exemplary manner. Please give her my compliments and assure her that no maid could have done better. Indeed, if this young fellow here has no need of such a one, I will take her into my own household, if she is willing to come to Holt.'

'You are most kind, sir' Mrs. Brigstone said. 'I will tell her, though I intend that she should stay here to finish her training, if only as a constant reproach to thoughtless men. Please sit and refresh yourself.

My master has spoken of you most warmly and I am glad to make your acquaintance. Perhaps a few lessons from a man such as you may even train him in a greater degree of politeness to his servants.'

It slowly dawned on Adam that both were having fun at his expense, though he had to own that he deserved it. 'I will speak to Molly myself later and endeavour to convince her that I mean her no harm. To be fair, I was deep in a most interesting letter when she came in and was thinking only of what it contained. Still, I own my fault and am ready to make amends. The compliments from our good friend here should go far to smooth ruffled feathers. Later, I will also submit meekly to your scolding, Mrs. Brigstone, as indeed I should. But let us not burden Capt. Mimms with my deficiencies as a master, many though they be. Will you take supper with us, sir? Better still, will you stay here tonight and continue to Holt in the morning?'

'I will take supper with you gladly, for I hope thus to know you better,' Capt. Mimms replied. 'Yet I am not so lacking in decency as to descend unannounced and expect to find a bed prepared. No, my good sir, I will stay tonight at The Black Boys Inn in the Market Place. Indeed, I have already left my chaise and horse with the stableboy there. I have also taken the precaution of securing a room.'

He turn once more to Mrs. Brigstone. 'Thank you for bringing me refreshment, Mrs. Brigstone. You also reveal the robust good sense of Norfolk people, mixed with the kindness I have always received from them.'

Mrs. Brigstone blushed at his words. 'I see you know how to charm, sir,' she said. 'When you were a mariner, I am sure you lacked for no female company in any port of the world.'

'Ah,' Capt. Mimms said, 'that was long ago, when I was a strapping lad out to taste whatever pleasures the world might offer me. Then I found a true and loving wife in Antwerp, brought her to Yarmouth, and forgot my roving ways. Alas, she is dead these ten years and I miss her as sorely as I ever did. But come, doctor, let us speak of happier things, for I came here for more than the pleasure of your company. I bring you news that has much bearing on the death of the Archdeacon of Norwich.'

'Then I will leave you to talk of that, masters.' Mrs. Brigstone said. And, with that, she left them.

Adam was usually the most patient of listeners. Today though his excitement at having someone before him to whom he could relate the taking of the smugglers at Gressington and the arrest of Garnet was too much for him. Before Capt. Mimms could open his mouth to relay his news, Adam began to explain what he had heard of the events of May. His guest smiled and held up a hand to stop him. 'Nay, sir. I know all about that news. Even now, Garnet is held in the castle at Norwich, awaiting transfer to London and trial before a judge at the Old Bailey. His passenger on that night is not with him though. None that I have spoken with are sure where he may be, but I do not doubt he too is held securely somewhere. War with France is coming again, I fear, which will be a sad blow for our trade.'

'Will Constable Garnet hang, do you think?' Adam asked.

'Most assuredly,' Capt. Mimms replied. 'You do not kill an officer of the crown—one victim is dead, another sore wounded—and walk away from the noose. Death may indeed come as a relief to the wretch, for I fear the authorities will have pressed him hard for as much information as they can. Now, my friend, let us speak no more of what is old news, for you will not have heard what I have to tell you.

'Since we met last, I have made it my business to visit many of my friends, acquaintances and business contacts in Yarmouth. It is no hardship, for most keep an excellent table and wine cellar. Besides, I assure myself that maintaining such acquaintance is sound business. I try to refrain from interfering in the way my sons manage our trade, but I can see no harm in helping them where I can. As you will understand, business relies on trust which is strengthened when people do business with those they know. My sons are young, but many of the most important persons amongst the merchants of the coast are now old, as I am. We find it easier to talk with those who share our memories.'

Through all this, Adam had been struggling to contain his impatience. Would Capt. Mimms ever get to the point? Before he wandered yet further into reminiscence, Adam ventured a question. 'Did you learn ought of interest from these men?'

Capt. Mimms regarded him with a benevolent smile. 'My good doctor, you are yet young and as impatient as all of your age, I see. Forgive an old man's ramblings. They did indeed have much to tell me. Old seafarers love little more than to share tales, unless it is a glass of good grog. To save you from becoming quite frustrated, I will tell you all, as plainly and rapidly as I may.

'My friends expected something to happen along this coast. The word had gone round these past three months that the government was taking a close interest in the whole coast from Harwich to Lynn. One, who has several ships plying the seas between here and the estuary of the Scheldt, noticed an increase in the number of navy ships lying at anchor in Yarmouth Roads. Another heard rumours of government spies abroad amongst the inns and drinking places most used by mariners. Such people are common enough, for the Revenue work hard to find where they might best send their riding officers to surprise smugglers. Yet now the number of spies had increased. All, it seemed, were seeking information about landings of contraband along the north coast. They did not show the usual interest in the creeks and beaches southwards to Orford. Instead they wanted to hear of gangs who operated between Hunstanton and Cromer—and, most especially, between Wells and Sheringham. There were also sudden searches of cargoes, ostensibly for contraband. Officers questioned ships' masters about any passengers carried. They were especially interested in those taking passage to and from the continent.

'As you may well imagine, this behaviour gave rise to much discussion. Those who make their living by trade and the sea are ever alert for signs of trouble. We have no love for the smugglers, nor they for honest merchants, but we manage to leave one another alone. Their interest lies in small, easily handled items of high value; ours in these parts mostly in grain, timber and cloth. If the inns sell liquor more cheaply as a result of these rascals' actions—and a neighbours' cellar contains good brandy and geneva spirits for him to dispense liberally to his guests—why should we complain?

'Your face tells me plainly that I am rambling again. Sadly, it is a common failing in the old. Very well, I shall return to the essence of my tale.

'The general opinion amongst merchants and shipowners was this. The authorities wanted information to let them seize people slipping spies and gold into England. The French want information about our military strength and readiness. That is plain. These revolutionaries also send money to support insurrection amongst the disgruntled and poor. France is in ferment, yet we, in England, are not so free from riot and disturbance that we may be smug. Scarce a dozen years ago, London was set ablaze by riots against the Papists. Of late, mobs have chanted 'for God and the King' in Birmingham, while destroying Unitarian meeting-houses and the homes of some noted men of science who are of that sect. I hear that the magistrates stood by and urged on the rioters, while the constables joined in the destruction. Men like Wilkes and Paine inflamed sedition, and the fire still burns.

'At first, too many of our men of influence ignored events across the Channel. Some even thoughtlessly welcomed the overthrow of the previous regime. They believed it would lead to more peaceful relations if our neighbour employed a constitutional system of monarchy like ours. Not a few reasoned that a France weakened by political upheavals would allow the growth of English trade. Without their interference, the extending of our empire could proceed without challenge.

'Now, it appears, France has overcome its first brushes with chaos and is building a new and more powerful army. In the first months of popular fervour, the French navy was laid low. Too many of its officers were noblemen. Most fled, others suffered a bloody death at the hands of the peasants. Yet now even their navy is being rebuilt and fresh officers found. The Frogs hate us, sir, and have a strong taste for seizing trading advantage from us, as well as our colonies in the Caribbean. No, war with France is coming again and both sides are manoeuvring for advantage before it breaks out.'

'And the death of our archdeacon? What of that?' Adam said.

'It is my belief, doctor,' Capt. Mimms replied, 'that the archdeacon blundered somehow into one or two French spies just landed on that stretch of coast. Thus he paid the penalty. They could not take the risk that he might have recognised what was taking place. I suspect they did not even know who he was. No, they saw only a gentleman, well-dressed, in an unexpected place. They cannot be blamed for making the obvious deduction that he must be an officer of the courts or the crown.

'This business of high politics might also explain the reluctance of those in power to allow the archdeacon's death to be investigated fully. They wish, sir, to keep any suggestion of what they know about the French activities from slipping out. To do so would hamper their efforts to discover the presence of spies and the identities of the people they meet with.

'And now we have proof enough, at least to my eyes. That seizure of the smuggling gang was carried out with a superabundance of forces. Thus it is impossible to doubt something more was expected than a boatload of laces and spirits. One clandestine passenger was secured, as I hear. Maybe they expected many more. Whatever else, they have blocked that rat hole. None will risk that route for a good while to come. I imagine they have also sorely frightened any more planning to offer passage to the continent in secret.'

The old sailor sat back and took a large mouthful of punch, then leaned forward again with a look of triumph. 'So, my good friend,' he said. 'What do you think of that?'

Chapter Thirteen

Frustration

Wednesday, 13 June 1792, Aylsham, Norfolk

MRS. BRIGSTONE PROVIDED THE TWO MEN with an excellent supper. She relished any opportunity to display her skill in the kitchen. As a bachelor, Adam rarely entertained at his home, so she felt her abilities as a cook had little outlet. Only when his mother came to stay was Adam moved to send out dinner invitations to the better class of people in the area.

That day, Capt. Mimms also proved a most agreeable guest. He praised Mrs. Brigstone's efforts at every turn and helped Adam do full justice to the dishes. The meal also made a large inroad into Adam's wine cellar. Adam was not a great drinker when alone. Now his store would need replenishment before he could consider entertaining again.

Growing merry, the two men talked of the state of trade, the prospects for a better harvest and the countryside ways of Norfolk. Then Capt. Mimms began on a series of tall tales of his days at sea, typical of mariners everywhere. He told Adam of his encounters with whales and of sailing amongst icebergs off the coast of Greenland. Then he switched to relating how he and his crew once fought a gang of pirates along the Barbary Coast. And, as was only natural, he described the delights of landing on exotic shores. How he once came close to bearing off one dark-skinned beauty to be his wife. And how glad he was after that he had not, when he found another even more wanton and voluptuous.

In all this, Adam proved the best of listeners, never suggesting any of it was more than the plain truth. Indeed, the talk was so brisk that it was late by the time the old man left for the short walk to The Black Boys Inn.

Adam was sad to see him go. His loud, good-humoured presence had filled the house, leaving it feeling somewhat empty and cold afterwards. It was with a heavy heart that Adam at last made his way to bed, rather more unsteadily that was usual.

The next morning Adam's head ached a good deal. His servants, perceiving their master not to be in the best of humours, went about their business softly and kept as far away from him as they might. They noted that he ate little, but drank a good deal of small ale—sure signs that he had over-indulged the evening before. Fortunately, he was engaged to visit several patients and left the house promptly at eleven. If he did not hear the sighs of relief that followed his departure, he surely should have done.

Whether his patients noticed any difference in his manner none of them said. Adam's way of consultation was always brisk and business-like and he liked to conclude his visits with dispatch. Some doctors spent many hours indulging their patients in discussing ailments and treatment. To Adam's mind, such close attention to their present problems too often encouraged patients to fall into melancholy. He preferred to raise their spirits by speaking and acting as if any current problems might be soon at an end. The mind was, in his experience, the most remarkable power in medicine. Let a person become sure of quick recovery and the chances of it happening were great. Let them dwell on their fears and the outlook became bleaker by the day.

Nevertheless, it was well into the afternoon when he made his way at last to Peter's shop. His temper was not improved when he found the place shut up and his friend also engaged on house calls in the neighbourhood. One look at his face when he returned home and his servants resumed the furtive movements they had set aside when he left that morning.

Thursday was no better. Adam had to leave early in the morning to visit a patient living almost ten miles distant. He had put if off for as long as he could, for the gentleman, though rich, was a hypochondriac of considerable experience and a niggardly host. Thus he returned in yet another bad temper, for it had proved a wearisome ride and a yet more wearisome consultation. Now there were letters to write and fresh supplies of medications to be gathered together to refill his medical bag. It was enough to try a saint's patience and Adam assuredly did not possess that.

Still, having been forced to set the matter of the archdeacon aside for a time, he did take a small step forward. During this time, when his personal search for answers to the thousand questions that bubbled in his mind had been suspended, it finally occurred to him to write to his mother in Norwich.

As a dutiful son, Adam wrote to his mother regularly with news of himself and his practice. He loved his mother dearly and often worried that she was too much alone since his father died. He had even thought of trying to find a practice in Norwich, so that he might see her more often. His limited means soon put an end to such plans, and he had to content himself with such visits as he could manage. It was fortunate therefore that Mrs. Eleanor Bascom was a regular visitor to both her sons' homes, being still on the right side of her fiftieth year and in excellent health. Nor was she any more content to be always alone than her son was to see her thus. Her last letter had brought the news that she had engaged a companion: a young lady of excellent accomplishment but slender means. She would arrive quite soon to take up residence.

'Thus she may be viewed and approved when next you visit me,' his mother had written. 'But I warn you that any failure on your part to offer her the welcome she deserves will incur my displeasure. I am quite decided that she will prove a dear friend, for she plays the forte-piano with uncommon skill and speaks both French and Italian fluently. I have already warned her that my two sons are rude, untutored men, barely able to speak English and quite without other accomplishments. Thus she will be prepared to endure your next visit with fortitude, if not pleasure.'

Adam knew his mother to be the most sensible and perceptive of women. He thus had little doubt that this female paragon of a companion would prove to be daunting in the extreme. Far from looking to show her a poor welcome, he was becoming nervous that she was quite unlikely to approve of him. His imagination drew a picture of a haughty, sharp-faced blue-stocking, who would take one look and dismiss him as unworthy of more than a distant courtesy.

Of course, he said none of this in his letter. Instead, he complimented his mother on her decision to engage a companion. He assured her he much looked forward to making the lady's acquaintance and would be affability itself when he did. Then, hoping he had occasioned a good mood in his parent with these words, he included a special request. Would she be willing to make some enquiries on his behalf amongst her friends? He assumed many must have known Dr.

Ross and his family personally. Might she therefore help him to discover what manner of man he was?

This was nearly the only positive thought that Adam had managed to make in the past two days. He could not sift and make sense of all the information he had on the man's death until he better understood the man himself. What was his character? What were his beliefs? Might there be any clue there to show why he was in Gressington churchyard?

AN UNLAMENTED DEATH

Chapter Fourteen

Bigotry Made Plain

Friday 15 June 1792, Aylsham, Norfolk

WHEN FRIDAY MORNING DAWNED, ADAM'S MOOD had lifted. He had
at last accomplished something. A servant would give his letter to the
carter who plied the dozen miles from Aylsham to Norwich most days.
Thus it would be in his mother's hand that evening, or the next morning at the latest. He also had a day free from business commitments.
Seeing their master enjoy his usual lavish breakfast, his servants
relaxed. Harmony returned to the household. After breakfast, Adam
stepped out into watery sunshine to make his way along the street
to the apothecary's shop. He was hoping that Lassimer might have
leisure to talk with him and he was in luck.

After a busy week, his friend was making up fresh stock. Adam
joined him in his compounding room, where Lassimer assured him
that he could listen and work at the same time. None of the remedies
he was making contained dangerous contents. None required the
most careful preparation.

'Most are simple nostrums,' Lassimer said, 'which do not harm. Indeed, they do little enough good, unless they are taken with total faith in their power. Our bodies and minds are, as I know you agree, closely intertwined. Thus the most feeble medicine may have a powerful effect on those who believe in it without reserve.'

They sat together as the apothecary worked, the room filled with the fragrant odours of herbs and the sharper scents of spices and oils. Lassimer called to Anne to bring them a jug of punch and, if she could persuade the cook, a few dainties to stimulate the appetite.

Once Adam began, Mr. Lassimer's response to his fresh news was again all any storyteller might wish. The young apothecary gasped, slapped his hand on his thigh and, on several occasions, cried out, 'Damn me, is it so?' and 'The Devil!' in his excitement. Then, when Adam had finished, he sat in silence. He seemed bemused by all he had heard, the punch untouched by his side. 'I thought I had news enough for you, but this quite o'ertops it. Spies! Foreign gold! Why, my friend, it is like the tales of adventure I loved to hear when I was still a boy. Not in some far-off land either, but right here on my own doorstep. I am quite dizzy with excitement.'

Adam had had more time to think over all that Capt. Mimms had told him. Thus he was gratified by Peter's response, but less ready to accept all at face value. After all, these were but rumours. Even so, information that circulated among successful merchants must be worth more than gossip heard in a tavern. Where Lassimer was excited, his own speech was more measured. 'Is this the answer, do you think? That Dr. Ross blundered into something quite unexpected and was either struck or stumbled and fell as he tried to make his escape? It sounds like enough, but it bears not at all on the great mystery that lies at the heart of this matter. Why was the archdeacon in that churchyard at that time to blunder into anything? Why did Mr. Harmsworthy take him there with so little curiosity about the reason. Why leave him there alone? I can make no sense of it.'

'Listen to what I have learned, my friend,' Lassimer said. 'It is not so momentous as your Capt. Mimms' discoveries, but may yet play its part. It too bears on events across the Channel.

'On Wednesday, I paid a call on an elderly clergyman who is a patient of mine. He lives to the south of here, along the road to Norwich. Nowadays, he keeps to his house a great deal, for he is much troubled by the gout. Yet he has kind and dutiful children. From time to time, they take him to their homes in the city to be within reach of old friends and attend sermons and lectures. He is a man of some learning and likes to keep his mind active, even though his body is failing him.

'He did not know of my interest in the archdeacon's death. Yet the death itself—and the likely candidates to be his successor—have been topics of considerable interest amongst the clergy. On a chance, I asked him if he had known Dr. Ross. At first, his answer seemed to offer no interest. He had not known the man, for he no longer has a cure of souls in any parish and so would not come to the archdeacon's attention.

'All was not lost. He had heard the man preach on more than one occasion. Our Dr. Ross was, he told me, a powerful and combative preacher in several of the city churches, as well as the cathedral itself. His sermons were of a strongly moralising tone. He often castigated the people of Norwich for their laxity in church attendance. He railed against their lives of indulgence and debauchery. He was loud against fornication, whoring and the like. He had a particular hatred of men who indulged in what he called 'filthy and unnatural perversion'. That he condemned many times.

'Such was typical of most of the sermons Dr. Ross preached since his arrival in the city. Yet of late—or so my patient had heard—he had preached in a different vein. Indeed, he had himself heard the man speak but a few months ago and noted that his views had become more political and more extreme. Not only did he consign all who questioned the authority of the Church of England to everlasting damnation. He also seemed to have developed a tremendous hatred of the revolution in France. Their rejection of the God-given authority bestowed on the King and the Christian church was, he said, the most rank blasphemy.

'According to his latest sermons, this rejection of God's chosen is but an aspect of a Satanic plot to destroy mankind. The overturning of proper respect for King, church and nobility, would loose anarchy upon us. Tolerance of dissent or seditious doctrines and writings is but the first step on the road to Hell. Anything that undermines orthodox belief should be anathema. All that stands between us and eternal damnation are the teachings of the Church of England. He issued violent denunciations of all who disagreed with him. Their views, he claimed, would soon bring revolution to England.'

Lassimer paused to give more effect to his final words. 'He seemed to see it as his personal duty, to fight the forces of dissent, rational religion and heresy wherever he found them. No discussion is possible with the forces of evil. Acceptance of different viewpoints was the same as surrender to the devil. He would have us believe dissenters, revolutionaries and freethinkers—even Wesleyans and Presbyterians—are pawns of Satan. He has let them loose to overturn the established order, deprive the King of his authority, the church of its power and the rich and noble of their property.'

Adam shook his head in wonder. 'You have done well, Lassimer. This is a vivid picture indeed. Dr. Ross, it seems, was a man of such extreme views that I marvel none had made an end of him earlier. Could he have somehow discovered that agitators from France were using places in his own neighbourhood to slip into England unobserved?

Would he have been foolish enough to seek to confront them alone? Surely, if had such knowledge, he would have gone to the authorities?'

'But what if he did,' Lassimer said, 'and they seemed uninterested? In no way would they have wanted such a one as Dr. Ross to know of their plans. From what I learned, he was far too likely to proclaim them from the pulpit in support of his own crusade. No, Bascom, their most likely course would have been to appear to take no great account of his words. They might even suggest he might be mistaken. For they would hope in that way to turn aside his attention into safer channels.'

'And if he preferred his own notions?'

'Why, then he would believe Satan had infiltrated even the government of the land,' Lassimer said. 'Armoured in his own invincible sense of self-righteousness, he would go forth to confront the Evil One and prove the authorities wrong.'

For a while, both sat in silence, absorbed in their thoughts.

Mr. Lassimer broke the silence first. It was clear he had decided enough had been said on the topic of the archdeacon's activities. 'I trust that you and your mother will take dinner with me when she visits you next. I dine generally at four and will be glad of congenial company. As you must have found, company in this town is necessarily limited—especially if you have no wife and are not a suitable catch for an unmarried daughter. I tend to find myself expected to be content with some stringy spinster whom no one expects ever to think of marriage. Many an evening I spend quite alone, for, after they have cleared away and set all to rights in the kitchen, Mrs. Brigstone and Anne go to their homes. Mrs. B sets me a cold collation on the table for my supper and I busy myself with reading or compiling my notes. Only the stable lad sleeps on the premises. Like you, I imagine, it is not unknown for me to be summoned to some sickbed during the night. Unlike you though, I have also known from time to time a summons to treat a lively widow for the symptoms of loneliness and other forms of deprivation. I deem it my duty to respond to both types of need in an appropriate manner.'

Adam quickly agreed that he and his mother would be most ready to take dinner at the apothecary's house. He also insisted that Lassimer must dine with them too, as soon as would be convenient. 'Only, I beg of you, make no mention of any nocturnal visits to widows. It would make my life extremely difficult, should my mother wonder whether my answering a night call might not be a truly medical matter. Mothers, like wives, do not always see a bantering remark as without some foundation in reality.'

Until now, opportunities to solve the mystery of Gressington churchyard's clerical corpse had been few. Now they crowded upon Adam, so that he scarce had time to ponder each fresh piece of information before more came to his attention.

The day after he had met with Mr. Lassimer found Adam sitting at his desk, absorbed in reading, when the maidservant brought the letters the carrier had delivered to the house.

Amongst the pile, two neatly folded papers drew his attention. On the one, he recognised his mother's handwriting. The other was also in a woman's hand, elegant and flowing, but not penned by any whose writing was familiar to him.

He took up his mother's letter first, surprised she had moved with such uncharacteristic speed to reply to him. She expressed no great surprise at his request for information about Dr. Ross. She wrote simply that she knew his curiosity only too well and had half expected to hear from him on the topic. Even the reports of the inquest in the newspapers had told her that the proceedings had been scanty. Indeed, amongst many in Norwich, she wrote, the inquest had been the major topic of conversation for a week or more. People were surprised that the unexpected death of such an eminent clergyman had passed off with such small interest. Where, they wondered, were the diocesan authorities or the man's family. Still, the public memory was short and, lacking further stimulus, speculation soon ceased.

Yet if he were to visit her the next Thursday, she had asked several of those who knew the archdeacon best to take tea. He might then ask his own questions and hear the answers first-hand. All she knew of the man herself, she wrote, was his reputation as a strict moralist. Most of that came from his letters in the papers, in which he constantly took issue with the city's dissenters and nonconformists. 'Norwich is a pleasant and sociable place,' her letter went on, 'in which all rub along in amity. We have no need of puritanical witch-hunts or theological arguments. I would never have allowed such a disagreeable man to call on me. Yet I know some of my acquaintances, more concerned than I to maintain their reputations as good Anglicans, might have felt forced to do so.'

So, Adam thought, I want information, they will provide it, but I must come in person to ask my questions. These ladies will have questions of their own. To get what I want, I will need to pay dearly and in similar coin.

'When you come,' his mother continued, 'I believe you will find my companion here before you. Be nice to her, I pray you. It will take her a little time to become used to our family ways. Giles can, at times, be too much of the rough squire. You, on the other hand, are prone to appear too severe and scholarly. I know both of you have good hearts, yet somehow I failed as a mother to give either of you any social graces. Still, I believe Amelia has taken Giles in hand on that score. Since you refuse to find a wife —or none will have you, which is just as likely—your solitude but strengthens a clumsy manner. My lady guests can take care of themselves, I do not doubt. It is Miss LaSalle I worry about.'

Ah, Adam thought, Miss LaSalle is both a bluestocking and a shrinking violet. How on earth will mother bear it? How will I bear it? Well, I have more important matters to attend to than nervous spinsters. Let her faint and have done with it, I say.

With such thoughts, he opened the second letter. In an instant, he had forgotten Miss LaSalle's feebleness, his mother's strictures and all else, for the message was from Mrs. Ross, the archdeacon's widow.

In it, she informed Adam that she had returned to her house in Norwich and asked him to wait on her as soon as might be convenient.

Well, he would take her at her word. He would accept his mother's invitation for Thursday next and ask if he might stay the night in her house afterwards. That would save him from the inevitable complaint from the groom, William, that it was unreasonable to expect Betty to carry him to Norwich and back in a single day. To leave early would be no hardship on a June morning. Thus he could reach Norwich in time to call on Mrs. Ross in mid-morning and return to his mother's house in good time to be ready when her ladies arrived.

Chapter Fifteen

Mrs. Ross Again

Thursday, 28 June 1792, Norwich

IT SEEMED TO ADAM THAT THE PARLOUR to which Mrs. Ross's maid showed him must always be gloomy. On that day, with the heavy mourning drapes over the windows, it was almost too dark to see his way. The woman who awaited him was near-invisible in the gloom, since she wore the black of deepest mourning. Only when he came close could he see his hostess.

Mrs. Ross was a short, slightly-built woman. Small of stature as she was, she now somehow shrank further within her heavy clothes as he looked at her.

Adam judged that she might be of a similar age to his mother, though the deep lines around her brow and mouth could have more to do with grief than the ravages of time. Once she would have been remarkably pretty. Now her skin was the colour of chalk and bore the faint sheen that reveals sickness within. As he took her hand and raised it to his lips, she looked at him with eyes ringed with the dark smudges betokening lack of sleep. Yet her voice, when she spoke, was firm enough. She motioned him to a chair opposite.

'Sit, sir. I am most grateful for your condescension in agreeing to visit me, for I do not think that I could manage the journey to your surgery. It took all my remaining strength for me to travel here from my daughter's home in Cambridge. She did not wish me to leave, such was her concern that I should not be alone in my grief. Yet I longed most for solitude, and by preventing me from meeting with you earlier, she has unwittingly increased my distress. There are questions I must ask you, Dr. Bascom. Though they may seem no more than the mental wandering of a woman laid low by grief, I assure you that your answers are of the greatest moment.'

Through all this, Adam sat silent. He was eager to know the reason why she had brought him to her house, yet his judgement told him that it would be best to allow her to approach the matter in her own way and in her own time.

'Your silence reassures me,' Mrs Ross said. 'It reveals a man more willing to listen than speak, and listening is what I need.'

'Forgive me, madam,' Adam said. 'I will indeed listen most carefully to whatever you wish to tell me. I will also answer all your questions to the best of my ability. Be assured of that. Yet both my conscience and my duty as a physician compel me to say something before you begin. It is clear to me that you are not well. I would not have you imperil your health further by speaking to me on matters which clearly give you pain. I am most willing to return at a later date when you feel more able to continue.'

'No, no,' she cried. 'I have you here now and I will not be able to rest until you have answered what I must ask you.'

'Then hear me too on this, madam,' he said. 'Our minds and bodies are one. Just as ailments of the body may cause great distempers in the brain, so the reverse is true. You are unwell in body, but it is

112

my judgement that the source of your weakness lies in matters of the mind. Grief and anxiety will ravage the body as badly as any fever. I will not wish to trespass into areas more properly addressed by your own physician. Still, if there is anything that I may offer from my own knowledge and ability that might alleviate your distress, be assured that I will give it willingly.'

'My physician—say rather the one appointed by my late husband, for he had his way in this as he did in all other aspects of my life—is a doctor of the old school,' Mrs. Ross said. 'It is beneath him to listen to his patients. No, he has but two treatments to serve in all circumstances: bleeding or cupping. When news reached him of my husband's death, he came here at once, his knives and dishes to hand. How I found the strength and courage I do not know, sir, but I ordered him from the house. Such is his pride that he will not return, I assure you, until I am willing to make the most abject apology.'

The faintest of smiles appeared. 'And that I will never do.'

'Now to business,' she continued. 'When I have asked my questions and heard your answers, I will submit to your professional ministrations. The Lord knows that I need them.'

Once again, Adam sat in silence, while she gathered her strength ahead of what she clearly expected to be a terrible ordeal.

'I was told,' Mrs. Ross said, 'that it was you who found my husband's body. I was not well enough to attend the coroner's inquest and, thank God, my presence was not required. But one who did attend told me that you gave evidence that you had found no signs that anyone else was present in the churchyard. Is that correct?' Adam agreed that it was.

'No one at all?' she said.

'That is not quite the case,' Adam said. 'At the time I gave my evidence, what I said was what I believed to be true. Later I learned that Mr. Harmsworthy, the magistrate, had taken your husband to Gressington. It seems that Dr. Ross arrived at Mr. Harmsworthy's house in some distress. His chaise had suffered a mishap on the road and needed attention that could not be given until next morning. Since he was most eager to reach Gressington that evening. Mr. Harmsworthy took him there, but did not enquire the reason for his visit.'

'Yes, he would be most eager,' she said, then was silent again.

'I cannot believe that the magistrate would take your husband to that lonely place and leave him there alone. Dr. Ross would have had no means to return after his business was completed. If my reasoning holds good, Mr. Harmsworthy must himself have been present for at least some of the time. I was not able to speak to him further on the matter after the inquest. Now he seems to have left the area, giving no date for his return.'

'I see,' she said, 'but you found no sign of a third person? No sign of any struggle?'

'None,' Adam said. 'I looked most carefully. Nor did I find the mass of footprints that I would expect had your late husband been set upon by thieves. I assure you, I found no signs of violence upon him, madam, save for the single blow that seems to have brought about his death.'

'And how was that blow caused, in your opinion?' she said.

'I cannot say for certain. There was no sign of any weapon. He may indeed have fallen and struck his head, for there were several large stones nearby. If he fell, he must done so backwards.'

'Fell…or was pushed?'

'Again, I cannot tell. The inquest found that it was an accident.'

'And you stand content with that?' she said.

Adam hesitated. He did not wish to cause her further distress, yet he could not bring himself to lie. 'To be plain with you, madam, I am not content at all. All that I have told you is true. I found no signs of violence. There was no indication that others were present at the time of your husband's demise. I would have expected the coroner to enquire into all of these matters, just as you have done. In particular, I thought he would want to know what brought your husband to that place. Yet he did not do so. When I tried to raise this question, he ruled it to be out of order.'

'You suspect the verdict was rigged?' she said. She might be sick, but her wits were sharp.

'If it was, madam, I do not comprehend the reason.'

'I do not either,' she said. 'Believe me when I tell you that I do not know why he went to Gressington on that day. I do have dark suspicions, yet they do not concern anything that would be of interest to the authorities. One day, perhaps, I will share them with you. For now, you have my thanks. You have not set my mind at rest completely— nor can you do so with honesty—but you have given me much ease. For the moment, doctor, I am too tired to continue with this subject. Would you be willing to come again, should I request it?'

'I would do so readily,' Adam said.

'Then, as I promised, I will submit to your ministrations. Your diagnosis was correct. I am greatly troubled in my mind, so that I have been unable to sleep and can barely touch any food. Can you also prescribe for ailments of the soul, my good doctor, for I feel that my soul is greatly injured?'

'That I cannot do,' Adam said. 'Indeed, I am not sure that such a thing as a soul exists, since, if it survives death, its substance must lie outside this natural world. No, madam, I leave the cure of souls to others. Mind and body present more than enough mysteries for any man of science.'

'A sceptic then,' Mrs Ross said, though her tone was light. 'No matter. I have had enough of certainties about the supernatural world to last me this lifetime and many others.'

Adam's detailed examination and questioning only confirmed what he had already suspected. Since the Archdeacon's death, his wife had eaten little, worried much and slept hardly at all. Yet he suspected that her grief came not from her husband's death, but from some other matter. Perhaps she would tell him in time, when she had learned to trust him more. Until then, he contented himself with giving her instruction on how best to regain her strength. 'You must eat, madam, whether you have appetite or no. Ask your servants to prepare you some good beef tea, adding perhaps a little bread. Then, as soon as you feel able, take some more extensive nourishment. It will be best to have whatever your fancy lights upon. Avoid large meals, for at this stage they will only induce nausea. Let your constant theme be little and often.

'For drink, I will give you a receipt for a good, strengthening herbal brew. You may vary this with a little ale and wine, but my advice would be to avoid tea or coffee until you feel your strength returning. I have also written here a receipt, which your servant may take to the apothecary. It is for a strong tincture of hops, poppy and valerian to help you sleep. Take two or three drops in a glass of wine when you retire for the night.

'Finally,' Adam said, 'I beg you take particular notice of these words: be kind to yourself. Whatever you feel is wrong, whatever you feel you have done that you now regret, do not punish yourself. Many wrongs may be righted in time, if we only have the strength to do it. Your basic health is sound and you have many years ahead of you. Look to the future and all may yet be resolved.'

So Adam took his leave, looking to the great clock in the hallway to reassure himself that he could be at his mother's house before her guests arrived. His visit had been more confusing than enlightening. It was clear that the Archdeacon's widow suspected that she knew the reason for her husband's visit to Gressington. It was this knowledge which caused her so much grief. Until she was willing to divulge more to him, he could not guess what lay hidden in her thoughts. So he tucked the puzzle away in the back of his mind and readied himself to deal with the challenge ahead.

AN UNLAMENTED DEATH

Chapter Sixteen

Ladies of a Certain Age

Early afternoon of the same day

WHEN ADAM HAD FIRST ARRIVED AT HIS MOTHER'S HOME that morning, he had surprised her by leaving again after but a brief greeting. Nor did he explain, but said only that he had some medical business to attend to and would return in good time to meet her guests. That promise he had fulfilled. The fewer who knew of his conversation with Mrs. Ross the better. He had no wish to waste time turning aside the inevitable questions about why she wished to see him. Especially since still he had no clear idea himself.

Now he was back, just in time to join his mother in her dressing room to take his final instructions.

'There will be five guests,' his mother told him. 'Mrs. Wellborne and Mrs. Transom, who are sisters. Then Barbara, Lady Grandison, The Honourable Jane Labelior and Miss Vastone, whose brother is heir-presumptive to Lord Maxstoke. All are prominent members of local society and knew the late archdeacon and his wife as well as any in these parts. They agreed to come readily enough, but do not be surprised if they hold back somewhat. The superstition is still strong that you should not speak ill of the dead. None will wish to be the first to share what they know. If you will be guided by me, you will look first to Lady Grandison. The rest will take their lead from her. She is old enough, and certainly rich enough, to set superstitions and conventions at naught. If she decides to trust you, you will learn all you wish to know. If she does not, your journey here will be wasted.'

Adam and his mother were still upstairs when he heard the maid go to the door to admit the first of the guests. His mother went down at once. She told Adam to wait until she sent the maid to call him, for she wished the ladies to be done with their greetings and settled, ready to talk, before she presented him.

It seemed an age that he waited. What on earth was taking them so long? Surely five rational women could greet one another and possess themselves of dishes of tea in less than twenty minutes?

Eventually, the maid returned and summoned him to the parlour, much like one of the early Christian martyrs being summoned to face the assembled lions in the arena. Allowing the maid to precede him, Adam gathered his wits and came in almost on tip-toes. His first impression of the assembled ladies was not one to give him confidence.

What he had expected, he did not know. Perhaps a group of neat, soberly-dressed women, sipping tea from fine-china dishes and talking in hushed voices. If so, he would have been disappointed. What faced him looked more as if the stock of several merchants were piled on the chairs. Rich heaps of ribbons, frills, furbelows and flounces adorned the ladies' clothes. They had their hair piled high in the latest manner, and fingers, necks and breasts carried more gold and jewels than he had ever seen before. The persons within this bounty were scarcely visible. But the noise! It seemed everyone spoke at once. When they did not speak, they laughed or cried aloud, and all in voices of such volume and power as would carry across the largest room.

'Ladies,' his mother shouted, for to do less would have been a waste of time. 'This is my son, Dr. Adam Bascom.'

The total silence which followed her words was more terrifying than the hubbub which had preceded them. Five pairs of eyes were fixed on him. Five faces showed their owners to be engaged in the closest examination of his dress and person. Five minds were weighing him against heaven knows what standards of acceptability. Adam had sat before some of the most learned professors in three universities and submitted himself and his knowledge to rigorous examination. Yet he had never felt so powerful a sense of being weighed and found wanting.

Adam's mother introduced him formally to each of her guests in turn and the usual pleasantries were exchanged. After that, there was something of an awkward silence while he wondered how best to begin.

Lady Grandison was the first to tire of this hesitation. Her clothes bore the greatest number of frills and trimmings. Her hair carried the most ribbons and curls. And her jewels so far outshone the rest that it almost hurt the eyes to look upon her, so much did she flash and sparkle with every movement. 'Well, young man, here we are. But before you say anything, let me ask you a question. We are all well aware that you found the Archdeacon's body in that churchyard. But what precisely is your further interest? Is it professional or personal? Your mother tells us you never knew the man—which you should, in my opinion, count a great blessing.'

She fixed her eyes on him and waited for his answer. Adam was not a man easily abashed, but he quailed before that gaze. He knew the course of the rest of the conversation would depend on what he said next. Almost without consideration, he chose honesty. 'A little of both, my Lady. Professionally, I am puzzled how he might have fallen and struck his head with sufficient force to cause death. Personally, I believe the inquest avoided the most pressing question: what was he doing in the churchyard at Gressington so late in the day? Until I can see a plausible answer to these questions, my curiosity gives me no rest.

'I should also, I believe, state at the outset that I have no proper standing in this matter,' he continued. 'I have no connection with his family or brief from the magistrate whose concern this should be. Indeed, he told me plainly enough to let the affair be forgotten. All that drives me on is my most regrettable curiosity and a sense that justice has not been done.'

Adam now held his breath, expecting to be sent on his way with a severe reprimand for his impertinence. The ladies continued to watch him gravely. At last, Lady Grandison delivered her verdict. 'I perceive that you find it hard to follow orders from those in authority, sir. That is as it should be. I have never done what I was told, merely because the teller claimed some right to direct my behaviour. If I am honest, I have never done as I was told, and there is an end of it. Many people have also said that I am as curious as a cat, though rarely to my face. I like your honesty in this matter.'

She now turned to the others. 'We may proceed as we agreed, my friends. Dr. Bascom is an honest man and I, for one, will give him my help freely.'

Adam bowed his head, murmuring his thanks. He felt as if he had unexpectedly been reprieved from the hangman's rope even while standing on the scaffold. 'I do not know what manner of man Dr. Ross was,' he said. 'That makes it hard for me to judge the likelihood of any of the situations presented to my mind.'

The ladies still seemed hesitant, looking at one another for reassurance. As his mother had predicted, none wished to be the first to speak and hoped for another to give the lead. Lady Grandison grunted with exasperation. 'What ninnies you all are. Surely you do not subscribe to the common superstition that you should speak no ill of the dead, lest they come to haunt you?'

She dismissed them with a shrug and turned to Adam. 'I have several characteristics that some describe as flaws, Doctor. I consider them essential virtues. Chief among them is this: I scorn to waste energy in the toleration of fools. Nathaniel Ross was a fool, and an unpleasant fool at that. He was pompous, bigoted, self-righteous and a bully. Though he was a clerk in holy orders, he was no Christian in my book. Our Lord bade us love our neighbours. If any about him were nonconformists or dissenters, he treated them only with hatred and derision. I loathed the man.'

There was some whispering when she paused, but no one spoke against her. She had not, moreover, quite finished.

'Nathaniel Ross's religion was ambition, young man,' she went on. 'He aimed to be a bishop, and that sooner rather than later. To achieve such a position demands support amongst those with influence on the government and the King. Having neither precise scholarship nor a talent for good fellowship, he planned another route to glory. He aimed to win over those who felt they had least in common with our Latitudinarian church leaders. I mean the remnant of the Jacobite tendency and the Tories of the deepest hue. These are the gentry most offended by change. Especially if they must accommodate themselves to seeing people in the merchant and professional classes become wealthier than they are. To that end, he preached blind obedience to authority and a continuation of the laws restricting dissenters from taking a full part in civic life. In short, sir, he was a snivelling toady. He would sell his soul in exchange for the chance to wear a mitre.'

Her tirade was over, to be greeted by nods of assent from the other ladies. As if released from any obligation to hold back, several now hastened to add their own criticism of the late archdeacon's character.

'The Lord Bishop's wife told me—in strict confidence you understand—that her husband could not abide the man,' Mrs. Transom said. 'He was punctilious in his duties, but did them with such strictness that he caused offence to many clergy of good standing. The bishop had constantly to smooth ruffled feathers.'

'I heard the same,' her sister, Mrs. Wellborne added. 'Mrs. Mannerly, whose husband is Rector of Great Binstead, said to me that her husband and Dr. Ross had a serious argument. The archdeacon criticised the Rev. Mr. Mannerly's willingness to dine with certain of his parishioners.'

'To dine?' Adam said. 'Surely that can be no sin?'

'Dr. Ross made it so,' she said. 'The persons with whom Mr. Mannerly dined are but occasional attendees at the parish church. Most often they are to be found on a Sunday amongst the Wesleyan congregation. According to the archdeacon, Mr. Mannerly should have refused all invitations so long as the man continued to stray from the Anglican church. Yet Mrs. Mannerly said the man and his wife were fine company and kept a most generous table.'

'He made fair to ruin the accord now existing between the Christians of this city and county,' Lady Grandison said. 'In place of tolerance and amity, he brought argument and confrontation. Many amongst the dissenting are good citizens, who contribute much to our society and prosperity. Indeed, my son, who is, as I have told you all before, most diligent in the improvement of the estate and its cultivation, speaks highly of certain Quaker merchants. Several such now both lend money and issue letters of credit to ease the inconvenience of conducting business in distant places. His agent may now buy and sell as easily in Antwerp or Edinburgh as in Ipswich. Their beliefs forbid them to lie or depart from plain speech. As a result, they have become trusted by all. He could not do without them.'

'Yet, for all his rhetoric, Dr. Ross took good care to speak out only when protected by a pulpit,' Miss Labelior announced. 'Whenever any of the labouring sort caused disturbance in the streets, he was sure to stay safe inside. In his sermons, he was most vehement in condemning riot and bidding all to be content with their lot. Beyond the church walls, it was another matter.'

'He was not alone in that. It is clear that a good many who feel themselves oppressed by masters and employers blame the parish clergy for siding with the rich and well-born,' Miss Vastone added. 'For any well-dressed clergyman to venture out when the mobs are in the streets would invite abuse, if not pelting with mud.'

'There's much in what you say, my dear,' Mrs. Transom said. 'Both the Acts to enclose the land, and the use of ingenious machines to replace labour, have thrown many men out of work. They blame those who benefit most from such changes. That includes the church. It cannot be otherwise, since squire and parson enjoy increases in their rents and tithes as a result.'

Adam sensed the conversation straying and moved to bring it back to the Archdeacon's character. 'Was Dr. Ross a friend to the poor and needy?'

The laughter that greeted this question was answer enough.

'More than once, as I heard myself,' said Miss Vastone, 'he preached that poverty was nought but God's punishment for laziness and shameless behaviour. Yet he also derided those who seek through education and encouragement to assist the poor to better themselves. His theme was ever that each was placed by God in his station in life and to change that was simple blasphemy.'

'The truth is, sir,' Mrs. Wellborne said, 'Dr. Ross was more apt to condemn than give comfort.'

'Even his own son…' added Mrs. Transom, then shut her mouth abruptly at the glances of accusation directed at her.

'His son, Madam? What of him.' Adam spoke gently, aware that too much curiosity might cause them all to take fright.

Once more it needed Barbara, Lady Grandison, to break the silence, her words as much a command as a source of reassurance. 'Oh, out with it, Rebecca. We all know, though some of you pretend you do not. We will not help this young man, as we agreed we would, by too great a delicacy. It is said, sir, that the archdeacon and his son had a most rancorous falling out of late. Mr. William Ross was brave enough to tell his father he would not follow him into the church. Thus his father disowned him and threw him out of the house. Young William has now disappeared, it is said. He did not even attend his father's funeral.'

'It was a foolish act,' Pamela Wellborne murmured, 'yet the boy is brave. It is said he is also handsome.'

'Said by you,' her sister snapped. 'Brave and handsome young men will be your undoing one day, sister.'

'Peace!' Lady Grandison commanded. 'Whether brave or not, it was honest. Mr. William Ross deserves credit for that. Now, Rebecca, finish what you have started.'

'Dr. Ross was determined his only son should follow him,' Mrs. Transom said, eager enough to continue her tale. 'He imagined a dynasty of bishops and archbishops, all named Ross. The young man, unfortunately, has neither a calling to the cloth nor any interest in the learning needed to aspire to a diocese. He was sent to his father's college at Oxford, but quite failed to attend to his lectures. After but one year, the Master sent him home, saying he was not suited. He did not drink excessively or carouse in the town, like many a son of noble parents. In the archdeacon's view his behaviour was worse. He spent his time with factory owners and the like, travelling even as far as Birmingham to talk with them. There he attended the science lectures given by Dr. Joseph Priestley, a notorious Unitarian. He also made the acquaintance of men such as Mr. Erasmus Darwin and Mr. Josiah Wedgwood. Both of them, as I am sure you must know, dissenters.'

'But these are eminent men of science,' Adam cried. 'They are also men of the highest repute. Most fathers would be delighted to find a son who had the honour to be accepted by them.'

'Not Dr. Ross,' Miss Vanstone said. 'He cared nothing for natural science or any other knowledge beyond theology. I have even heard him say the world would have been a better place had Sir Isaac Newton never been born.'

Adam merely shook his head at this. He knew Dr. Ross was a bigot, but this was rank stupidity.

'Young Mr. William Ross wished to study natural science and mathematics,' Mrs. Transom concluded. 'From his earliest youth he had a rare skill with numbers. It seems he neglected his university studies only to pursue others better fitted to his mind.'

'His father must have been furious,' Mrs. Wellborne said, perhaps considering her sister was garnering too much attention. 'I feel sure he would have lectured his son on the duty of obedience. Never mind his own wishes, he must do as his father required, like it or not.'

'Besides,' Miss Labelior added, appearing to choose her words with both care and considerable relish, 'there was the other matter.'

'That was just tittle-tattle,' Miss Vanstone said.

'Not at all, Letitia.' Miss Labelior sounded affronted. 'I was told by one well-placed to know.'

Adam prompted her gently. 'The other matter?'

Miss Labelior favoured him with a warm smile and a playful pat on his thigh. He had given her back the limelight and she was going to take full advantage of it.

'Mr. William Ross had formed an unsuitable attachment,' she said, in the tones of one passing on a great secret. 'The girl is, I believe, remarkably pretty and rather shapely...' Both were plainly attributes

Miss Labelior claimed for herself. Her quick look towards him told Adam he had best agree, which he did with a slight inclination of his head. '…and also rich enough. But…' a dramatic pause worthy of Mrs. Siddons herself. '…her family are dissenters.'

'If every young man who formed an unsuitable attachment was disinherited, Jane,' Lady Grandison said, 'only daughters would ever be mentioned in wills. I myself formed several in my youth. Had I had courage enough to stay with them, I dare say I would have married more happily—though perhaps with a lesser fortune than I enjoy today.'

Adam's mind struggled with the idea of Lady Grandison ever lacking courage to do whatever she wanted. But this intervention had broken the pattern that led to such openness from the others—as she may well have intended—and quickly brought the topic to a close.

'Well, Dr. Bascom?' she said. 'Have we given you information enough?'

Adam assured her this was indeed the case and added profuse thanks.

'Good,' Lady Grandison said. 'Now it is your turn to answer questions. Tell us—in full detail I say—how you found the archdeacon's body. What state was he in? What did you next do? Full answers, sir. We cannot have an eyewitness before us and go away lacking proper information in any respect. I will not allow it.'

At the inquest, Adam wished for a full questioning and had none. After these genteel and high-born ladies had left, he felt lucky to have at least most of his skin still about him. Never had he endured such an hour. But when he ventured to make complaint to his mother on the matter, he met with scant sympathy.

'Those who choose to meet with dangerous creatures must expect a few scratches,' she said. 'You did well enough. You survived. Barbara Grandison has devoured many stronger men than you, I assure you. I would not doubt the others have consumed not a few as well. Do not assume that every woman with the title 'Miss' knows little of the ways of men or the pleasures they offer. Letitia Vanstone has had as many lovers as hats, they say. And Jane Labelior was especially grateful that you supplied her entrance line. If you had not, your skin might show yet more wounds than it does. No, Adam, I fear they liked you. Had I not been present, you would not have escaped several most pressing invitations to dine—ones it would be most imprudent for any young man to accept. Now, it is time you met Miss Sophia LaSalle, my new companion.'

AN UNLAMENTED DEATH

Chapter Seventeen

Sophia LaSalle

Later that day

MISS SOPHIA LASALLE, NEEDLESS TO SAY, proved neither a vinegary blue-stocking nor a frightened mouse. The woman who awaited them in his mother's small parlour was probably of much the same age as Adam. She was neatly dressed and neither tall nor short, with a pale complexion and dark hair. Adam found her decidedly pleasant to look upon. Her face was not beautiful, but she had fine, large eyes and a good figure. He greeted her with grave good manners and she replied with equal formality.

It was too much for Adam's mother, who proved unable to contain her laughter. 'I imagine a condemned criminal and the hangman would show more warmth in their greeting than the two of you,' she said, wiping tears from her eyes. 'You are, I declare, as solemn as owls. Come, relax as friends should. I am not asking you to wed one another, merely to be comfortable in the other's presence.'

'I am quite comfortable, mother,' Adam said.

'As am I, madam,' Miss LaSalle added.

The silence that followed proved well enough that both were lying. Adam had never possessed any talent for small-talk. He was effective in dealing with his patients, so long as the subject-matter of their discussions was clear and lay within his area of knowledge. With others, men or women, he found himself often at a loss for words. Now, since it seemed his mother was not willing to help him, he tried again. 'Ah...um...LaSalle. French name. Bonjour, Mademoiselle.'

'Bonjour, Monsieur,' she replied. 'My name is indeed of French origin, as you surmise. My grandfather was called Martin la Salle and certainly spoke French. He was of a Huguenot family from the Austrian Netherlands and a silk-weaver of some repute, like his father before him. When persecution came yet again, he fled to England. Thus I was born in Ipswich. I am almost as English as you, sir. Both my grandfather and father took English wives, so at best I am but one quarter Huguenot.'

Adam felt a little discomforted by her response. 'I beg your pardon, Miss LaSalle. I merely sought to make polite conversation.'

'Now you are annoyed with me. Do not be so. Your mother warned me to expect a scholar, not a courtier. For that, I am grateful. I much prefer to talk of matters of moment. All the flowery graces and compliments in the world cannot compare with an honest sharing of ideas and observations. Let us forget the conventions and talk rather of sensible topics. I believe that you have studied in Leiden, Dr. Bascom. Do you still maintain contact with people in the university there?'

'I do indeed, madam.'

'You cannot imagine how much I envy you. In our society, an educated woman is too often treated as a freak, rather than a person who seeks to develop the gifts Providence has given her.'

'I do not think thus,' Adam said. 'Nor, I believe, do some at least of the dissenting faiths. Only a few days ago I was speaking with a

Quaker merchant who has taken great pains to see his daughter has a fine education. But you do yourself an injustice, for I believe you speak both French and Italian with some fluency. That is a trick I was never able to master. I spent a year in the United Provinces and never gained more than a few phrases of Dutch.'

'My grandfather and father taught me French, doctor, and one of my brothers has an Italian wife. I take my opportunities where I may.'

'I believe what decided Sophia to come to live with me was less my character than the quality of my cases of books and the excellent libraries in this city,' Mrs. Bascom said. 'She rather reminds me of one of my own children, whose head was always buried between the pages of a book.'

'Now you mock me a little, madam,' Miss LaSalle said. 'I would never willingly consent to spend one hour with a person whose character I disliked, far less live in their house. Your dear mother, doctor, has already shown me great kindness and regard. I am delighted to be here and feel sure I will find being her companion a most pleasant experience. But come, I am all agog to know what you made of your mother's guests. Did you like them? They are all, I understand, ladies of a most superior sort.'

Adam smiled at this. 'Like is not a word I would have considered using,' he said, 'but I suppose I did like them to an extent. Once Lady Grandison had approved of me, they were happy to tell me what I wanted to know—though later I had to pay heavily for their confidences. By the end of their questioning, I felt like one of those unfortunate rabbits you see hanging outside a butcher's shop. My skin was gone and my inner parts had been scraped quite bare.'

'Do not let him fool you, my dear,' Mrs. Bascom. 'He was in his element. He loves nothing better than to worm information from unsuspecting people. If they turned the tables on him at the end, it was no more than he deserved.'

133

Adam realised Miss LaSalle might well not know why he wanted to meet these grand ladies, so he hurried to explain. 'By the merest chance, I became involved in a puzzling matter concerning the late Archdeacon of Norwich …'

Miss LaSalle interrupted him. 'You need not bother with tedious explanations, doctor. Your mother has explained to me the reasons for you coming here today. But tell me. Did you learn what you wished?'

'I wished to know more of the archdeacon's character,' Adam said, 'hoping that might help me make more sense of the rest.'

'And has it?' Miss LaSalle asked with great eagerness.

'I have discovered, alas, that he was a most disagreeable person. I hesitate to say so much of a clergyman, but all I have been told is consistent. I must judge him to have been narrow-minded and self-righteous to an extreme. He was also exceedingly ambitious to rise higher. Even so, such vices are common enough in this world. None of them seems sufficient to offer a reason for him going to Gressington. Nor for any to seek to compass his death.'

'It was to meet someone,' Miss LaSalle declared. 'Nothing else makes sense.'

'The churchyard was certainly a secluded-enough place for a secret meeting,' Adam replied. 'But why travel so far? Are there not places closer to Norwich that are equally private and deserted?'

'But you have answered your own question, doctor. Logic dictates that if the place for a meeting is inconvenient for one party, it must have been chosen because of its great suitability for the other.'

Adam stared at Miss LaSalle in amazement. Why had such a simple piece of reasoning escaped him? He did not know what to say.

'I warn you, Adam,' his mother said. 'Once she has some piece of knowledge in her sight, Miss LaSalle has the determination and hunting instincts of a terrier after a rat. She will drain you dry before she gives you rest. But that is enough for tonight, children. I wish to hear no more of deaths and secrets. Let us turn to happier matters. Did I not hear, Adam, that you have encountered your great friend Mr. Lassimer again? Is he well? Does he prosper in the medical profession as you do?'

Since his mother had changed the subject so firmly, Adam had no choice but to bow to her wishes. He therefore embarked on the story of Mr. Lassimer's life since they had last been together in Glasgow. His mother listened attentively, nodding sadly at the point where misfortune fell upon Mr. Lassimer Senior. Then she brightened again as Adam explained how Lassimer had found his place in the world as an apothecary. Naturally, he made no mention at any stage of widows or servants. When Mrs. Bascom asked if Mr. Lassimer was yet married, Adam simply said he was not.

At this point, Mrs. Bascom turned again to her companion. 'I only met Mr. Lassimer once, Sophia. Then he seemed to me to be the kind of man many a young woman would judge a most suitable husband. His spirit is cheerful, he works hard and he is a generous and kindly friend. I am sure he will soon find the right lady. My elder son, as you know, has been married some years. Of the one before you, I sometimes despair. He has reached thus far in life without displaying any interest in marriage at all.'

'Not every young person sees marriage as a desirable state,' Miss LaSalle replied. Then she fell silent, as if to speak further risked exposing more of her thoughts than she wished.

The clock now struck the hour of four and Mrs. Bascom announced that it was time to dress for dinner. And so, being dismissed, each made their way to their chamber and prepared themselves for the evening.

AN UNLAMENTED DEATH

Chapter Eighteen

The Alien Office

Friday, 29 June 1792, Norwich

ADAM WAS ENJOYING A LEISURELY BREAKFAST with his mother and Miss LaSalle the next morning when a housemaid came in with a visiting card on a small tray. Mrs. Bascom naturally turned to take it, looking surprised that any should call so early in the day, but the maid moved it from her reach. 'Beg pardon, madam, it is for Dr. Bascom. I have asked the gentleman to wait in the small parlour.'

Mother and son looked at one another in surprise. 'Who knows I am here?' Adam said, 'and has the temerity to call at such an hour?'

'Take the card and see,' his mother said. 'What is the name on it?' So great was Adam's puzzlement that he merely passed her the card.

'Mr. Percival Wicken,' she said. 'Do you know him? The name means nothing to me.'

'I know nothing of him,' Adam said. 'Whoever can it be?'

When Adam entered the small parlour a few moments later, he knew the answer immediately. The tall, elegant man standing before

137

him was undoubtedly the one Capt. Mimms had pointed out to him at the inquest. Then he had been in company with the bishop's chaplain and much interested in what happened.

'I am pleased to make your acquaintance, sir,' Mr. Wicken said, holding out his hand in a most affable way. 'Please forgive me for calling on you so early and give my equal apologies to your mother. I arrived from London late last night and must return as soon as possible. I am unable to delay until a more polite hour.'

Adam retained just enough presence of mind to take the proffered hand, but there his manners deserted him. 'How did you know I was here, sir?' Why have you sought me out thus?'

Mr. Wicken seemed neither surprised nor insulted by Adam's directness. 'I would be poor indeed at my business if I had not known, doctor,' he said. 'You came to Norwich early yesterday morning and paid a call on Mrs. Ross. Then you returned to this house. Shortly after, your mother received some of the more prominent ladies of the city. I assume you joined them and the topic was Dr. Ross's death. You have also talked of late with Capt. Mimms, an elderly merchant of these parts. He has been making enquiries amongst his business acquaintances in Yarmouth. All these were quickly reported to me.

'You are a man of considerable intelligence and even greater curiosity, sir. You are also most persistent in seeking to satisfy your questions about that regrettable event in the churchyard at Gressington. I suspected at the time that neither the pedantry of Mr. Allsop, nor the clumsy bluntness of Mr. Harmsworthy, would persuade you to lessen your interest. Sadly, I was much pressed for time and allowed my need to be back in London to override my judgment. Since then, I have had even less leisure to handle the matter in person —for I soon realised that nothing less would serve.'

Adam would have spoken then, but Mr. Wicken raised his hand to prevent it. 'Hear me out, sir,' he said. 'I have not come here to tell you to mind your own business, as I suspect Mr. Harmsworthy did. I certainly will not try to dismiss your thoughts as irrelevant, as Mr. Allsop. I am here to answer as many of the questions which puzzle you as I may, since our activities in these parts are now complete. You should take it as a sincere tribute to your skills as an investigator that I have done so. My praise in such regard is not given lightly, nor set against any but the highest standards.'

'Who are you, sir? What are you rather?' Adam asked. 'For I know not which is the more appropriate question to ask.'

Mr. Wicken smiled at that. 'Who I am you know: Percival Wicken, from London. What I am is not so easy to explain. Perhaps I can best put it like this. I am in charge of part of the Alien Office. That institution rarely features in the newspapers, entirely by design. On the surface, it does the most mundane tasks associated with persons from other countries who wish to visit our shores. Behind the scenes, it collects information. I am an investigator, of a sort, but one who spends nearly all his time in and around Whitehall. My task is to give advice to His Majesty's ministers on the activities of certain people of interest. Many play significant parts in events beyond this country's borders and we must decide how best to respond to them. To that end, I utilise many who collect information for me, some knowingly, others less so. Such information I weigh and analyse, just as you do when making a diagnosis. Indeed, if you will not consider it impertinent, I could say that, as you are concerned with the health of the body, my concern is the health of the body politic.'

'I regret that you will find me very dull of wit, but I am no wiser, sir,' Adam said.

'Perhaps you may be when I have finished my tale. May we sit, perhaps?'

Adam was mortified. In his surprise at seeing Mr. Wicken, he had neglected common courtesy. Then, learning that Mr. Wicken both knew where to find him and had come from London specifically to talk to him, he had failed to right his error. Mr. Wicken had risen, naturally, when Adam entered the room. Both men were still standing.

'My apologies, Mr. Wicken,' he said now. 'I have quite forgot my manners. Please be seated. I still wonder that you knew where I might be today, since I am not at my own home. Have you had me followed all this time?'

'No great wonder, sir; and no, I have neither the people available, nor the inclination, to have you followed. You would have to seem a great deal more of a threat to the stability of this country for that to be an action I would authorise.

'Let me answer these minor points first then, since they seem to distract you. Any government needs information to guide its decisions. Often, it is concealed with great care. Those who wish to harm the state do not advertise that fact. Those who seek to discover information which our government wishes to keep secret act likewise. Messages, letters, even people, are constantly smuggled between our enemies and rivals and their agents in this land. These include some whose dearest desire is to overthrow our government and institutions. Others wish to disrupt our trade or steal our inventions. There are also home-grown rebels, seditious groups and dangerous radicals. Please be patient, my friend, for I see you are eager to deny that you belong to any of these bands of rogues.'

Adam had indeed half-risen in shock, his mouth open and denials ready on his tongue.

'I never thought you did, doctor,' Mr. Wicken continued. 'I mention them only to make plain my role. I act on behalf of His Majesty's government to collect information to reveal the plots and stratagems of England's enemies. I concentrate on matters that take place within our borders. Others do similar work abroad. To that end, I use agents to seek out what I need to know.'

'Spies,' Adam said, still shocked that he had in any way come to the attention of this man.

'Indeed, spies,' Mr. Wicken continued. 'Some such reported to me that your Capt. Mimms was visiting various inns and houses in Yarmouth. He had pointed questions about what had taken place recently in Gressington. They could not understand why a respected merchant and mariner, now of advanced years, should be so interested in smuggling. They thus communicated their puzzlement to the usual persons to whom they give information. From there it came to me.

'Knowing of your curiosity in the matter of the archdeacon's death, it was not hard for me to conclude that you had talked with Capt. Mimms and stimulated his interest. Whether he was seeking fresh news on your behalf, or merely wished to spring a surprise on you with some novel revelation, I did not know.'

'It was the latter,' Adam said. 'We had talked, but I had no idea he would look for further revelations in the way that he did.'

'Indeed,' Mr. Wicken said. 'Well, no matter. My reasoning that you were still dissatisfied with the outcome of the inquest on Dr. Ross was not so remarkable. I have decided it will be best to visit you and tell you what you wish to know, as far as I can. Our activities in this area are complete, as I said, for the time being at least, and there is no reason to prolong your curiosity further.

'I have taken a long and twisting path to give you an answer to your first question: how did I know where to find you? It is simple, I instructed my watchers to find out and report to me. When they did, I hurried here. I must thank you, doctor. By choosing to visit Norwich today, you have saved me the extra journey to Aylsham.'

If Mr. Wicken had expected his revelations to quiet Adam's concerns about this visit, he was wrong. From what he had said, it was clear that Mr. Wicken moved in exalted circles. He was far more important than his presence at the inquest had suggested. Had he given up his time—and made a journey of more than one hundred miles—to gratify some country physician's curiosity? No, it could not be possible.

As usual, Adam preferred directness. 'I am indeed sensible of the time and trouble you have taken to be here today, sir. I will be glad to have my questions answered, for they have nibbled away at my mind as mice do at cheese. Yet I cannot but wonder why such an important personage as yourself should act in this way. I am no one. I have no personal standing in this matter. No, sir, I am merely the unfortunate who stumbled over the poor man's body in that churchyard…'

Mr. Wicken interrupted him. 'And, given what I have told you about my work, your mind worries that I have some ulterior reason for my actions unbeknownst to you. Probably a reason that you should either fear or seek to avoid. Am I right?'

Adam assented. He felt as he had done on more than one occasion when the master at his school had reason to reprimand or punish him for some misdemeanour.

Mr. Wicken, however, appeared delighted with Adam's admission. 'My dear doctor, your candour is as refreshing as your reasoning is swift. As you can imagine, I spend a good deal of my time with those who would conceal all their thoughts from me, if they could. Some are inside our own government, I may add. It is delightful to find one who speaks what he thinks, even if it is wrong—as it is in this case, I assure you.

'What brought me here is something like admiration, doctor. As I understood the way you have reasoned in this matter, I found myself most impressed. That is a rarity, I can assure you. No, sir, I have come to have the pleasure of meeting you for myself and showing you how close you have come to the truth of this matter. Though, if I am to repay frankness with frankness, I must own to a curiosity of my own.

'There are still some aspects that escape me. I can no longer devote my scarce resources to their resolution. Indeed they probably have no bearing on the duties of my office. However, it occurred to me that I might be able to persuade you to go just a little further on your quest and satisfy my curiosity as I hope to satisfy yours. When I have told you what I can, I will return to this and we will see if we can strike a deal. Is that acceptable to you?'

The thoughts and questions in Adam's mind were moving so fast that he could scarce focus on one before it was displaced by the next. His answer, therefore, came from instinct, not rationality. Perhaps that was a blessing, perhaps not. Only time would tell. Yet one thing was clear to him, even through the fog swirling in his mind. He had a patient whose future health and ease—perhaps even her life—depended on his ability to lay her fears to rest. To walk away from the puzzle of the archdeacon's death now, regardless of what Mr. Wicken could tell him, would be the gravest dereliction of his duty as a physician. He would never be able to live with himself.

'I accept, Mr. Wicken,' he said, 'though I cannot see how my fumbling efforts may succeed where your superior knowledge and skills have not.'

'We will see, doctor,' Mr. Wicken said. 'It seems I have more faith in your ability that you. Well, I am willing to back that faith. I do not believe you will prove me wrong.'

They were interrupted now by the arrival of a servant bearing a tray with a jug of punch, glasses and two small dishes of sweetmeats. 'Begging your pardon, sir,' the girl said to Adam. 'The mistress thought that you had perhaps forgotten to offer your visitor refreshment.'

It seemed Adam was fated throughout this morning to be found wanting in matters of simple hospitality. The thought had never crossed his mind. Blushing with embarrassment at his woeful lack of politeness, he told the girl to set down her burden. Then he asked her to convey his fullest thanks to her mistress for making good his absence of manners, however belatedly. As the maid poured glasses for them both, he thought he detected a grin on her face, though she quickly hid it, sensing he was observing her.

When she had gone, he would have offered more apologies to Mr. Wicken, but his guest gave him no opportunity. 'As I said, doctor, I must return to London as quickly as I may. Please thank your mother for her kindness and tell her I was glad of what she sent. Now, with your agreement, let us return at once to the matter in hand.'

'Earlier, you mentioned spies,' Mr. Wicken continued, after taking a long draught of the punch. 'What you may not have realised is that such persons come in many forms. Some, as the popular imagination insists, are disreputable personages from the lowest ranks of society, who frequent vile inns and bawdy-houses to pick up what rumours they can. Some are honest tradesmen and artisans in contact with colleagues infected by radicalism, revolutionary fervour or simple greed. Mariners are needed to move undiscovered amongst mariners. Labourers observe labourers and so on. Like is needed to pass unnoticed amongst like and observe their thoughts and actions.

'At the end of last year, our attention was drawn to the parts of this coast northwards of Norwich. First, we picked up rumours of a group of gentlemen meeting in secret. No more than that. Then word reached us that certain groups in which we have an interest talked of a secret pathway to and from the other side of the German Ocean; a pathway that began on this same part of the coast. Many seek to enter or leave England unobserved, doctor, and we are ever trying to stop them. Since 1789 and the outbreak of revolution in France, we have redoubled our efforts. Not all who seek to enter our land are nobles fleeing the guillotine and the mob. Men like Paine wrote openly about beginning a similar revolution on this side of the Channel. Indeed, we are well aware that the French have been sending many spies here, both to foment trouble and to report back on the state of our ability to withstand invasion.'

'So war is coming again,' Adam said.

'Almost certainly,' Mr. Wicken said. 'My own judgement is that it may be as soon as the end of this year or shortly after.'

'These two rumours—the secret meetings and the pathway across the seas —were they linked?' Adam asked.

'We did not know then and do not know now,' Mr. Wicken replied. 'All I can say is that any such route needs secure places along the way where those using it may wait to move onwards. Yet our spies found none, though they questioned innkeepers and livery stable owners most carefully. It seems this route was not using any of the usual types of staging point. In country areas, strangers are quickly noticed and cannot easily pass themselves off as other than they are.'

'But visitors to gentlemen's houses need not worry,' Adam said. 'They might be described as visiting friends or distant family members. No one would ask anything further.'

'Exactly,' Mr. Wicken said, smiling. 'I said you were of quick mind, did I not? Now you have proved it. If the rumoured secret meetings of gentlemen were linked to this pathway, could they be discussing amongst themselves where the next people passing through should stop to rest?'

'But gentlemen, sir,' Adam replied. 'Can we believe such as these would act against their own king and country?'

'Why not? The Jacobites joined in outright armed rebellion. Wilkes had to flee to France because of his disloyal outbursts.'

'So you had your spies look there,' Adam said.

'Not just there,' Mr. Wicken said. 'There is another sort of person who may move easily from place to place without arousing suspicion. Our land has many dissenting preachers and evangelists who are constantly travelling from congregation to congregation.'

'Of course!' Adam cried. 'That is why you needed the archdeacon.'

'You are far ahead of me,' Mr. Wicken admitted. 'You are right, of course, but give me leave to explain a little more before we come to him. To place spies amongst the gentry is almost impossible, save by using their servants, which would be abhorrent to all decency. Amongst men of God, it is no easier. What we required were people in a position to ask questions without attracting attention. Clergymen and ministers of religion move amongst the rich all the time. Now, before you protest that none would consent to act as spies, however worthwhile the cause, let me add this. Not all those who supply us with information know that they are doing so. It is often better for us to use an intermediary who can solicit information without appearing to do so. Many men gossip when at ease, as do many ladies. Might it not be worthwhile to have one or two present at such relaxed times to pick up snippets and make sure they reach the right ears?'

'Who might do that,' Adam asked, 'yet not be a clergyman, preacher or gentleman himself?'

'I will give you the name and address of one right here in Norwich before I leave,' Mr. Wicken said. 'Indeed, I have warned him to expect your visit, for I hope to have you speak with him to see if I have missed anything in his tale. But let us return to Dr. Ross.

'The Archdeacon of Norwich was well placed to know what was happening in the parishes under his supervision. It was also known that he had a strong dislike of dissenters and non-conformists and was ever alert to what they might be doing. He seemed perfect for our purpose, since he was also an ambitious and vain man. Such people love nothing better than to show off their knowledge, especially if they believe it must exceed what others know. All that was needed was to arrange for a suitable person to urge him on and supply the admiration he so craved, then listen to what he revealed. Thus we might gain some insight into the gentry and wandering preachers at the same time. If some of these were offering shelter and silence, we might discover them.'

'I understand, sir,' Adam said. 'Yet Dr. Ross, from all that I have heard, might as easily alert suspicion as disclose it.'

'One aspect of my work is paramount, Dr. Bascom,' Mr. Wicken replied. 'I need to be a most sound judge of men and women. In this case, I failed miserably. I often seek out those with weaknesses of character. Such are of the greatest use to me. I thought I understood enough of Dr. Ross's weaknesses to use him for my purpose. I did not. I thought I could control his actions. Again, I was wrong. Worst of all, I thought I could use him in a limited way, without his knowledge, and leave him much as before. Instead, I may have provoked his death. Yet, please believe me, I neither intended that outcome nor had any part in bringing it about.'

Mr. Wicken paused to take a second great draught of punch, for he had been speaking almost without a break. Adam was fascinated by the tale that was unfolding. He did not doubt that it was true, just as he believed at once Mr. Wicken's assertion that he had not planned, nor brought about, the archdeacon's death. Whether what was being revealed to him was the whole truth…well, that was another matter. For the moment, he would wait to discover what more his visitor had to say.

Since Mr. Wicken now seemed reluctant to go on, Adam assumed that everything he had said so far was of small importance. What came next must be the crucial element of his story. He had to call up considerable resolve to proceed. 'Dr. Bascom. What I am now going to relate is of a most secret nature. Most of those with whom I work would believe me mad even to go as far as I have. Yet if we are going to assist each other, as I hope we will, you must understand the situation in complete detail. Still, I must needs point out that what you will learn here is of the gravest importance to the defence of our country against vicious and implacable foes. If they knew how far we understood their purposes, they would change their strategy and we would need to begin again. I am trusting in your good sense and discretion. If my trust is misplaced, it will ruin us both.'

'Your words are far from comforting, sir,' Adam said. 'Part of me wishes to avoid such a heavy responsibility and would have you stop at once. Yet another part, probably the strongest, is so intrigued by your narrative that to walk away without knowing more feels unbearable. Proceed, Mr. Wicken. I am a loyal Englishman. I am also well used to hearing matters that demand total silence on my part.'

'Thank you again for your honesty, doctor,' Mr. Wicken replied. 'If you did not feel uncertainty of the highest degree about the wisdom of allowing me to continue, I should mistrust you at once.

Chapter Nineteen

The Archdeacon Unleashed

The same day

AGAIN, MR. WICKEN PAUSED AND DRANK. He seemed totally immersed in the recollection of this period of frustration and indecision. It was as if he had forgotten Adam's presence. Now he was talking to himself, reviewing for the thousandth time what he knew, what he reasoned and what still lay beyond his grasp. Adam imagined his mind running over the meagre facts again and again, looking for anything missed, inferences passed over, links ignored. The silence grew longer.

At last, he spoke again. 'By means I need not disclose, we found that the activity of our mystery group was focused on a small area in the north of this county. It seemed to cover the coast between Wells and Cromer, with a focus on Gressington. Their actions were purposeful, but we could make little sense of them. We also knew the local smugglers used places around this area to bring contraband ashore from larger vessels standing well out to sea. The German Ocean is large, doctor, and full of dangerous shoals and sandbanks. Ideal waters for any ship that wishes to be unobserved or elude capture.

'Our only hope was to find where the people in whom we were interested assembled before being taken out to sea. We needed someone who might pick up rumours of hidden comings and goings from amongst the great houses in the area. Someone who might also remark on any sudden increase in the passage of so-called preachers or dissident ministers. We needed someone like Dr. Nathaniel Ross, the recently appointed Archdeacon of Norwich.'

'Could you trust him?' Adam said, amazed. 'From what I have heard that would be risky indeed. The man was, if you will pardon my frankness, a most contumacious, narrow-minded and damnable bigot.'

'You have him captured, sir. No, of course we did not trust him. Indeed, we went to great lengths to make sure he knew nothing of our existence. Our intent was to make use of him to flush the group into the open. He had no need to know what I have told you. We did not wish him to do anything he did not do already. All we wanted was for him to continue to stir up controversy and damn all who questioned the status quo. Revolutionaries are hot-headed. We hoped that they would not be able to restrain themselves from fighting back. We have found from our experience in Ireland that open denunciations of Popery are always met with a violent response. Thus the Irish rebels reveal themselves to us. Maybe this group would do the same.

'Our plan was to have Dr. Ross talk openly about what he saw and heard to the person we had instructed to become his friend and confidant. That was our mistake. We should have known—I should have known—how unwise it was to assume anything of the actions of someone so obsessed.'

'You mentioned a confidant,' Adam said.

'That is the person I am asking you to visit, doctor,' Mr. Wicken said. 'He may tell you about his part in this in greater detail, if he trusts you. For our purposes at that time, nothing mattered save that Dr. Ross should look out for any group meeting in secret, especially one holding views he would find unacceptable.'

'He took your bait.'

'Indeed he did. Sadly, it seemed not so much to sharpen his attention as to inflame his passions. He began to preach ever more wildly of the evils of dissent. He accused all manner of persons of the most heinous crimes against God. Instead of directing his gaze towards groups of a clandestine nature, he hurled his venom everywhere. Wesleyans, Quakers, Unitarians and anyone not of his opinion on theological matters were fair game. We should have stepped back and had no more to do with him. It was plain that he was more like to scare the quarry away than point to their presence. My only excuse is, I own, a poor one. I was desperate; at the end of my resources. In my stupidity, I tried to recover what I should have abandoned. I told our agent to suggest to Ross that he had heard of one group of ill-minded persons, based somewhere around Gressington.'

'So Dr. Ross went off to Gressington to find them,' Adam said.

'Worse than that. He seems to have gone to confront them himself. He fed his ambition and pride on fantasies of catching the criminals and parading his cleverness to the world. What better way to discountenance his detractors? How he thought he had identified these persons I cannot say, for he told no one.'

'Whoever he found, the result was his death.'

'Perhaps. That remains unclear. What was most glaring was that his death, with the subsequent enquiries it must bring, would frighten away the people we most wanted to apprehend. Now I am sure you can see why your questions—reasonable as they were—had to be discouraged so rudely. It was essential that our quarry should believe we accepted a simple explanation for the Archdeacon's death. That we would investigate no further. The local constable, Garnet, suggested a way. From the start, he was determined to brand the death an unfortunate accident. Since we did not suspect him of any other motive than laziness, which is a near-universal trait in parish constables, we followed his lead. I instructed Dr. Allsop to use the law to bring in a plausible verdict of accidental death. In doing so, he came near to overstepping the mark. Yet you did not press your doubts and I had no idea you would do more than complain to one or two friends of the stupidity of country coroners. I expected trouble from Dr. Ross's wife and family about the verdict. None came and I was grateful. Only later did I wonder what kept them so silent. Mr. Harmsworthy was also told to accept the verdict. He too agreed, though now I also wonder about him.'

'My brother said he was a most diligent magistrate,' Adam said.

'You add to my worries, doctor, but I have no time to pursue that concern. I am almost at the end of my tale and it becomes pressing for me to take my leave.'

'Proceed, Mr. Wicken. I promise to restrain my curiosity.'

'Most of the rest you must know. We allowed time for those concerned to believe we had lost interest, or never had any. That part of my plan worked, as did the careful attempt to direct interest far away to Lynn. We knew the smuggling gang we suspected of involvement was planning to bring ashore a large consignment of contraband at Gressington. In time we knew when. The trap was set. When it was sprung, we had the whole gang and their ship offshore, plus a good deal of contraband to please His Majesty's Revenue. That was our cover. What we were seeking was a lone boat containing a few passengers. We found that too, though the people on board fought hard to escape.

'The constable and the Frenchman,' Adam said.

'The constable indeed. We had not suspected him of anything, save idleness and the kind of accommodation with smugglers typical of his kind. Now we discovered he was the key to the operation. He was the man who collected people in his boat, landed them secretly, and took others back to the ship. Just as we had done, he was using the smuggling operation to conceal his true intentions.'

'So the smugglers were just that?' Adam said. 'Smugglers?'

'Precisely,' Mr. Wicken replied. 'They were well paid to take no notice of any strangers aboard the ship and what became of them.'

'And the constable's 'cargo'? The lone Frenchman?'

'Now you please me again, doctor. We could hardly pretend there had been no small boat and no passenger. One of our men was dead and another sorely hurt. The Frenchman we felt we could admit to, given the fears now abroad. But that was all.'

'There were others?' Adam said.

'One other. An Irishman. A notorious member of that hot-bed of sedition the United Irishmen. It seems our good constable had quite a business, for he would arrange the secret movements of any who might pay him enough. Our net was closed. The prey was taken. But it was not the prey we wanted.'

'That was all?'

'Not quite. When taken, Garnet had about him a bundle of letters to and from various French agents in England. Again, a most useful haul, but not what we sought. Believe me, we have questioned Garnet with some rigour, but he denies knowing anything about the people he carried. He claims he never knew from where or why they came. He never met the person who arranged his involvement. His instructions came by letter only, without signature. When the deed was done, he would be instructed where to find the cash that was his payment.'

'You believe him?' Adam said.

'I do. This group is far too careful and well-organised to put any trust in a greedy fool like Garnet. He will hang for what he has done and they will, in time, find another such person. For the moment, this route is blocked and our quarry scattered. Who knows where they may be found next time?'

For a while, they sat in silence, each absorbed in the events of the past. Then Mr. Wicken stood up. 'You know, that constable was a most enterprising fellow. When we searched his house, we found a package, neatly wrapped and hidden. In it were four books containing stories and illustrations of an extremely lewd nature. He must have had an extra business in the import of pornography. I would have believed such material was easy enough for gentlemen to find in this country. Still, this was pornography of a most particular nature. Perhaps those with tastes of this kind soon tire of what they can find in England, especially in a country district. However, enough of that. Now I must take my leave, as I said, but first I must ask for your help.'

'How can I help you, sir? I have neither skill nor knowledge in these matters' Adam said.

'What you have is better than that,' Mr. Wicken replied. 'You have a sharp mind and abundant curiosity. I can spare no more resources to continue to watch this area. I had to beg for what was made available to me last time. Thank goodness my haul included enough to please my masters. I will get no more to pursue what one called 'Wicken's chimaeras' for a long time. Yet, as I hope I have shown you, all my efforts produced nothing with regard to my primary objective. No, my friend. All I want of you is what I wanted of Dr. Ross: information garnered by careful observation. In your case, I have told you all I can, so that you may watch and listen with knowledge of what I want and why. There will be no intermediary this time either. What you find—assuming you agree to aid me—I wish you to communicate to me alone, either by letter or, if the need warrants, in person. I know where to find you. I will tell you where to find me. Guard the information well, I beg you. There are those who would pay much for it and thus bring about what they most desire: my death.'

Without saying more, he gave Adam a small piece of folded paper. Then he hurried out, calling back over his shoulder that he knew the way and required no servant to show him to the door. Adam, too stunned even to speak, let him go.

The front door banged, footsteps could be heard descending the steps to the street, and Mr. Wicken was on his way.

A moment later, a maid hurried into the room. 'Has your visitor gone, sir? I thought I heard the front door.'

'He has gone.'

'But the mistress gave me most particular orders to listen for signs of departure and make sure he was escorted from the house in a polite manner.'

'Do not worry, child. I will explain all to my mother. He desired no politenesses and would wait for none. It was not your fault.'

'Thank you, sir,' the maid said. 'Will you join your mother in her parlour? She said to tell you she has asked cook to send up your favourite pastries.'

Adam smiled, but declined. Time enough to endure his mother's questions, for her curiosity was as great as his own. He suspected the same of Miss LaSalle, who would doubtless join them. 'Please tell your mistress that I am most cognisant of her kindness, but I must sit alone for a while. I will join her later, perhaps. Oh and…what is your name?'

'Ellen, sir.'

'Well, Ellen, please be ready either to take an urgent letter for me yourself or send someone else who can do so. It will not need to be taken far, but I will want the messenger to wait for an answer. Do you understand?'

The girl nodded and he waved her away. What he needed now above all was silence and solitude. He had much to consider.

On a sudden, he remembered the paper Mr. Wicken had given him. What it contained was an address in London where he might find Mr. Wicken, together with another name and address. Well, he would go and see this other man before he left Norwich. Whether it would serve any better purpose than curiosity, he did not know.

Chapter Twenty

Preliminary Diagnosis

Later on Friday, 29 June 1792, Norwich

ADAM SAT IN SILENCE, TURNING OVER AND OVER what Mr. Wicken had told him. Every turn produced fresh combinations of what he knew. As he did so, he upended each piece and combined one part with another. Then he fitted together accounts from different sources and and sometimes took them apart again. Inferences and deductions were made, considered and rejected. Guesswork filled gaps and was pulled out again. Occasionally facts and ideas fitted together with such precision that he knew they had to form part of the truth. Yet even now the full solution eluded him.

The archdeacon was not a stupid man. Did he guess that he was being led on? Would vague rumours of dissidents and freethinkers be sufficient to draw him deep into the Norfolk countryside. Would they be enough to take him there late in the afternoon, to a lonely spot like Gressington? He must have been intending to meet someone. Who was it? Did they meet, or was he dead before the other person could arrive?

Feeling disgusted that he knew so much and yet understood so little, Adam felt disheartened. Even Mr. Wicken, with all the resources at his command, had made little headway. How could he, a country doctor, hope to do better? Why should it matter to him anyway? It was not his problem. His job was to heal the sick.

As Adam said those words to himself—'my job is to heal the sick'—something happened which he could never explain afterwards. It was as if his mind was filled with a brilliant light, and his body convulsed by an electrical charge. If he had been a superstitious man, it might even have made him think about divine intervention. As it was, he sat up suddenly, slapped his hand on his thigh and shouted, 'Damn my boots! What a fool I have been!'

His shouts brought the maid, Ellen, hurrying into the room, but before she could even open her mouth, Adam was issuing his orders.

'Pen, ink and paper!' Adam said. 'Hurry, girl! Quick as you can.'

The maid stared for moment, clearly wondering whether her mistress's son was in full possession of his reason. Then she hurried off as she was told, and returned in but a few minutes with the writing materials.

'The mistress says…' she began, but got no further.

'Quiet! Let me think. I am going to write a short note that I want you to take immediately to the house that I will tell you. Wait there for the reply and hurry back as fast as your feet will carry you.'

The maid bobbed uncertainly and stayed silent. The gentry could be extremely strange at times, and it did no good to antagonise them. While Adam wrote, she did her best to become invisible.

'There,' Adam said. 'Take this at once to the archdeacon's house in the cathedral close. Make sure that those within hand it immediately to their mistress. Then wait, as I told you, and bring the reply back to me.'

The girl hastened to the door, slipping through just as Adam's mother entered.

'Adam!' His mother said. 'What on earth is going on? You have an unknown visitor at breakfast time and spend nigh an hour with him, ignoring even the most basic duties of a host. Next, he leaves without any ceremony and you sit alone in here for another half-hour, leaving everyone wondering what is happening. Then you shout loud enough to wake the dead and send my maid running to get you pen and paper. Now, I perceive...' They heard the front door bang shut. '...you have sent the poor girl on some errand, I know not where. My dear boy, I know that I have urged you in the past to treat my house as your own, but do you not think this is going too far? Would it not have been polite to ask if you could command my staff in this way?'

'I apologise most humbly, mother,' Adam said, 'but there is not time. It is of the greatest importance that I speak again with Mrs. Ross before I have to leave Norwich.'

'Mrs. Ross? The archdeacon's widow? I did not know that you were acquainted with her.'

'I spoke with her yesterday morning, at her invitation,' Adam said. 'Something that I have just learned may be of tremendous importance to her. She is sick in mind and body, and will not be cured until she is able to resolve certain matters. I will do what I can, but much depends on me being able to speak to her quickly, then act on what she says. I cannot be sure, you see. It all seems to make sense, but I have been wrong before. Now, before Ellen returns, I must ask you a vital question. Do you know a Mr. Jempson, a prominent merchant in Norwich, I believe, and a Quaker? Where does he live?'

'I am more amazed than I can say,' his mother replied. 'Yes, of course I know of Mr. Jempson. I imagine that everyone in this city does. If it were not for our foolish laws, by now he would be an alder-man and probably Lord Mayor. He has done much for those who live here and brought great prosperity. Yet I am not acquainted with him personally—as it seems you are.'

'I recently had occasion to save him from footpads,' Adam said, 'but that is of little matter. Things he told me then seem to fit with things I have heard today, and others I was told by Capt. Mimms. Do you know where he lives, mother? I must try to meet with him as soon as I may. Oh, and may I stay here tonight? My return to Aylsham must be delayed.'

'Your last question is probably the only one I have understood,' his mother said. 'Yes, of course you may stay. You really had no need to ask. Sophia and I will be glad of your company for another evening—at least, if this wild mood leaves you and you are fit for our company again.'

'Do not be cross with me, mother. I will explain as soon as I am able, for I know that I have inherited much of my curiosity from you.'

'I am not cross, merely bewildered. However, enough of that. I do know where our admirable Quaker lives and you shall send Roger, the stable-lad, there with your message. It is a good way off and poor Ellen will undoubtedly need to recover her breath and her wits when she returns. I had not marked you for such a sly-boots, Adam. You are plainly involved in some urgent enterprise, yet you have made not the smallest mention of it to your own mother. Your brother Giles is so like his father. He is a plain, solid, country squire, with neither the wish nor the imagination for adventures. Well, I cannot say I was not warned. Before you were seven years old, your grandfather said to me that, one day, you would surprise us all. What he had marked in you, he did not say, and I paid little heed. I was wrong. It seems all our family's adventure, inventiveness, boldness and nerve—so long absent on the family tree—are concentrated in your person. Now they are showing themselves in full. It takes my breath away.'

Adam grinned at that. 'Well, mother, you always said there must be a black sheep in every family.'

She laughed. 'No,' she said, 'you are no black sheep. You have too wise a head and too good a heart for that. Yet I begin to wonder if you do not have something of the wolf in you. I perceive you are engaged in a hunt that I must not impede. Ah, Ellen is back.'

Almost at once, the maid came into the room. Her breathing was laboured and her face quite pink from the effort she had made to return with all speed.

'Mrs. Ross says...' but she had not the breath to continue and must needs gasp in air in a most comical manner. 'Mrs. Ross says...'

'Stop! Breath a little first. If you fall down in a faint, as you are like to do,' her mistress said, 'we will never know what the poor lady said.'

Ellen did as she was bid and stood there for several moments until her breathing and her colour were more normal. Then, straightening her back, she presented her information in a rush. 'Mrs. Ross says you may call on her at any time, sir. She will be most pleased to see you and she is quite taken aback by the urgency of your message. But she had already determined to tell you all just not so soon...sir.'

'Thank you, Ellen,' Adam's mother said. 'I am sure my son is most grateful for your diligence in returning in peril, so it seems, of your own well-being and decorum. He is, as usual, too preoccupied in thinking about what you have said to tell you so himself. Go to the kitchen, sit down, and tell cook I say to give you a pot of small ale and some food to revive you. Oh...before you sit, please step into the yard and tell Roger I have an urgent errand for him. He is to come here immediately.'

As the maid left, Adam was already on his feet and moving towards the door. 'I cannot wait for Roger. Please, mother, tell him to go this instant to Mr. Jempson's house. Let him present my compliments and ask if I may have opportunity to speak with Mr. Jempson in person and in haste. Then bring back the response at once. Something like that. I am sure you can word the message more politely. What matters is that Mr. Jempson receives my message as quickly as may be and is apprised of its importance.' With that, Adam was out of the door and away, leaving his poor mother standing once more in a state of the greatest shock.

Chapter Twenty-one

An Unhappy Union

Still later on the same day

WHEN ADAM WAS SHOWN INTO HER PARLOUR, Mrs. Ross stood to welcome her visitor. She must feel less frail, Adam thought.

'I had not expected you to call again quite so soon, Dr. Bascom,' she said, 'though I am glad to see you. Thanks to the draught you gave me, I slept well last night and woke much refreshed.'

'I am delighted, madam,' Adam said. 'As I said to you yesterday, more than anything you need to allow your mind and body to recover. You have endured a period of great unhappiness. I hope that I may be able to ease your mind still more, as a result of some information that came to me unexpectedly only this morning. I will soon return to my home in Aylsham, so I wished to take the opportunity of being in Norwich to call upon you and deliver my news in person.'

'You are most kind, sir. As I told your mother's maid, I was myself determined to ask you to call upon me again when you were next in this city. It seems the opportunity for both of us has come immediately.'

Adam cast around for some way to introduce the reason for his visit as gently as he could. Mrs. Ross's state remained fragile. He had no wish to startle her or cause her further distress.

'Mrs. Ross,' he began. 'Forgive me for making what can only be an assumption based on certain comments you made when we talked last. I do not usually listen to gossip, but in this case—where it seemed to bear on the welfare of a patient—I felt I had no choice. I have heard that there was a falling out between your husband and your only son, not long before the tragic events at Gressington.'

'You have heard correctly, Doctor. That is an event that weighs heavy on my conscience. When we spoke yesterday, I was quite unable to tell you of it. That was, I now believe, an error. I excused myself by noting that you were a stranger to me, and that I had no need to add to my distress by recalling things I would much rather forget. Yet your diagnosis of my condition appeared all too accurate. If you recall, you suggested that the ills of my body might well be produced by malignant workings of my mind. At that point, I almost blurted it out. I am ashamed to say that my courage failed me, as it has done so often in the course of my life. Maybe this time I will not be so punished for my cowardice, for you seem to be my guardian angel in this matter.'

'No angel, madam, I assure you. But I may be able to bring a message of comfort nonetheless. Were your recent fears centred on the thought that your late husband may have gone to Gressington churchyard either in pursuit of, or for a meeting with, your son? Did you imagine that his death was linked to something that passed between them?'

To Adam's horror, Mrs. Ross's face became as white as any ghost's and she fell back into the chair behind her, gasping for breath.

'Mrs. Ross…madam…are you unwell?' Adam said. 'A thousand apologies. I am such a clumsy fool. I have startled you and, as a doctor, I should have known to avoid that. Sit still, please. Compose yourself. Shall I call for a servant? I ran from my mother's house with such speed that I did not bring my medical bag with me. How I curse myself for what I have done! I came to bring you relief, as I imagined, and I have brought hurt instead. I do not deserve forgiveness…'

In his distress, Adam must have continued to condemn himself for several more minutes, had not Mrs. Ross held up her hand for silence.

'Please, Dr. Bascom. Do not blame yourself. I was taken aback for a moment, that is all. I am quite well, I assure you. The accuracy of your diagnosis and deduction amaze me more than I can say, for you have struck the nail fairly on the head.'

'Dear lady,' Adam said, still inwardly cursing himself. 'Let me continue at once, since I know now that the news I bring can cause you only relief. Why your late husband went to Gressington on that fateful evening I still do not know for sure. Yet what I can tell you with assurance is that it was neither to meet your son there, nor to pursue him in any way. Whatever happened to cause Dr. Ross's death, accident or not, your son had nothing whatsoever to do with it.'

In the lengthy silence which followed, Adam stood and stared at his hostess, quite unable to decide on what he should do. She shut her eyes and held one hand to her mouth, becoming quite still. Gradually her breathing seemed easier and some colour returned to her cheeks.

At last, her eyes still shut and tears staining her face, she spoke. 'Please sit down, doctor, for I can sense you looming over me. If you do not move away a little beyond my reach, I may not be able to prevent myself from jumping up and kissing you. And that would be most improper.'

Adam sat, though he still leaned forward, ready at any moment to spring to aid his patient.

After a little longer, the lady opened her eyes. 'You cannot imagine what relief you have brought me, Dr. Bascom, and what gratitude I feel. I can still scarcely speak from it. But sit still and I shall explain all. First, let me recall my proper duties as a hostess and call the servant to bring us refreshments, for I see from the clock over there that it is already past noon. I imagine that you would take something, sir? My appetite has returned on the instant and I find myself more thirsty and hungry than I believe I have ever been before.'

'Thank you, madam. Some small refreshment would be most welcome, for breakfast feels to have left me some long time ago. I am delighted that you feel ready to accept nourishment again. Only, I beg you, be moderate at the outset, whatever you feel. Even the best of food and drink may be rejected by a stomach that has lain empty, or near so, for some time.'

Neither wished to go to the dining room, so Mrs. Ross bade her servant bring them some cakes and a pot of good chocolate for herself. Adam chose chocolate also. He feared that ale or punch might make him sleepy, for he felt quite worn out.

'Please forgive my impertinence, doctor,' Mrs. Ross said, when the dishes and plates had been cleared away. 'I believe that I see in you a physician who should give thought to healing himself also, for you appear quite tired out.'

'You are as able at diagnostics as I am,' Adam said. 'I am indeed tired, for much has happened in these two days. Yet I am not so tired as to be unable to listen to your tale. As so often, my curiosity will, I vow, give me no rest until I do.'

'Then I will begin at once,' the lady said. 'Our marriage was blest with but two children, the elder a girl and the younger a boy. There was a third, another boy…but he did not long survive. Our daughter is now

166

married and is raising a fine family in their house near Cambridge. She is a most dutiful and happy wife, I am glad to say. I was the first, but never the second.'

'Never, madam?'

'That is how it seems now, doctor. But my trials in the uncertain landscape of marriage are not so much to the point and I will pass over them for the moment. I need say only one thing, for that is essential to understand what I will tell you and the part I played in it. I was totally dominated by my husband. His wishes became mine. His actions I could not question. I now see that was destined all along to cause great grief. Our son, William, is a fine young man, sir. At school he was an able scholar, excelling in mathematics and all subjects bearing on things mechanical. Yet almost from the day of his birth, my husband had destined him for high office in the church. What my husband wished was unalterable law in our household.

'When his school days were ended, William pleaded with his father to allow him to study at a Scottish university. They are, I believe, better disposed to mathematical and similar subjects than the more conservative universities in England. His father would have nothing of it. William must attend the university at Oxford, as his father before him. Nothing less would fit him for swift ordination and a smooth path to a bishopric. When William protested that he felt no vocation to the church, that too was dismissed as something that would come in time.

'William went up to Oxford at the start of the Michaelmas term last year. He did not wish to go, but his father fell into a violent temper and ordered him to do as he was told. He even preached him a powerful, extempore sermon on the need to honour one's father. Mothers were not mentioned, since my husband had long assumed I would subordinate myself to him—as indeed I did, God forgive me. Needless to say, William fared poorly at Oxford. He avoided the studies he found so irksome. Unlike the sons of the rich, he did not waste his time in gambling or drinking. Instead, he travelled to Birmingham to meet with some of the leading citizens there. They are men of great mechanical and business ingenuity, I believe, and held in the highest regard by many. Of course, that counted for nought with my husband. Especially when he found the majority to be dissenters.

'At the end of the Hilary Term, in April of this year, a message came from William's tutor that he should not return. In deference to my husband's standing in the church, and his position as a graduate of the university itself, it was most discreetly phrased. His tutor wrote that William might not yet be ready to embark on the studies his father had arranged for him. Perhaps, given a gap of a year or so, he might take up his studies there again.

'I will leave you to imagine the scene between father and son. Each spoke in the most intemperate language; each doubtless hurt the other badly. What finally caused a break was when William announced that, during a visit to Birmingham, he had encountered a young lady and fallen in love. Her father had brought her to meet a Dr. Joseph Priestley, a man of great reputation as a natural philosopher. Father and daughter had then shown friendship and condescension towards my son. As happens in such cases, youth and shared interests soon led to a more tender attachment. Before the end of the week the father and daughter spent in Birmingham, my son was smitten.

'All this he explained, adding that he had maintained a correspondence with the young lady, with the full approval of her family. He hoped, he said, to ask her to be his wife, once he was in a position to support her.

'If he thought this might pacify his father, he could not have been more mistaken. At once, my husband's fury increased and he shouted that no son of his should ever marry a strumpet he had met by chance. Of course, our son sprang to the defence of his love, saying that she came from an excellent family and a wealthy one. Her father, it seems, is a most respected merchant and banker. The boy never got to say his name, for at the word 'banker' my husband at once demanded to know if the family were dissenters.

'It was the final blow. No son of Archdeacon Ross, no son of a man destined to be a bishop of the Church of England, could ever marry a dissenter. It would destroy my son's prospect of high church office. Worse, far worse, it would harm my husband's career also.

'William was ordered from the house at once and told never to come here again. He was not even allowed to speak with me before he went. Indeed, my husband only told me of his action well after the boy had gone. It was when he sat at his desk, writing to his lawyer to cut William out of his will. When I asked where William would go, the only answer I received was that he could go to the Devil himself, for all his father cared.

'I thought I had loathed my husband before, but now I found that I hated him with every fibre of my being. Yet still all those years of subservience held me in their chains.'

Mrs. Ross was weeping freely now and Adam would have stopped her continuing with her tale, had she not thrust out a hand to signal him to stay where he was. 'No, sir. Do not ask me to stop. Until I tell someone all, this poison will continue to wrench the life from me. I am not a wicked woman, I believe, merely a weak one. Now I have been punished for that almost more than I can bear. Let me seek redemption and a new life. The events I have described happened scarcely two days before my husband left this house, never to return. He is dead, sir, and though his God damn me to burn for eternity for saying so, I am heartily glad of it.

'When the news came of his unexplained death, I feared the worst. Oh, not that my son would willing kill his father—never that. Yet perhaps they had met, continued their argument and some accident had thus been brought about. I expected my son to hear of what had happened and hurry home. When the days passed and he did not, I thought I should lose my wits. I played the part of the grieving widow, prostrated by her husband's death, since that was what people expected. To my secret joy, it even served to absolve me from attending that monster's funeral. I vowed on the day my son was banished from his own home that I would never again act as a dutiful wife. Nor would I cross the threshold of an Anglican church, if I could by any means avoid it. As soon as I have found fresh lodgings, doctor, I will leave this house and have no further dealings with any part of my former life.'

'Have you heard from your son?' Adam asked, as gently as he could.

'Not one word,' she replied. 'I believe my daughter must have some idea where he is, for they were always close. If that is so, she will not tell me. All she will say is that he is alive and well under the protection of people well-disposed to him. He may have forbidden her to say more, for I am sure he must blame me in part for what happened to him. I could—God knows I should—have sought to reverse my husband's actions. I did not and my silence must have seemed to betoken full support.'

'I will not tell you not to blame yourself, madam,' Adam said, 'for it is too late for that. Nor will I blame you in any way for your feelings about your husband's death, since he bore the majority of the blame in this matter. In the same circumstances, I must have felt the same. Still I can perhaps offer you a glimmer of hope.'

'You have heard of my son?' she asked, sitting up and leaning across to grasp his hand.

'Not that,' Adam said. 'Not quite that. Now, I must ask you to bear with me and summon up your courage, for all I can offer at this stage is a hope, nothing more.'

'I will do as you say, doctor, and it can be the start of my path to a better life. I have always been a coward. No longer. Men say that faculties grow with use. Thus I will use my stunted courage and hope, in time, to see it grow stronger.'

'You have my profound admiration, Mrs. Ross,' Adam said, and meant it. 'I will not say that I pray for you, for to be truthful, as I think you guessed at my last visit, I place no credence in prayer to gods of any kind. Rather I will say that I believe you to be far stronger than you think. I am sure you will be capable of withstanding the blows fate has dealt you and recovering from them.'

'What is it you hope then, doctor?' Mrs. Ross asked.

'I have realised information I received some time ago, but could make little sense of at the time, now points me in a certain direction,' Adam said. 'Before I came here, I sent a message to a person I met completely by chance. He is a dissenter, as he told me freely, a Quaker. But from my own observation and all I have heard of him since, I judge him to be an honourable and good man. I hope to enquire of him whether he has any knowledge from within his community and contacts of where your son may be and his state of mind. My hope is thus to gain more certain information for you. Yet it is possible he knows nothing. If that is so, I will ask him to make enquiries on my behalf. I am sure he will do this, for we parted last on the best of terms and I have no doubt he will aid me in any way he can. Now, madam, be patient. None of this is certain. My hopes may be sound or they may not. All I can promise is that I will tell you the outcome, plainly and honestly, whatever it may be.'

Mrs. Ross still held Adam's hand. Now her grip tightened and she pulled him towards her, reaching her face up to kiss his cheek. 'There, I have done it and you will brand me a shameless woman. I could not prevent myself, though I hope you will not feel you have to confess my actions to others. None has shown me as much kindness as you, sir, in many a year. If I possess any power of blessing, it is yours in full measure.

'Now, my most dear friend—for you see my shamelessness knows no bounds—I must ask you to leave me. I am exhausted beyond measure and must sleep. For the first time in this whole sorry business, I feel hope that will make my sleep the sweeter. Whatever happens next, I will never forget what you have done for me. When I am well, I shall make it my business to seek out your mother and tell her what a fine son she has. I have a fine son too. Thanks to you, I can now think of him again without any shadow falling over me. Should I see him again or not, I will never forget that either.'

Chapter Twenty-two

A Musical Interlude

Later that afternoon

ADAM WAS DESTINED FOR A CONSIDERABLE DISAPPOINTMENT when he returned to his mother's house. Roger had come back with the message that Mr. Jempson was away. He was on a visit to oversee some of his business interests in Lynn and would not return until later in the following week. Being by nature impatient, Adam felt the disappointment keenly—so keenly that only action could relieve his mind. He determined to go at once to see the man whose name Mr. Wicken had given him. Thus, to the amazement of all at his mother's house, he turned around and left again.

The name on the paper had been Tobias Sulborne; the address in one of the small streets that ran between the Cathedral Close and the river. It was, of course, quite possible the man was about his business somewhere. Yet since that weighed less with Adam than his need to be active rather than fretting at his mother's home, he went there just the same.

Mr. Sulborne's house proved to be a neat dwelling, not large but in good condition externally. It lay in a good situation, for it was closer to the majestic bulk of the cathedral than to the wharves and warehouses along the river bank. As Adam approached, he could hear a fortepiano. Someone must be at home, though it might rather be Sulborne's wife or daughter than the man himself. As he got closer, it was plain that whoever sat at the keyboard was no common performer. The music was rich and complex and the manner of playing both assured and dextrous.

A young maid answered the door, ushered Adam inside and hurried off, taking his visiting card. At once the music ceased, so she must have gone to whoever had been playing. When she returned, she told Adam the master would see him at once. Then she led him into a pleasant room, not overly large, containing both the fortepiano he had heard and what must be either a spinet or harpsichord. Mr. Sulborne himself proved to be a man of middle age, middle height and middling stature. The kind of man you might pass ten times in the street, yet fail exactly to recall on the eleventh.

After the usual introductions and pleasantries, Sulborne ushered his guest to a chair by the fireplace. The maid was sent for coffee.

'My wife and children are out, Dr. Bascom,' Sulborne said, 'so you have chosen a propitious time to make your visit. The Good Lord has seen fit to bless us with abundant increase, all healthy and full of energy. My youngest child is yet but four years old, while the oldest is now fifteen. When all are present, the house can seem quite small, though they are well-schooled to stay quiet when I have a pupil come here.'

'You are a music teacher then,' Adam said.

'In part,' Sulborne replied. 'I see Mr. Wicken neglected to tell you more about me.'

'He told me almost nothing,' Adam said. 'He gave me a slip of paper as he left on which he had written your name and address.'

Sulborne smiled. 'I fear Mr. Wicken is often distracted by weight of business. But you are not of this city, or you would know my name at least. I am the cathedral organist and master of the choristers, sir. Yet even such an ancient and magnificent see as this pays its organist but a meagre stipend. I am forced to supplement my income by giving music lessons in the city. I teach fortepiano and spinet, together with singing. My pupils are the daughters of merchants and professional men such as yourself. Indeed, sir, I taught Miss LaSalle, who I believe has now become your mother's companion. She is a most accomplished pianist and has a lovely singing voice. Occasionally, she even pays me a visit and we play and sing duets together.'

It seemed to Adam that all people sang Miss LaSalle's praises, so that he might even have come to dislike her, had he not met her first.

'But you have not come here to talk of such trifles I know,' Sulborne continued. 'Ah, here is Betty with coffee. Refresh yourself, sir, and I will tell you what you want to know.'

At the start, Mr. Sulborne's tale repeated what Mr. Wicken had suggested. The only surprise to Adam was that Mr. Wicken had been born in Norwich. In his early twenties, he had been a tenor in the cathedral choir. That was at about the time Sulborne had first come to assist the previous organist. Shortly after that, Mr. Wicken had moved to London, though he had remained in occasional contact.

'It was through his most kind endeavours,' Sulborne said, 'that I met both Mr. Handel in his old age and Mr. Haydn during one of his visits to the capital. Percival Wicken has ever been a friend to me. So I am naturally ready to assist him when I can —which is but rarely, for he is become a great man, while I remain but a humble organ-player.'

It was in January, Sulborne said, that Mr. Wicken had first asked him about Dr. Ross. That was when he suggested that Sulborne should strike up an acquaintance with the man. It would be of service to him, he sad, and those who employed him.

'I knew him, of course,' the organist said, 'as all did about the cathedral. Yet I suspected I was beneath his notice. He was not an agreeable man, doctor, as I am sure you have been told. At first, he rebuffed my efforts. Yet I think even Dr. Ross had at last come to realise that none would associate with him if they might avoid it. Not even his own colleagues in the church or the Chapter. He was both arrogant and narrow-minded, but he was also lonely. And like many such, instead of mending his ways, he became bitter towards a world that he felt had rejected him. It only made matters worse, I fear. Where he had warned, he now denounced. Where he had been merely domineering, he became an outright tyrant.'

It was Dr. Ross's loneliness that had been the means of Sulborne finally becoming an intimate of this stern and difficult man. Once accepted, Dr. Ross told him of the great hatred he had for non-conformists and any who rejected the established ways. Sulborne also discovered that the man's self-righteous moralising had arisen, at least in part, from his failure to find acceptance and warmth in his own household.

'He knew even his wife and children had come to dislike him,' Sulborne said. 'Yet he seemed unable to deal with this by any means other than forcing them at least to obey him.'

Thus matters had continued until, of a sudden, Ross had become excited. Some contact had been made with him: contact that would, he said, allow him to prove he had been right all along about the rottenness infecting society. He would not explain much more. All he would say was that he must go somewhere on a certain date. At that time, his contact would reveal all to him. Then he would have the means of uncovering a most damnable group of men engaged in the extreme of perversions. All was arranged and he only had to await the call.

'Did he mention revolutionaries or the French?' Adam asked. 'What you say sounds like something more related to morality than the political world.'

'No, sir,' Sulborne said. 'As I told Mr. Wicken, he described whatever and whoever it was he was seeking to reveal as wicked, filthy and depraved. He said nothing of a political nature. Indeed, it was my own belief that he was not especially interested in political events. He abhorred the revolutionaries of France, but on moral and religious, not political, grounds.'

Then, according to Sulborne, Dr. Ross's world tumbled into chaos about him. 'He told me —these were his very words,' Sulborne said, '—that he had done a most damnable thing, for which he would suffer for the rest of his life. He had driven his only son from his house and intended to disinherit him. The lad had first disgraced him by being sent home from Oxford University, then defied him by refusing to enter the church. Worse, he had announced he would take a wife of his own choosing, a young woman of good fortune, but of a dissenting family.'

'Yet all might have been resolved in time,' Adam said. 'Was there really cause for such an extreme response?'

'He knew he had done wrong, doctor,' Sulborne replied. 'He knew he had allowed his passions to rule him. Yet he had been unable to resist flying into a rage. The words were out before he had stopped to consider what he was saying. I believe he still hoped he might talk with the boy again and try to set things right between them, but it was not to be.'

'Why not?'

'He did not know where his son had gone, nor how he might make contact with him. Even his wife had finally said she would have no more to do with such a husband. He was alone, facing the ruin of all his hopes and knowing that he had brought this calamity on himself.'

For a moment, both men were silent. Until now, Adam had assumed Dr. Ross so firm in self-righteousness that the banishment of his only son would mean little. Now the picture was rather of someone torn apart by guilt, yet unable still to set aside the habits that had brought him to disaster.

'In the midst of this, his contact sent him a message to come for a meeting,' Sulborne went on. 'In a way, it must have come as a relief to have something to do, even though he ought to have ignored all save mending what he had done. He went in great haste. I did not see him at that time, but I heard that he disappeared, speaking to no one. Only when the news of his death reached us did we have the smallest information about his destination. Of his purpose, most knew nothing at all.'

'So this rapid departure had nought to do with his son?' Adam asked, more for the sake of final certainty that any other purpose.

'Oh, no,' Sulborne said. 'As I told you, he had no idea where the young man had fled. Nor would his pride yet have allowed him even to enquire. It was a terrible death that awaited him.'

'Why so?' Adam asked. 'If all is as it seemed, he died in an instant, and from a single blow.'

'Because he died unforgiven of his sins, doctor. He died without proper repentance and the opportunity to make reparation. None of us know the time when God may call us to His judgement. Dr. Ross died, as it were, in the midst of his sins. He must have faced the Lord thus. Only one outcome would have been possible, I fear. Hell awaits the unrepentant sinner, the Bible tells us. Hell and all its terrors.'

Adam did not believe in Hell, but now was not the time to enter into theological dispute. Instead, he asked the other question that had bothered him for so long. 'I wondered at the time why the authorities of the church seemed to accept the verdict of accidental death so easily.

Even if that was correct, would they not have wished to discover why one of their dignitaries was in such an unlikely place?'

'I cannot answer for them,' Sulborne said. 'I know the bishop sent his chaplain to observe events. I also know that the story of the arch-deacon's quarrel with his son, and the action he had taken, was common knowledge about the Close. It is my belief—no more than that, mind—that the church authorities were becoming embarrassed by the archdeacon's behaviour. He was upsetting too many people of power, wealth and influence, which are all much the same thing. To have engaged in a public quarrel with his son would have been the final straw. When his death was ruled accidental, and his own family raised no question at that, I suspect there was a collective sight of relief. The man could be buried and forgotten.'

'A sad epitaph,' Adam sad.

'Sad indeed, doctor. I never liked Dr. Ross. Indeed, I would have avoided him like all the rest, had not Mr. Wicken asked me to do otherwise. Still, by the end I pitied him greatly. There was much about his fate that should be a warning to us all.'

For a moment, they sat in silence again. Then Mr. Sulborne seemed to recall something. It caused him first to take out his watch and ascertain the time, then to jump up in alarm. 'Forgive me, doctor. I do not wish to suggest any rudeness towards you, for I have found talking with you most helpful for easing my own conscience in this matter. Yet I have quite forgot the time. I have a pupil who will be here in but moments and nothing is ready. Will you excuse me, sir? I demand punctuality of those who come to me for teaching. It will never do to be late myself.'

Adam rose at once, full of his own apologies for arriving unannounced and taking up Mr. Sulborne's time without prior arrangement. And so, with repeated apologies from Sulborne and profuse thanks from Adam, the two men parted.

AN UNLAMENTED DEATH

Chapter Twenty-three

Discretion and Trust

Early evening the same day

THE DAY HAD BEEN A LONG ONE, for Adam arrived back at his mother's house with scarcely enough time to change before dinner. However, his talk with Mr. Sulborne had made him forget his disappointment over Mr. Jempson and so his good temper was restored. He determined not to mention talking with Mr. Sulborne, at least for the present, since that would provoke questions—especially from Miss LaSalle—that he had no idea yet how to answer. He was not able to visit his mother as often as either would like. Now the opportunity to spend another evening in her company—and that of Miss LaSalle—was most welcome. Why spoil it by inviting any situation where he must, in all conscience, refuse to answer their questions?

Over dinner, as if by some unspoken agreement, they each avoided any return to the events of the day. Instead they conversed of generalities and the many friends that his mother had made in the city of Norwich. Later, family matters predominated. Giles was at last getting the finances of his estate into order. While it would be many years be-fore he could pay off all the mortgages, it was good land. He had high hopes of soon restoring his income to a more acceptable level. By sell-ing his father's most extravagant purchases for the Hall, he had raised enough money to start on the most urgent repairs. Improvements to the various farmsteads would follow. The tenants had been pressing his father to undertake this work for some years. That was why most had resisted any increase in rents. Now, with the tenants happier, Giles's land agent would be able to bring the rentals up to a more satisfactory level.

In like vein, Adam was able to tell his mother that his medical practice had increased substantially since he saw her last. He would no longer be so dependent on carrying out inoculations to bring in a basic income. The benefits of this process were now more widely recognised. In several localities, the town council, the Boards of Overseers for the poor, or even local charities were paying for people to receive inocula-tion. But while Adam applauded such improvements in public health, it made it impossible for him to charge reasonable fees for the same service. It was fortunate that he could now find profitable employment in other fields.

To all this Miss LaSalle listened most attentively, though she spoke little. It must all be new to her, Adam thought. How interesting that she had the good sense to stay silent and absorb the new ideas. Many ladies seemed to feel ignorance of a topic should be no barrier to expressing their opinions.

Once the servants had cleared away the remains of an excellent meal, Adam and the ladies retired to his mother's small parlour. The arrival of hot water, teapot and dishes for taking tea would, he knew, signal the start of her questions. He could expect a prolonged and most detailed investigation of recent events. Would Miss LaSalle contribute? Or would she stay quiet, listening and thinking? He could not resist hoping it would be the latter.

He had considered what he would say as he changed his clothes before coming down to dinner. There were certain matters that he could not in good conscience reveal. It was clear he must try to direct the conversation into safer areas.

Adam began by revealing how Mrs. Ross had first written to him. This visit to Norwich had been the earliest opportunity for him to call on her as she had asked. Thus he had gone to her house by arrangement yesterday morning. He had expected, he said, her wish to hear first-hand all he could tell her about the circumstances of her husband's death. What he had not anticipated was the delicate state of health in which he had found her. As he knew it would, this tale brought several exclamations of the most profound sympathy from both ladies.

Next he explained how he had done his best to allay her worst fears and left her with the best medical advice he could. After Mr. Wicken left, it had suddenly occurred to him that he might do more. That was why he was so eager to see her again, before he returned to Aylsham. Thankfully he had found her somewhat improved.

As his mother knew, he said, the matter of the rift between Dr. Ross and his son had been mentioned to him. Now, on this second visit, she had told him of it herself and how she had been unable to intervene. It was his firm opinion that grief over this event was caus-ing great injury to her health. She feared her son's continued absence meant that he was not able to forgive her for appearing to take his father's part.

'I always disliked Dr Ross,' his mother said at this point, 'but now I find that I have nothing but the most profound contempt for the man. What a loathsome creature! To be such a tyrant to his poor wife and family. If indeed, after death, we face that strict judgement which he so often proclaimed, he resides now in one of the lower depths of Hell.'

Then Miss LaSalle spoke. As Adam had hoped, she had stayed silent until now, absorbing his words without comment. 'I wonder that so many parents see marriage as the natural end of any daughter's existence. Some unions, I own, bring much joy. It would be best had others never taken place. My own father was horrified when I renounced any intention of marriage. Yet your tale, doctor, offers ample proof that I may yet avoid great sorrow by my choice.'

'Do not judge all men by the standards of one, my dear,' Mrs. Bascom said. 'Yet I cannot but agree that a bad marriage is like to be worse than none at all.'

Adam wondered at Miss LaSalle's words. She was still young. She was comely enough and undoubtedly capable and intelligent. What might have brought her to such a firm decision to remain single? Sometime, he might be able to satisfy his curiosity on this matter, but not now.

For the moment, Adam excused himself from explaining more about Mr Wicken's identity and the reasons for his visit. Instead, he said, he would note only this. Mr. Wicken came from the Alien Office in London and his interest in Adam and what he had seen stemmed from certain questions asked at the inquest on Dr. Ross. The detail was, he said, confidential and he was not at liberty to divulge what he had been told in that way.

However, part of what Mr. Wicken had said made it clear that there was no connection between the death of the archdeacon and his falling out with his son. On his second visit to Mrs. Ross, Adam was able to assure her that her fears on this count were baseless.

It took a moment for his mother to make the connection herself, then, her hand pressed to her mouth, she stared him in horror. 'Oh… it cannot…not murder! She cannot have imagined that! Oh, the poor woman. That must be enough to destroy the most balanced mind, let alone one already weighted down with shock and grief.'

'In such a situation,' her son said, 'human beings are rarely able to consider matters in a rational way. No, I do not think she ever believed it was possible. I think she was so sick with guilt at her own inactivity and submission to her husband, that she feared the greatest of all punishments. What drove her mind to near total distraction was remorse, not a belief in her son's real capability to commit murder.'

'It must be so,' Miss LaSalle murmured. 'No mother would think that.'

'Even though, in her heart, she knew her fears must be false,' Adam continued, 'she could not set them aside. Rather she used them to punish herself for what she had done—or rather not done.'

'She has no guilt,' his mother declared, speaking with total firmness. 'All this is on her husband's head, not hers. Whether it was chance or another's hand that sent Archdeacon Ross from this world, it has but rid us of a foul hypocrite.'

'Aye, madam,' Miss LaSalle added. 'What you say is true. That man must prove a most shameful stain on the church that he claimed to serve. I am glad I never encountered such a one.'

For a time, none of them wished to speak further. Their hearts were too full of pain and anger. It was Adam who sought to lighten their mood.

He explained that he hoped by contacting Mr Jempson to set enquiries in train that might serve to locate young Mr. William Ross. If that proved possible, he would next send a message imploring him to return home and set matters right again with his mother. Only then, in Adam's opinion, would she be able to return to full health. His mother applauded this action warmly and Miss LaSalle too smiled upon him. To his surprise, he found he liked that very much. Finally, he turned again to the matter of Mr. Wicken.

This was the subject on which he felt he must tread with most care. He did not doubt that Mr. Wicken had told him things which he should not share with anyone else. Yet he had also assured Adam that matters regarding the smuggling gang—and the business of ferrying people in and out of the country in secret—were completed. Adam had spent some time before dinner considering how he might best explain Mr. Wicken's visit on that basis alone.

Thus he now began. First he told his mother how the archdeacon's death had been a most inopportune event for the plans to seize the smuggling gang. How the authorities had feared that too close an investigation might scare the criminals away. And how, when it appeared the death might be accidental, they seized on this as the best way to calm suspicions. Mr. Wicken had, he said, assured him that his questions at the inquest had been appropriate both from a legal and a logical point of view. Only the overriding need to preserve the planned operation had made them seek to suppress his curiosity. His visit today was a belated explanation and an apology for what had happened.

'I suppose that was kind of Mr. Wicken,' his mother said at this point. 'Yet it was no more than your due.'

'This Mr. Wicken seems a most important person,' Miss LaSalle added. 'I wonder that he came so far to do what he could have done in a letter. Was there not more to his visit than this?'

Adam's startled glance at Miss LaSalle when she said this must have conveyed more than he had intended, for she blushed and hung her head.

'Pardon me, doctor,' she said. 'I interrupted you with my curiosity. Pray continue and I will hold my tongue. In some matters, I suspect, discretion is worth more than I guessed.'

Adam was discomfited by her sharpness of mind. But since she must have realised he was editing his story a good deal, he was still more grateful she had the good sense to assume he had reason for doing so. Miss LaSalle, he decided, was even cleverer than he had first imagined.

His mind relieved, Adam continued after the briefest of pauses. Mr. Wicken, he said, had next told him the smugglers had all been captured, thanks to the deception the authorities used to direct attention to the area around Lynn. Best of all, they had also been able to seize a man who was involved in the secret passage of spies and other undesirable people into and out of England. That was none other than Constable Garnet.

The circumstances of the archdeacon's death had no connection with the smugglers. Indeed, Adam told his little audience, Mr. Wicken had no idea why Dr. Ross went to that place. Nor had any signs or information emerged that pointed to any other person being present. It was this latter news that he had carried to Mrs. Ross with all dispatch.

To his enormous relief, his mother seemed satisfied with what he had told her. Aside from one or two questions about Mr. Wicken himself, which he was able either to deflect or to answer in innocuous ways, she seemed content to let the matter rest.

In Miss LaSalle, he could only trust to that discretion she had praised. For several moments, the young woman was silent and seemed to be struggling with some internal debate. Then, having reached her decision, she smiled at him again and thanked him for letting her stay to hear his tale. His ordeal was over.

Still, as Adam lay in his bed that night, he could not help but wonder whether Miss LaSalle would let him off so easily. He was certain she guessed something of how much he had omitted. She had also owned to being of a curious disposition on most subjects. Yet even if she pressed him, he would not be able to go further. His last thought as he drifted into sleep he would later recall with amazement. At that moment, it seemed, he felt nothing would be more agreeable than to win her trust in him, in this matter and in many others.

AN UNLAMENTED DEATH

Chapter Twenty-four

A Puzzle Shared

Monday, 2 July 1792, Aylsham

ADAM DID NOT, IN THE END, RETURN to his own house until Sunday afternoon. His mother's company acted as balm to his mind after the stress of the past few days. Even Miss LaSalle seemed to grasp his need for relaxation. Whatever questions were still in her mind stayed there.

Though the weather continued to deny that summer had arrived, the ride back to Aylsham was uneventful. He had no fears that his absence might have proved a problem. Mrs. Brigstone was entirely capable and trustworthy, well used to taking full charge of household matters.

Amongst the letters waiting for him was a brief letter from his brother Giles. A servant had brought it over on Friday from Trundon Hall. Giles must have received a similar letter from their mother to the one she sent to Adam. Now he expressed some surprise—and not a little apprehension—at her decision to find a companion. Like Adam, he must have imagined some withered and embittered spinster, who might mar the good relations that had always marked their family, even in the worst days of their father's financial woes.

Adam immediately wrote in return. He related his visit to his mother and commented on her continued health and high spirits. He was also able, he hoped, to set Giles' mind at rest about Miss LaSalle. 'She is a delightful, modest young woman' he wrote. 'Her conversation is good, her mind well-developed and her manner entirely appropriate.' He did not notice his failure to describe her appearance in any way.

Of course, his sister-in-law Amelia saw this at once. When the letter was shown to her, she told her husband that Adam must be 'quite smitten' with Miss LaSalle to be so quiet on this score. Still, as she and Giles knew well, Adam had been smitten with several young ladies in the past and had shown no inclination to suggest matrimony to any.

Beyond writing that he had been spurred to go to Norwich by gaining a new patient there, Adam said nothing about the rest. It would be time enough to tell his brother about other matters when the puzzle had been either cleared up or finally set aside.

This Monday Adam rose late, put on his favourite morning gown and enjoyed a lengthy breakfast. He also caught up with reading the newspapers the carrier had brought from Norwich the previous week. Adam was an avid reader of the news. His mother scorned to buy any journals, labelling them all as purveyors of scurrilous scandal.

Thus it was that he arrived finally at Peter Lassimer's shop nearly at the noon hour. He found his friend with several customers waiting for his attention. Adam was not one to miss any opportunity to ingratiate himself with potential patients. He therefore took the chance to exchange greetings and local news with all those who waited. Maybe fifteen minutes passed in that way until the final customer had been served. Then Lassimer pointed to the door to his compounding room.

'I have much work to do, doctor,' he said with a grin, 'even if lordly physicians like yourself can afford to work but one day in each week.'

Adam replied in kind. 'Naturally, my friend. A physician's cures work the first time. An apothecary's patients must return many times until he hits upon a remedy by chance.'

The antagonism between university-educated physicians and the more lowly apothecaries was well known. It had served many time as a suitable source of banter between them.

Adam was happy to talk while his friend worked to replenish his stock of medicines. Too close attention to the version of events he believed it was safe to share might reveal the gaps and holes in the tale.

The story he told Lassimer was essentially the same as the one he had given to his mother. Lassimer was a good friend, but prone to gossip. Adam could, he knew, have sealed Peter's mouth by the simple expedient of asking him to treat all as confidential. Yet he had his own reasons for wanting the apothecary to spread abroad much of what he heard in this case. Gossip given leads to gossip received. Adam hoped Peter's friends, acquaintances and customers might be useful in bringing further information.

When he had finished, he relaxed in the chair Lassimer had set for him by the compounding table and waited for his friend's reaction.

'Well,' Lassimer said at last, 'it was most odd that Mr. Wicken was willing to come so far just to apologise for what happened at the inquest. I wonder if he had any other reason for seeking you out? I never met the man, but he sounds a most unreliable type of gentleman.'

This was far too close to dangerous territory and Adam acted at once to direct Peter's attention elsewhere. 'He did not say he had come to Norwich just for that purpose,' he said, as casually as he could. 'I expect he had other business in the city. Maybe he was intending to be present at the assizes when the smugglers are tried. I believe Constable Garnet, being of greater villainy, is to be brought before a judge at the Old Bailey.'

'There's another fellow of whom I have many doubts,' Lassimer said. To himself, Adam breathed a sigh of relief. 'I wonder why he and Archdeacon Ross planned to meet.'

Adam, sat up in an instant. 'Why do you say that? Could there have been links between such an important churchman and a gang of smugglers?'

'I never imagined there was,' Lassimer replied. 'But they must have had some contact with one another. You proved it by your own words. Did you not tell me, at the start of this business, that the constable showed no surprise when told the corpse in the churchyard was the archdeacon's?'

At this, Adam started violently, then struck the heel of his hand against his own forehead.

'Bascom, you addle-pated nincompoop!' he shouted. 'You veritable prince of asses! Lassimer, I thank you. You are a paragon of reason. I should be ashamed to be here, wasting your time. Of course! He showed no surprise at all. Yet anyone, especially a parish constable in a tiny village, should be amazed. Imagine a body, lying in their churchyard, being a person of such rank. He must have expected the archdeacon to be in Gressington.'

'So they met?'

'No. They cannot have met,' Adam said, 'whatever they planned between them. Now you have set me on the right tack, that is plain. Garnet appeared surprised at the news that a dead man had been found, not that it was a gentleman in fine clothes. Unless he is an actor of the calibre of Garrick or Kemble, which I much doubt, his surprise was plain. It was not feigned, I would stake my life on that. He simply overlooked, in his surprise, to pretend to be staggered at the identity of the dead person.'

'I thought I had solved it,' Lassimer said in a plaintive tone. 'So, let me have this right. They arranged to meet and Garnet either killed Dr. Ross or they had a struggle and Ross fell. Then Garnet ran off to avoid being linked to the dead man.'

'No. That is not right,' Adam said. 'It cannot be so. Garnet may have been expecting the archdeacon, but for some reason no meeting took place. It is not just the evidence of my own eyes that points me to such a conclusion. All we know of Constable Garnet proves he is greedy for money, and not at all concerned how he may come by it. Not only was he paid by the smugglers, I am sure, to stay quiet about their actions. He was also captured in the act of ferrying someone in secret to their ship. Even under close questioning, as Mr. Wicken calls it—I cannot imagine Garnet's treatment to have been gentle—he maintained he had been seeking his own profit.

'Had he been there when Archdeacon Ross fell and rendered himself unconscious, he would have robbed him before running away. If he had killed the man, the same would be true. Thus he would have garnered a significant amount of money and saleable goods. He would also have made it almost certain the man's death would be attributed to some cutpurse, robber or vagabond. It was the fact that the corpse had not been robbed that first produced suspicion.

'Oh, he was quick to give the answer of an accidental death, I warrant you that. He would be terrified that someone investigating a homicide would enquire in too much depth. Why was a high dignitary of the church lurking in that churchyard? Whom might he be meeting and why? Even Mr. Harmsworthy claimed to be puzzled by the archdeacon's determination to reach Gressington that afternoon. When his chaise was badly damaged, he went to great pains to find another to take him.'

'So Archdeacon Ross had an arrangement to meet Constable Garnet,' Lassimer said. 'Or Garnet and someone else.'

'Indeed he must have,' Adam replied. 'Yet, for some reason that meeting did not happen. Instead, either the archdeacon stumbled on others, who attacked him, or he wandered about and fell by chance. No. No,' he went on at once. 'Had he met others and been attacked, we would have seen signs of that. Nor would they, if they were smugglers or other felons, have failed to rob him. Perhaps he did stumble and fall by chance. Perhaps it is as simple as that.'

'Perhaps it is,' Lassimer said, 'but we are, it seems, no further forward in discovering why Constable Garnet and Archdeacon Ross had arranged to meet. All we know is that must be the reason which took Dr. Ross to Gressington in the first place.'

'If I write to Mr. Wicken right away, perhaps Garnet may be challenged with our knowledge of the arrangement and led to explain,' Adam said.

'That will not serve, I fear,' his friend said. 'You said Mr. Wicken left London when the constable was about to stand trial. Unless things have changed, I expect we will read in the newspaper, either tomorrow or the day after, that the court sat last week. Garnet would have been found guilty and may be hanging at the rope's end even as we speak. No letter from here would reach London in time for your friend Mr. Wicken to stay the course of the law. Not even if you carried it yourself.'

'Then the matter is at an end and we will never know,' Adam said.

His despondency must have sounded in his voice, for Lassimer stopped what he was doing and came over to clap a hand to his shoulder. 'Not at all. Cheer up and start reasoning it out with me. We both doubt that Archdeacon Ross had any interest in seeking out smugglers. What was he eager to discover then? What else might he have thought the constable could tell him?'

'Yes,' Adam said, becoming animated again. 'More than that, what information would he have been willing to pay for? I doubt Garnet would consent to disclose anything without receiving a fat fee first.'

'I have it,' Lassimer said in triumph. 'The archdeacon was always obsessed with rooting out immorality and heresy. He must have suspected some group were meeting in secret near Gressington to conduct Black Masses and violate innocent virgins. People like those fellows associated with Dashwood and Wilkes some years back.'

'A Hellfire Club? Surely not. Not in rural Norfolk! Besides, even that lecherous group did not violate any woman who was not paid well to allow them to do it. I heard that they brought whores from London to serve their needs. They may have carried out some parodies of sacred rites, but it was never proven.'

'Would that have mattered to the archdeacon?'

'No, probably not. His kind of over-zealous nature rarely waits for proof before reaching conclusions. But…'

'No 'buts',' Lassimer said. 'You will see that I am right. Some whisper of lechery and blasphemy had reached the archdeacon's ears and he was hot on their trail. Maybe Constable Garnet had genuine information. Maybe he was pretending, so that he might cheat the archdeacon out of money. Either way, Archdeacon Ross believed he could find out when and where the meetings took place. Knowing that, he could act to seize them. I will make it my business to listen and ask careful questions on the matter. If such rumours reached Norwich, they must reach me.'

'You will ignore me, I know,' Adam said, 'but I urge you to have a care. If such a desperate group exists, they will not stoop from calling down the most terrible curses on any humble apothecary who stands in their way.'

'Now you make fun of me,' Lassimer replied. 'Have it your own way, When I am proved correct in my reasoning, I will remember your derision and make you beg humbly for pardon.'

Adam should have left matters there, but he could not resist making a final observation. 'It is just…can you imagine any of the gentlemen of these parts as members of a Hellfire Club? Most are dullness personified. They are the epitome of English country squires, addicted only to the pleasures of table and bottle. Indeed, a good many are well past their sixtieth year of age. Even if their minds still run hot with lust for maidens, I doubt their bodies could come near to matching those urges. The only fine flanks their hands run over now are those of their hunting horses and hounds.'

'Say no more,' Lassimer said. 'You have expressed your disdain. Of course, you forget that dull squires have hot-headed sons. Still, that will be your loss. I will wager you a dozen bottles of finest port wine that I am proved correct. Will you accept my challenge?'

'I will,' Adam said, 'Though buying such wine will harm your purse, while seeing me drink it will injure your pride still more. Now, sir, enough. You have patent cures to concoct and I have serious medical business to pursue. Let us each to our own tasks. I will await your reports with eager anticipation.'

Chapter Twenty-five

Mere Thoughts and Speculations

Wednesday, 4 July 1792, Aylsham

WEDNESDAY DAWNED BRIGHT AND CLEAR. For a moment or two, Adam's waking mind could not grasp the reason for his bedroom being so light. For weeks before, each morning had brought cloud, rain or even, on one or two occasions, fog. Yet that day the sun shone, the sky was a pure blue, unspotted by cloud, and the air promised a first taste of summer's warmth.

It was a day not to be wasted lying long in bed. Adam rose and rang the bell for the maid to bring water and shaving materials. Then, his face clean and free from beard, he dressed in a clean shirt, his favourite breeches and an old, but much-loved waistcoat. Over it all, he drew on a coat of equal antiquity. He was going walking, he told himself, not visiting the quality. Even so, he knew Mrs. Brigstone, if she happened to see him, would shake her head and tell him he looked like a poor farmer on his way to market. But today he would dress as he wished, whatever she thought.

Going downstairs, he avoided the kitchen with care. That was where Mrs. Brigstone would be. He may have resolved to do as he wished, but that did not include provoking her criticism. Though the thought of breakfast aroused his hunger, he would not stay to eat. Time enough later for that, when he had sharpened his appetite by a brisk walk in the morning air.

Stopping by the back door, he drew on an pair of strong boots and let himself out into the garden and thence into the street behind.

It seemed all Aylsham was of the same mind. The street was already busy. There were people walking and on horseback. There were farmer's carts and the handcarts and wagons used by tradesmen to deliver their wares from door to door. No one, as it appeared, wished to be abed on such a morning. The inn chaise stood ready outside The Black Boys to take customers to Norwich. Even the horses looked alert and ready for the off. Few of the gentry of the town shared his liking for early walks, but many had sent their servants to the bakers to purchase fresh morning rolls. He could smell them, hot from the oven that Mr. Stipping and his apprentice would have lit not long after midnight. His stomach rumbled but he continued with resolution. If he stopped now, he might never get started again.

Sunshine is a sovereign way to raise the spirits and each person he passed greeted him merrily. The better sort raised their hats and bade him, 'Good morning, doctor. A fine day at last.' Artisans and tradesmen touched their hands to hat-brims or foreheads and called him 'sir' or 'master'. Servants bobbed curtseys or clumsy bows, careful to keep their eyes cast down. Only Peter's maid Anne, looking as pretty as the morning itself as she swept the path outside her master's shop, looked him full in the face. She smiled and wished him, 'A pleasant walk, Dr. Bascom, and a fine morning for it.'

Without thinking, he smiled at her in return and raised his hat. Then blushed and hurried on, uncomfortable that her beauty had drawn from him a response more suited to the mistress of a house than a servant-girl.

Leaving the busier part of the little town, Adam headed for the river. The Bure is no great stream, but its waters run clear and fast. Good fish, he knew, waited in the deeper pools for any angler skilled enough to tempt them. Strangers seemed always to expect the whole of the county to be flat meadows or marshlands. In this northern part of Norfolk, the landscape was more of a pattern of low hills and wide valleys. Here rivers flowed strongly enough to power a good many mills along their length.

The constant rain of recent days had swollen the streams still further. Now the Bure, although it retained its clear water, bustled along swiftly. Hidden rapids and obstacles dappled its surface, while fierce-looking dragonflies patrolled the banks. In the water meadows, sleek cattle watched Adam pass. The morning milking time was nearly upon them and the milkmaids would soon come to call them into the barns and yards. A herd of bullocks ran up to inspect him, unused to seeing anyone abroad at such an early hour. Then all scattered in con-sternation as he clapped his hands and shouted at them.

Inevitably, Adam's thoughts strayed again to that morning in April, as fine and windless as this, when he had purposed on a similar walk from his brother's home. That was the day that began the puzzle that taunted him still. The day he stumbled on the body of the arch-deacon, lying in the grass of the churchyard. Could it be only three months ago? So much had happened since. It seemed at least a year must have passed, but no; it must be three months more or less to the day.

As he walked, he tried to review what he had learned since then. He knew that the archdeacon had died from a blow to his head. A blow almost certainly caused by falling and striking the back of his head against a stone or part of a tomb-marker. Whether that one blow was the only cause of his death was unclear. He may have suffered an apoplexy at the same time, or shortly afterwards. His end may have been due in part to the effects of lying unconscious all night on cold, damp ground. The truth might never be known, for the body was duly buried some months ago.

He was almost sure that there had been no scuffle and no large group of people present. Both would have left signs. There were none. One other person might have been there. It was impossible to say.

No one had robbed the body or disturbed it after the fall. That argued against a footpad or the rascally constable. No weapon had been found. The archdeacon had not been struck on the head while standing upright. That too seemed beyond argument.

A heron sprang up from amongst the grasses at the edge of the river and flew away with a harsh cry. It had been hunting, Adam thought. If only he could also know where to pursue his quarry. All he could do was return again and again to what he knew, hoping to flush out something missed before.

The inquest had been arranged to record a verdict of accidental death, he told himself. Thanks to Mr. Wicken's visit, he knew why it had been so. He also knew why Dr. Ross's family had accepted the verdict so meekly. Mrs. Ross secretly feared her son might have been involved in some way. Everyone else, assured that there were no signs of murder or robbery, found the verdict quite satisfactory. The Bishop and the church authorities, he assumed, felt the same. Too much enquiry might stir up scandal, which no one wanted. Besides, the saddest part of the death of Archdeacon Ross was that no one mourned or missed him. People had soon forgotten their surprise at his death. When he lived, he had made himself universally disliked. In a few years, his memory would be altogether gone. So much he knew. Now, what yet remained to be explained?

Though his purpose had been to enjoy the beauty of the morning, in truth Adam had noticed almost nothing in the last quarter mile. He was so deep in his thoughts he might as well have been walking the streets of Norwich or pacing up and down in his room. Now he noticed on a sudden that he had already gone farther than he intended and must needs turn back. The way ahead was too overgrown for easy passage.

Turning back, he tried once again to direct his attention to the natural world about him: to the butterflies, and flowers they rested upon, and to the birds, his first love. It was useless. Within a dozen paces, his thoughts were back with those characters and events that now seemed to occupy his mind through most of his waking hours.

He still had no idea why Dr. Ross had been in Gressington churchyard. That, most of all, gnawed at him. Theories abounded, yet all were based on nothing but imagination. Hellfire clubs, Black Masses and blasphemous gatherings were nonsense, in his view. The stuff of excitable scribblers in cheap broadsheets, not sober reasoning. Thanks to Peter's words, Adam was almost certain the archdeacon had arranged to meet Constable Garnet. His own reasoning told him no actual meeting took place. What was the meeting for? Why did the constable fail to keep his rendezvous? Both were mysteries. Was the archdeacon so delayed the constable had already gone away? Did Garnet fear a trap? Did he come then see Mr. Harmsworthy, the magistrate, there with the archdeacon? Might he have assumed it was a trap and he was about to be arrested? He could not have known that Mr. Harmsworthy was there only by chance and he must have recognised him.

That started another thought. The meeting with Garnet was, presumably, meant to be secret. Yet Dr. Ross must have realised what would happen if the constable saw him arrive with the magistrate. In such a case, no informer would say or do anything that might incriminate him. When the Archdeacon's chaise suffered damage, was Harmsworthy's house the only place he could go? Might he not instead have taken the horse from between the shafts and ridden it? A man such as he seemed to be would hardly have cared whether that might leave a coachman with a long walk on a dark evening. Was there a coachman anyway? Adam was almost sure Mr. Harmsworthy had made no mention of one.

Adam's stomach growled, reminding him that he had yet to break his fast. That spurred his pace, but did little to calm the thoughts rushing through his mind. What was the Archdeacon's purpose in meeting Garnet? To gather information for his own reasons? To find some proof that his dreadful warnings of moral decay, so derided by most, were true after all? And why involve Mr. Harmsworthy? It seemed the Archdeacon had demanded, not a fresh horse to ride, nor the loan of a vehicle, but that Mr. Harmsworthy in person should take him to his meeting.

Were Dr. Ross and Mr. Harmsworthy in league in some way? Was Mr. Harmsworthy in league with Constable Garnet? Garnet had been confident that he could aid the smugglers without being suspected. Worse, he could also carry on his own 'trade' in taking spies and letters to and from ships offshore. Was there someone powerful to protect him? Then there were the pornographic books Mr. Wicken had found in Garnet's house. Was this yet another business venture? Looked at in this way, the man must have been supremely confident of his own skill in evading the authorities. Either that or, more likely, to have found some means of persuading the local representatives of justice to look the other way.

Adam shook his head. He was becoming as mired in speculation as everyone else. Without more facts, he could answer none of these questions. Yet Garnet and Dr. Ross were both dead. Mr. Wicken had assured him he knew nothing of the archdeacon's purpose in going to Gressington. And now Mr. Harmsworthy was gone away, none seemed to know where.

Time to lay it aside, he told himself yet again. His priority must be to see whether he could start a process of reconciliation between Mrs. Ross and her son. The young man had no part in his father's death, of that he was sure. If Mr. Jempson could discover where to find him, Adam might send a message in which he would detail his mother's poor health. Add the remorse and guilt she felt for her previous inaction and it would be a hard-hearted son who refused to come to his mother's help. The only conclusion he could reach today was that until Mr. Jempson received word of Adam wishing to talk with him, he could go no further.

Adam had left his house set on enjoying a good walk on a fine morning. He had walked even further than he intended on that glorious morning, yet returned home in sombre mood. Despite all his inner reasoning and analysis, he was no further forward. Only the scent of a fine breakfast restored a little of his spirits. As luck would have it, Mrs. Brigstone was busy somewhere in the house, so he managed to slip up to his room. By dressing in a more suitable morning gown before she saw him, he could avoid any remarks about his unseemly appearance.

AN UNLAMENTED DEATH

Chapter Twenty-six

The Quaker's Daughter

Thursday, 5 July 1792, Aylsham

ADAM WAS TO GET HIS WISH TO TALK with Mr. Jempson sooner than he thought. After his frustrating walk the morning before, he had given his mind to business for the rest of the day. He dealt with correspondence, and he composed a suitable announcement to place in several local newspapers. All physicians, apothecaries and surgeons needed to advertise. Indeed, some newspapers might carry almost a whole column of such announcements. The business of tending to sickness was crowded. Apothecaries like Lassimer at least served a proper apprenticeship. Others merely announced their self-taught abilities. Such were the many barber-surgeons, local midwives, drug peddlers, and sundry charlatans. Amongst these, the skills of the huckster often counted for more than medical knowledge.

To Adam's satisfaction however, society now expected the modern physician to be a proven man of science and learning. Physicians needed to establish their credentials as members of the upper, educated classes as well as clinicians. His own university career was impeccable and would stand him in good stead. Yet he must still advertise his services and acquaint the neighbourhood with what manner of person he was. He had written and rewritten with care, stressing his qualifications first, then his practical skills. Some physicians aimed to treat all types of sickness amongst a given group of people. Others hoped to do better by specialising. Based on recent events, Adam decided to pursue this latter course. His announcement thus emphasised his skills in treating all manner of nervous and melancholic complaints. Melancholy had become known as 'the English disease' through its sheer prevalence, so it should offer excellent opportunities.

Tired by his concentration, Adam had then gone to bed early. He hoped for another fine day on the morrow. If so, he would, he resolved, once more begin with a bracing walk in the fresh air. Only this time he would set aside his puzzles and focus on Nature's beauties.

Sadly, it was not to be. It seemed the weather gods had exhausted their meagre store of sunshine for the time being and Thursday's dawn brought dull and misty weather once again. Still, that matched his mood. All the excitement from his time in Norwich had drained away. His review of the few sure facts about Archdeacon Ross's death had brought no fresh insights. His speculations, far greater in number, only convinced him that it would most likely prove impossible to resolve.

Such sour thoughts took away his appetite, whether for breakfast or for the impending consultation with Mrs. Bremerson. This wealthy widow of the neighbourhood showed a pleasing eagerness to request expensive visits and treatment. Yet this was matched by the inventiveness with which she concocted fresh ailments to bring to him. The reality was that she enjoyed rude health, despite being now in her fortieth year, as she told him one day, with a look of such archness that he was hard put not to laugh aloud. He would have placed her nearer sixty, despite her made-up face and the fashionable clothes she had sent from London. Whatever the truth, she paid her account promptly, which was rare in these parts. Even better, she sang his praises to all who would listen, and was thus the kind of patient most doctors would envy him for having.

Usually she called him to her large house on the road towards Cromer. Today she had sent word that she was visiting friends in the town, so would come to him instead. Once seated in his consulting room, she kept him talking of trifles while she took note of the room and its decorations. Her friends would have a full account later of at least part of their doctor's house and his taste in furniture and fitments. Now, at last, she was ready for business.

Her stomach, she told him was greatly upset. Indeed, she had convinced herself that she had contracted some dangerous nausea from eating a dish of jugged hare. It was presented to her, she told him, by 'that dear Lady Nestonbury'. Although the lady's heart was kind, she thought her chef, being French, was seeking to destroy the British upper classes. His method was to add some diabolical poison to the food he prepared. She had been awake all night after eating the hare and had since felt nauseous on several occasions. Would the doctor need, perhaps, to take her pulse or—here she giggled—place his hand where he might feel how distended her stomach was? Could he offer her something to ward off the effects of whatever evil potion had been in the food?

Dr. Bascom did not need to accept her invitation to leave his chair and venture closer, it seemed, nor did he need to lay his hands on her. A few questions would suffice. She pouted at his words, but assented. Thus she revealed that she had eaten almost the whole hare.

'It was quite delicious, you know,' she said. 'The poison must have been one of those undetectable by the victim. The kind the Borgia family invented.'

She had washed down the hare with one or two glasses (more like four or five) of an excellent Portuguese wine Mr. Haston, that paragon amongst Norwich vintners, sold.

Her response to his last question affirmed his diagnosis.

'I accompanied the hare with a few simple vegetables: early peas and carrots, a little cabbage,' she said. 'Oh, and new season potatoes, of course, and then some apple jelly made with the last fruits from the store. Nothing more, unless you reckon some stewed quinces and a small handful of walnuts.'

In the end, Mrs. Bremerson was sent away as happy as she could be since Adam had remained in his seat throughout the consultation. He gave her a receipt for some medicine for indigestion to take to 'that nice Mr. Lassimer' down the street. Then added the advice to eat lightly for some while, until 'the poison' should have cleared from her system.

'But doctor,' she complained, 'I eat like the tiniest bird! If I eat less, I shall waste away. You can see how thin I am.'

The doctor could see nothing of the sort, but was too polite, and too aware of her worth to his practice, to do other than nod assent.

It was shortly after noon that Hannah, his parlourmaid, disturbed her master's reading to announce that a Mr. Jempson had called. Would the doctor be able to receive him? His book forgotten, Adam sent her on the instant to ask Mr. Jempson to join him.

As the grave-looking Quaker entered, it occurred to Adam that he had not seen the gentleman at his best on the only other occasion of meeting him. Even after he had returned with Adam to his house, he had seemed pale and shaken by his ordeal. His clothes too bore signs of him being thrown to the ground by his attackers.

Today, however, he was in fine fettle and quite recovered from any after effects. His clothing might be in the sober style required by his Quaker beliefs, but even the most cursory glance revealed the fineness of the cloth. That and the skill of cutting and sewing together spoke of tailoring of the highest excellence. The man standing now before Adam, holding out his hand with every expression of delight, could not be taken for anything but a most prosperous merchant.

They exchanged greetings and compliments and Adam, remembering his duties as host, ascertained that Mr. Jempson would prefer to take a cup of coffee to a glass of punch. They engaged in the usual small talk of people who liked one another, yet knew little of the other's background. Then, after Hannah brought a pot of fine coffee and cups, and it was tasted and pronounced delicious, it was time to get down to business.

'I apologise for being absent when thy messenger called at my Norwich house,' Mr. Jempson began. 'I was away on business in Lynn. I have been fortunate enough to conclude that business a little earlier than expected. Thus I determined to return home via Aylsham. My daughter is busy arranging the new house to her satisfaction and desires me to give my approval.

'To be plain, my friend. I would not dare to do otherwise. My daughter, Elizabeth, has the kindest of hearts, but greater determination than any man I know. Whatever she sets her mind to, that she accomplishes without fail. It is a brave fellow who questions her choices—and a foolhardy one who seeks to change what she has done. She has cared for me since her dear mother died. Now she is set on retaining that task, though I have urged her on many occasions to seek a suitable husband. I can easily afford to have as many servants as I want and my wants are few. She need not fear for my well-being, should she set up a home of her own.

'My man sent word to Lynn that thou hadst called and wished to see me urgently, but I had left before his message reached me. Fortunately, he had sent a similar message to Aylsham, in case I made a detour on the route back to Norwich. That message awaited me when I arrived last evening. Thus here I am.'

Adam's impatience had been mounting steadily through this preamble. Yet he had taken care to smile and nod and show no sign, he hoped, of the turmoil within his mind. Now, when Mr. Jempson paused, he could contain himself no longer and moved at once to the heart of the matter.

'When we met last,' he said, 'you were returning from Lynn, as now. You also said that, on your outward journey, you had been escorting a young couple travelling there. The man, you told the clerical gentleman who was amongst our party, had recently joined your Society. Before that, he had been a member of the established church. Was his name perhaps Mr. William Ross? It is most important that I know.'

Mr. Jempson appeared stunned, both by the nature of the question and the abruptness with which Adam presented it. 'Mr. William Ross? No, his name is not William or Ross. Why shouldst thou have thought so?'

A third person, had one been present in the room just then, could not have avoided laughing aloud at the sight the two presented. Mr. Jempson looked bewildered. Adam, betraying in his face the most acute disappointment, had thrown himself back into his chair and clutched the arms as if his life depended on it. For a moment, neither moved, then Mr. Jempson recovered himself and leaned forward.

'There is a story here, friend. Unfortunately, thou hast determined to start it part way through. Now, return to the beginning and tell me why it should be so vital for thee to know about this Mr. William Ross. I cannot offer thee my aid, which I am most ready to do, unless I know what thy purpose is in seeking this man out.'

210

Sick at heart as he was, Adam could see the sense in what Mr. Jempson suggested. As briefly as he could, he explained all. First how he had found Dr. Ross's body and become concerned that the man's death was too easily attributed to chance. Then why he was now convinced that his fears on that score were unfounded. He decided not to stray too far into the detail of Mr. Wicken and the raid on the smugglers. Mr. Jempson could have no interest in that affair, beyond the one common to all who traded by sea. Instead, he turned to the messages from Mrs. Ross and his meeting with her in Norwich.

'She is a most unhappy woman, sir, and this is affecting her health,' Adam said. 'It is my firm opinion that her remorse is wholly sincere. All I have heard, from several sources, confirms that her late husband had a most domineering nature. He would have suffered no arguments from a mere woman. He was, to be plain, as great a tyrant at home as he was a demagogue and a ranter in the pulpit. I have told her that she bears no great guilt, for she could not have changed his mind whatever she had done. Still, she is unable to forgive herself for the way her son, William, was treated and her refusal at the time to take his part. Now, poor woman, she believes she has lost him for ever. That loss, Mr. Jempson, is tearing her heart in two.'

'This is indeed a most unhappy tale, friend,' Mr. Jempson replied. 'I knew of Dr. Ross, as all did who are of our Society—aye, and many others of a dissenting cast of mind as well. Of his personal nature, I am ignorant, though I can well believe what thou hast said. In his public life, he was bitter and cruel in his enmity towards all who were not of his mind. Where he might harm us, he did. Where he might sow rancour and stir up hatred towards us, that he did too. When the news of his death reached me—a death by accident, as all believed—I felt only relief. No, a little shame too, for no man should rejoice in the death of another, however base that person may have been.

'Be assured, friend, that no Quaker had any hand in this matter. That is most certain, for we reject violence towards any, let alone causing death. Our young men will not fight in any war nor become soldiers or sailors. However much we might have feared and disliked Mr. Ross, none would have lifted a hand against him.'

'I do believe that, sir,' Adam said, 'and that is not why I have told you this tale. Mrs. Ross told me that her son had confessed to his father that he had formed an attachment to a young woman. Now he wished to marry her as soon as he might be able to support a wife. For him to have said so much would, as she explains it, have infuriated her husband. He demanded to choose whom his children should marry, without regard to their wishes in the matter. Yet worse was to come, for the young lady concerned is, it seems, of a dissenting family. It was this news that provided the final provocation. It caused Dr. Ross to disinherit his only son and forbid him the house or any contact with his own family.'

'And so,' Mr. Jempson said, 'thou didst link this in thy mind with my tale of accompanying two young people to Lynn. Thou didst believe that these were young Mr. Ross and his new bride.'

'I did,' Adam replied. He felt quite foolish now.

'But friend, if young William knew he must wait to speak of marriage to the young lady on whom he had set his heart before, would it not still be important to hold his peace? When he told his father of his wishes, he was still the heir. He might be clear in his own mind that God was not calling him to the ministry of his father's church. But surely he hoped to find another course in life suitable to one of his background; one which would provide a basis for marriage? If he so antagonised his father as to cut himself off from family and fortune, where was he to earn a living to support himself, let alone a wife? To have married in that state, even if the girl's parents would have permitted it, would have been unthinkable. Besides, though thou hast not

212

said how old the young lady is, did I not gather from thy story that Mr. William Ross had only just completed his first year at the university? How old must he be? 19? 20? He is not of age to marry without his parent's consent. He must have known that would not be given.'

Mr. Jempson paused at that point, then broke into loud and hearty mirth. 'My dear friend,' he said, when his laughter had subsided enough to allow speech. 'How I wish thou couldst see thyself! Thou art the perfect picture of an errant schoolboy! One who has failed to con his lesson and must now stand to endure the punishment of the master and the derision of all his fellows.'

'How could I have been so stupid?' Adam said. 'I was so sure I knew all and would be able to help Mrs. Ross recover her son. I see now how what few wits I have were taken up. It was with the most vain imagining of her gratitude and the way that I would shine in others' eyes for my intelligence in bringing facts together to produce an answer.'

'Thou hast learned a most valuable lesson, friend. It is pride that so often leads to each of us straying from the path of reason and truth. That is, in part, why members of our society will have nothing to do with ranks or titles. Never believe that thou dost deserve to be set above other men in some way. By doing so, thou wilt open the path to every kind of thoughtless and presumptuous action.'

'It is a bitter lesson indeed,' Adam said.

'Nay, say not so. Only thy pride has been hurt. Thy purpose—to help a fellow creature who is suffering great pain and unhappiness—is noble indeed. Besides, thou art not wholly wrong in thy reckoning. I may well be able to get word to the young man you mention. If so, he will be urged to set aside his bitterness and hurt and hasten to be reconciled to his mother. That too is a noble purpose and one I will be most willing to assist. Perhaps, between us, thou and I may even be able to repair a small amount of the harm let loose upon the world by Dr. Ross. Like you, I must hold him to blame for all that has come about. He is beyond redemption in this world, it is true. Let us hope that God may yet be able to bring about what to us seems impossible and restore him to a state of grace.'

'You can help?' Adam was almost afraid to put his hope into words.

Mr. Jempson spoke carefully, unwilling to raise greater hopes or certainty than the facts warranted. 'I mentioned my daughter, Elizabeth. Earlier in the year, she went north to Edgbaston, a village near to Birmingham, to visit her aunt. Many of our Society have settled in that area. It is becoming a centre of industry and innovation in manufacture, and there is also a need for those who can finance new ventures. We of the Society believe the Creator has placed a spark of His Divine Light in everyone, rich or poor, young or old, male or female. It is our most solemn duty to use that gift to live a good life. We also hold the education of all those in our Society to be essential, so that this Light may be enhanced and used to best effect. Some of this takes place each Sunday in our meeting, as we sit in silence to wait upon God and the inner promptings of the Light. Men need no priests or ceremonies, friend, since God speaks plain to each one in the silence of his heart, if he will only listen.

'When Elizabeth returned, she spoke eagerly of all she had seen and done. In particular, she had made it her business to attend a series of lectures given by Dr. Priestley. He is a man of great learning and science and a firm favourite amongst all in those parts who value the search for truth and understanding. She also said that she had met another young woman at those lectures and recognised her from the Sunday meeting she had been to with her aunt. Being both of the same background, these two girls sought each other's company and arranged to meet at each lecture. In a short time, they became firm friends and, as is the way of the young, happily talked together of what was dearest to their hearts.

'Thus Elizabeth learned that a young student from Oxford had been coming to Birmingham whenever he could. He also wished to listen to the many men of science and industry who give lectures there. That itself was unusual, for those who have access to the universities, as we do not, often show little interest in any kind of study. It seemed this young man was also of quite slender means, his father keeping his own hand tight on the purse-strings. He could not be absent long from his college and to purchase passage on the stage for the distance from Oxford to Birmingham and back, even outside, is no small thing. Seeing his eagerness for knowledge, coupled too often with hunger, one or two of the gentlemen took pity on him and offered him food and accommodation in their own dwellings.

'So also had this young woman's father done. The young man had proved a most welcome guest. He was modest and polite in all things and eager to listen to anything of the way of learning his host might relate. It is unusual amongst the young, friend, to find one more willing to listen than speak—aye, and amongst the old too, my family would tell you.

'These visits had begun before Christmas. By early spring they were near weekly occurrences. The daughter of the house and the student had spoken often and had, as is the way of things, come to develop an affection. In public, he was always most careful of her reputation. If he escorted her to the lecture, he took care to sit apart from her, lest any should take their amity amiss. To the world, he was no more than a young man repaying her father's kindness by acting as protector to a young woman going abroad.

'By now, friend, thou must know that I suspect this student to be none other than the Mr. William Ross thou hast spoken of. My daughter has maintained her correspondence with her friend. I will at once ask her to write and enquire whether we are correct in assuming his identity. If we are, the friend may well know where he is. In his pain and need, he may even have fled where he received kindness before and be living somewhere in Birmingham. I do not know.'

Adam would have piled praise and gratitude on his guest for his thoughtfulness, but the other would not allow it.

'No, friend. I deserve nothing as yet. Thou dost not even know if any good may come of this. Even if it does, give thy thanks rather to whatever power thou thinkest directs events in this world for bringing it about. Thou art not in my debt in any way. In comparison with thy rescue of me from the thieves and the kindness thou didst show me afterwards, I have done nothing.'

The two men talked a little of other matters after that, but it was not long before Mr. Jempson took his leave and hurried to find his daughter. He left Adam torn between hope and fear. Might he at last be able to find Mr. William Ross? And, if he could solve at least one of the mysteries involved in the archdeacon's death, might he not solve more?

Chapter Twenty-seven

Back to Holt

Thursday, 12 July 1792, Aylsham to Holt

ADAM SET OUT IN THE EARLY MORNING, intending to arrive in Briston before noon. An idea had come to him earlier that week and he was delighted that he had been able to arrange matters as he wished. Sometimes, even for him, being alone in his house save for the servants had became irksome. The evenings in particular opened before him as long tunnels, too often devoid of interest or amusement. By day he could busy himself with his patients. His practice was growing swiftly, thanks to several recommendations. Yet, once the last piece of business was complete and dinner eaten, he found little to occupy his mind that was pleasant or relaxing.

Adam had even been cheated of long talks with his friend, Lassimer. He too was becoming a busy man. So much so that he had persuaded his silent partner and nominal master apothecary, Mr. Gerstone, to employ an apprentice to assist him in the business. A suitable lad could probably be found locally. Though Mr. Gerstone would still be master for the purposes of the Worshipful Company, Lassimer would be in charge as the most senior. Fresh discussion with the Master of the Worshipful Company had born fruit. He had agreed to ask the Council to bring forward Peter's entry to the freedom of his profession by six months.

As a result, Lassimer was committing much of his scant free time to these changes. He had started talking with several lads seeking apprenticeships and arranging the lodgings, for an apprentice would sleep in the attic of his house.

Much of this had begun before Adam had left for Norwich and he realised he had been naïve to assume it would be completed before he returned. He had imagined taking dinner with his friend at least once or twice most weeks. It was not to be. Lassimer was so often busy in the shop or out on the road that he was usually too tired for company of any kind.

It was while mulling over this sad turn to events that Adam had first conceived the plan he was now on his way to carry out. What he intended would allow him to lessen his loneliness by visiting his brother, while combining business and pleasure along the way. He would ride first to attend on a patient of good standing in Briston. Then he would discharge his promise to Capt. Mimms in Holt to keep him informed of new developments. Finally he would travel on to Trundon Hall, where he might spend a day or so with his brother's family before returning to Aylsham.

He had thus written letters to Briston, Holt and Trundon Hall. Mr. Kalloway, an elderly patient at Briston, replied that he would be delighted by a visit. Alas, Adam feared only death would cure the condition that troubled the old man. He was only able to bring some relief from the pain. As before, he would renew his patient's supplies of the powerful draught that alone gave the respite of sleep. In too many cases, treatments for serious conditions produced unpleasant effects such as violent purging or vomiting. That strong disease required strong cures was the conventional view. Yet he had often seen men and women suffering from their last illness hastened to death as much by their treatment as by the disease. He sometimes wondered whether milder doses given less frequently, but over a longer period, might work as well. If the patient was destined to die anyway, was it not better to allow his or her last days or weeks to be as comfortable as they could be? Why seek to prolong a life attended only by violent suffering?

Determining to test out his ideas by experiment, he had therefore selected a few suitable patients. To these he applied lower doses of the normal remedies, accompanied by suitable draughts to kill pain or induce sleep. Mr. Kalloway was such a patient. Study of the detailed notes on each patient that he kept in a ledger had quickly convinced him that his approach was sound. Mr. Kalloway, in particular, suffered far less pain. He even enjoyed some reasonable measure of restful sleep. It remained to be seen whether his progress towards death would be any faster as a result. Yet Adam was content that he had a grateful patient and could feel he had provided some aid in a hopeless situation.

Capt. Mimms had also responded eagerly to Adam's request that he might be received later today. Indeed, he had gone further. Not only was Adam invited to dine with the old mariner, but Capt. Mimms insisted he should stay at his house for the night, proceeding to Trundon Hall the next day.

'It would be a sad thing for you to arrive to greet your brother and his family so late in the day,' he wrote. 'I am only too familiar with the state of tiredness and disarray that accompanies a lengthy ride. You will also be wearied by the additional burden of attending a patient along the way. I am alone in a house far too large for my needs. Several bedrooms stand empty and it would be my honour to offer you such accommodation as I can. Besides, I can also offer you some diverting entertainment. Not perhaps up to the standard of the city, but enough to while away an hour or two most pleasantly.'

It seemed a troop of travelling players were to set up in a barn behind one of the inns in Holt. There they would present plays for the amusement of the local populace. Performances would take place on Thursday, Friday and Saturday. After that, the troop would pack up their things and move on to the next town.

Adam loved the theatre. Naturally, this show would fall well below the standards he had enjoyed in Oxford, Glasgow and at the Theatre Royal in Norwich. The latter was a large building, able to contain a thousand in the audience it was said. Thus it attracted many of the finest players from the grand theatres in London and Dublin. He had even seen Mrs. Siddons on its stage. Still, most of the actors and actresses who were now famous had started out in travelling troops, such as the one setting up in Holt. What matter if the scenery was poorly painted and the costumes worn and patched? The plays on offer were often farces or comic entertainments well suited to an audience that would include rustics as well as a smattering of the better sort. Adam was well-pleased at Capt. Mimms' suggestion and at once sent word that he was happy to accept.

Adam rode along with a light heart and a keen sense of anticipation for the days ahead. Only the weather, as so often this year, was glum.

After he arrived at the house in Briston, Adam examined Mr. Kalloway carefully. He listened to his descriptions of his state of health, noting all down to add to his patient ledger later. Even though he knew there was no hope, he felt it only right to bestow his attention as readily on Mr. Kalloway as on any other patient. The old man seemed to take comfort from such care and it should on no account be denied.

Even so, his visit lasted little more than an hour. The effort of talking had so worn out his patient that it would have been unkind to continue further. Thus he was in good time for dinner with Capt. Mimms.

He found his host in fine spirits and eager for news. Adam related his well-practised version of what he had learned from Mr. Wicken, leaving out those parts which he felt honour-bound to keep secret. To this he added an account of his talk with Lassimer. Capt. Mimms agreed at once. The facts all pointed to Constable Garnet as the person the archdeacon had arranged to meet in Gressington churchyard on the night of his death. Lassimer and Adam were correct about the constable.

'There's a rogue for you,' Capt. Mimms said. 'It is well known that many a parish constable in a coastal village thinks it prudent to turn his eyes away from his neighbours' nocturnal activities. Some may even accept payment from the gangs to warn them when Revenue men are to be abroad. But few, I think, are as avaricious and greedy as Garnet. To think he was not only staying silent about the smugglers, but also using them for his own purposes. Of course he will say he did not know the manner of persons he was doubtless paid well to convey in secret. Still it takes little enough thought to fix upon the most likely answer. I declare he must have known, or guessed. That makes him a traitor, doctor, as well as a most cunning criminal.'

'I agree with you,' Adam said. 'He must deny such knowledge if he seeks to avoid the terrible punishment the law lays down for treason. He knew he would hang anyway. He did not wish to suffer worse. It also explains why the wretch was willing to fight—aye, to kill too—in his effort to escape.'

For a while, both men sat in silence, preoccupied with their thoughts about Constable Garnet. Then Adam sat erect and gave a loud exclamation. 'Damme! There it is. That I should have been so dull of wit not to have seen it before!'

'Calm yourself, my young friend,' Capt. Mimms said, 'for I dare hope I may call you such after enjoying your company once again.'

'Of course you may,' Adam replied, 'and I hope you will allow me the same level of intimacy in our dealings together. But when I tell you what I have grasped only this moment, you may regret claiming friendship to any as stupid as I must be.'

'Never!' Capt. Mimms declared. 'Now, pray tell me at once what has so disturbed your composure.'

'It has just become clear to me why Garnet did not fulfil his arrangement to meet with Dr. Ross. It is simplicity itself.'

'Not to me,' Capt. Mimms said. 'I cannot guess.'

'He did fulfil it—or tried to!' Adam cried. 'What do we know of Garnet? That beside his greed and contempt for all law and decency, he is cunning. He would not walk calmly into the churchyard and greet the archdeacon like a friend. No, he would most likely take care to go to the churchyard before the appointed time. There he would conceal himself to spy out the land before showing his face. Recall that the hour of their meeting was set for late in the day. That would make it easier to hide somewhere about.'

Capt. Mimms stared, but did not speak, so Adam plunged onwards. 'I imagine he had instructed Dr. Ross to come alone. He was taking some risk in revealing himself, though I expect he assumed the archdeacon would not know him. He may even have muffled his face to avoid recognition, should he ever encounter the man again.'

Adam paused again. His brain was racing ahead of his speech. He needed a moment or so to arrange his thoughts sufficiently to aid explanation. 'Dr. Ross was late—of course he was! His chaise was damaged and he had to seek help. Mr. Harmsworthy told me the archdeacon was wild to reach the churchyard, fearing he might be too late for whatever he purposed there. Garnet must have become apprehensive at the delay. If so, he would be even less willing to take further risk of being seen by any save the one he intended to meet. He had too much to lose. The smugglers' grand landing of contraband, and his own arrangement to take those people out to a ship, were to happen shortly. They were only delayed through concern over the archdeacon's death and the enquiries that might result throughout the area.'

Another pause. 'Now think, my good friend. What did he see?'

Capt. Mimms stared at him, his face a picture of total incomprehension. 'I have no idea,' he said. 'How is it possible to know what might have served to frighten him off?'

'But we do know,' Adam cried. 'We have known almost since the start. He saw Archdeacon Ross enter the churchyard, and he also saw that he was not alone. He had the magistrate with him. To a criminal mind, that would suggest only one thing. Dr. Ross had betrayed him and planned to have him seized by Mr. Harmsworthy and taken into custody. Garnet failed to meet the archdeacon because he feared arrest. It is as simple as that.'

'So he waited until Mr. Harmsworthy left,' Capt. Mimms said, 'then stole up on the unfortunate Dr. Ross and took his revenge.'

'No. That I do not think, nor is there any evidence to suggest it. Far more likely that Garnet would try to get away as fast as possible. I doubt that he had given his name to Dr. Ross when the meeting was arranged. He would specify only a time and place. Perhaps they had some token or password by which each could identify himself to the other. So long as Garnet could remain unseen, he was safe. You can be certain he would determine to have no further dealings with Dr. Ross, but there was no need to kill him. His own carefulness and suspicion had saved him, as it must have done many times before.'

Another piece had fallen into place. Yet, once his momentary euphoria had passed, Adam admitted that it was but a minor piece of the puzzle. It led to no further revelations. Nonetheless, he and Capt.

Mimms ended their meal happy and the older man was more than warm in his admiration for Adam's powers of deduction.

Chapter Tweny-eight

A Theatrical Interlude

That same evening, The Feathers Inn yard, Holt

IT CAN BE IMAGINED IN WHAT A FINE MOOD Adam and Captain Mimms set out to walk the short distance to the temporary theatre where the evening's entertainment was to take place. Many other people were taking the same direction, so the players were going to have a good audience. Such travelling troops relied on the box office takings for all their needs. Most of the actors were not paid. Their reward came by an occasional 'benefit performance' at which the takings would be theirs.

The programme, Capt. Mimms had explained, was typical fare for an evening in a small town. Nothing of the grand tragedies or solemn historical plays you might find at a city theatre. Here the diet was one attuned to a less sophisticated audience. It was also more likely to be within the compass of the players themselves.

Tonight they would begin with a spoken monologue on the theme of the trials of love. That would doubtless be proclaimed in a most affecting voice by whichever of the actresses was deemed the prettiest. Then there was to be a 'comic entertainment of dancing, performed by two famous dancers lately arrived from Italy'. Adam doubted these would have come from further than Cambridge or Ipswich, but kept that to himself.

The main dish of this theatrical feast would then follow. A 'grand melodrama, entitled Forkbeard's Curse or The Pirate's Revenge upon a Villain'. That should allow for a good deal of the kind of stage fighting and effects with fireworks for which such companies were renowned. Finally, the evening would end with a farce. Today it was to be 'The Contrived Maidenhead', and would naturally involve a comely young whore and a rich old fool. She would convince him of her virginal innocence to raise the price of her favours. Meanwhile, she would be entertaining herself with several handsome young blades behind his back. Everyone would be able to guess the plot in advance, but it would matter little. The real purpose of the play would be to allow for a mass of double meanings and bawdy humour. Adam was expecting a fine evening of entertainment.

The opening monologue, The Trial of Love, was indeed delivered by a pretty girl. Adam judged her to be scarce fifteen years old. Yet she already showed signs of the dark-haired beauty she would doubtless become. It may even have been her first appearance on the stage, for her voice at the start was barely loud enough to carry more than halfway down the room.

Some wag called out, 'Speak up, me darling! You make a damn pretty picture, but we'd like to hear the words as well.'

But if he hoped thus to put her out of countenance, this girl was made of sterner stuff. 'You shout loud enough, sir,' she called back, 'but I dare say you ain't pretty! Now let me get on and have done with your nonsense.'

The audience erupted in laughter and cheers.

The girl, much emboldened by their support, now spoke out loudly, winking at the audience as she did so. The end of her performance was thus signalled by loud applause—mixed with many shouted suggestions of how certain patrons would like to make trial of her love in particular.

The dancers came on next, dressed in costumes doubtless last used for Harlequin and Colombina. Those clothes, and the dark hair of both man and woman, were probably the limit of their claim to have 'lately arrived from Italy'. And if their dancing lacked somewhat in grace, they went to it with such enthusiasm and enjoyment that they too won the audience over. Their act was ended with wild applause. During her bows, Colombina made sure each was deep enough to allow the better class of patrons, seated in the front rows, a fine view of her firmly-rounded breasts.

Now came the melodrama, which the most experienced of the players undertook. The first scene took place in the secret lair of Forkbeard, a notorious pirate. Forkbeard himself entered, telling the pirate with him that a ship of the Royal Navy had trapped and destroyed his pirate vessel. Thus he must now flee to save his own life. At those words, two sailors entered, led by a dashing young officer, who called on Forkbeard to surrender in the King's name. A fight ensued between pirate and officer. At first, Forkbeard seemed to be winning. He even managed to wound the officer by a sudden trick (loud boos and hisses from the audience). Yet the officer recovered and fought back, while the sailor accompanying him put the second pirate to flight. At length, the officer darted at Forkbeard and ran him through. The pirate chief fell (huzzas on all sides) and the young officer declared that the seas were now safe for English ships again. Finally, he instructed the sailor with him to see Forkbeard properly buried. He might be a villain and a pirate, the officer said, but he had been born an Englishman and deserved respect (loud cries of agreement).

The second scene opened with the sailor left to bury Forkbeard ransacking his room, in hope of finding treasure. All he found was an old box, too light to contain gold or jewels. As he began to open it, he started back in alarm: Forkbeard was not dead!

Raising himself on one arm, the pirate chief branded the sailor a thief and a villain, ready to stoop even to robbing the dead. Pointing a shaking hand, he pronounced a curse on him, saying that if he opened the box he was holding, he would die a foul death. For a moment, the sailor stood in amazement. Then he leapt forward, drew his knife and stabbed Forkbeard to the heart. Finally, declaring he gave no credence to curses and such nonsense, he rushed from the room.

The second act followed after an interval, in which the sounds of scenery moving could be heard from behind the curtain. When the curtain rose, it was no surprise to find the location had moved to a room in England. Here a pert doxy was telling her mother, an amazingly ugly hag, how she had entranced a young fool of a gentleman into making her his mistress. All that stood in the way of a fine life of wealth and leisure was her wretched sailor husband. She always hoped he would fail to return from his voyages, but she suspected him to be an arrant coward who took good care to avoid danger of any kind. Now, she declared, he should not spoil her plans. At that, she pulled a small bottle from her pocket and showed it to her mother. It contained, she said, a powerful poison that she had obtained from the apothecary by telling him her home was overrun with rats. If her husband returned again, she planned to drop some into his drink as soon as she could.

At that moment, the door opened, revealing the sailor last seen killing Forkbeard. In a loud aside, the doxy exclaimed that this was her husband, who had once again returned, damn him! This would be the last time. At once, she turned back to the sailor, all affection and attention. She was overjoyed, she told him, that he was home with her again. Had he brought her a present?

Her husband then put Forkbeard's box on the table and told her that he won it in a fight to the death with a powerful and notorious pirate (loud cries of 'liar!' from all sides). Unfortunately, all he had found inside was an old book of parchment, written in some strange, foreign tongue. Opening the box, he now took out the book and showed it to her, saying he could see no value in it.

His wife at once branded him a fool. Were there not learned men eager to buy worthless books and papers, so long as they were old? All they had to do was to find a way of letting several such people know of this book, then sell it to the highest bidder. At once, her husband was full of resolve. Saying he had the perfect one in mind, he left to speak to the local rector, whom he described as an old fool much given to fancies of that sort. If he did not want the book, or could not afford their price, he would assuredly know who could. As he left the room, the curtain came down again.

This time, the gap between scenes was short and the curtain rose on the same room. The wife was now revealed in the arms of a foppish young man, lavishing kisses and caresses on him. After a moment, the lover broke away from her hold, announcing that his parents were set on him marrying some dull girl. It was just because she had a fortune, whereas he would far rather marry the woman now before him. It was clear that she had not told him she was married already.

In another aside, the faithless wife now told the audience that this young fool was better than nothing. Yet she doubted that he would stay out of debt long enough to give her the life she wanted. She would therefore help him spend his new wife's money, then find another protector as quickly as she might. Spotting the pirate's box on the table, she asked the fop if he knew of anyone interested in old books and the like.

He told her that his tutor at the university—an old dodderer who thought himself a great scholar of the occult—would be wild for such

229

an object. Seeing an opportunity, the sailor's wife told him to send the man to her. She had something that he would pay handsomely for. It was a strange book full of secret writing 'a sailor she knew' had brought back for her as a curiosity. Turning once more to the audience, she declared that she knew well she could dispose of the book for far more money than her husband. Once she had rid herself of him, that money would be hers. Her current lover had proved to be less generous than she hoped, once he had from her what he wanted. She would thus use the money to set herself up in a fine house and attract richer prey.

The final act opened again in the sailor's house. Entering, the sailor told the audience that he had agreed to sell the box and the book to the rector for the sum of twenty pounds. The rector would soon arrive bringing the money, but he would tell his wife the sum agreed was only ten pounds. The rest would afford him plenty of grog. It would also buy the favours of young Nancy at 'The Ship Inn'. She, he declared, was as fancy a young piece as he had ever set his eyes upon and far more attractive to him than his complaining wife.

This same wife now entered from the other side of the stage. She too made an aside to the audience. She had sold the box and book to the young fop's tutor for the sum of thirty pounds, which he had promised to bring her shortly. Seeing her husband, she tried first to induce him to leave, so that she might meet the tutor alone. He, of course, was expecting his own visitor and refused to budge, trying instead to persuade her to go out from the house.

After some argument, husband and wife sat down with their backs to one another. Now there came a thunderous knocking at the door and two men came in, both obviously irate.

These were the rector and the tutor, who had met in the lane outside. Eager to draw applause from a fellow enthusiast, each explained to the other about their intended purchases. Thus they found that the couple were in the process of selling the same object twice. Now they had come to demand satisfaction. They had sent for the constable to take both husband and wife before a magistrate.

While the sailor blamed all on his wife, saying he had not known of her treachery, she slipped from the room. In her absence, the sailor next tried to set the two antiquarians to bidding against one another for the box and book, but they refused. At length the wife returned, bearing a tray with three cups on it. Affecting a tone of sweet reason, she said she was sure it was all a misunderstanding. If they would be willing to sit and refresh themselves with a glass of her punch, matters might be resolved to everyone's satisfaction.

Her husband, still angry, snatched up the glass and drained it at a gulp. Rector and tutor also took glasses, meaning to drink in a more seemly fashion. Indeed, the rector had the glass against his lip when, on a sudden, the tutor gave a great cry. He threw his own glass upon the floor and dashed the other from the rector's grip. In a fury, he told the amazed clergyman that he knew something of physic from his alchemical studies. Thus he had recognised the distinctive smell of a powerful poison in his glass. As both men turned to face the wife, her husband gave a great groan and clutched his stomach.

What followed was the typical death scene of such plays. The husband cursed his wife, snatched up the box and book and threw both into the fire. Then, with much groaning and sighing, he expired upon the hearth. Meanwhile, the other two had seized the wife and held her. When the actor playing the husband decided the audience had received proof of his ability to drag out a death scene, the constable entered. The wife was accused of murder, bound and led away to await the hangman's noose.

When the curtain fell on this last scene, the audience might have been forgiven for thinking the play at an end. However, the curtain quickly rose again on the empty room, now lit from the left by an eerie, greenish light. Amidst the sounds of chains clanking and the groaning of tortured souls—doubtless supplied by the rest of the company behind the scenery—the ghost of Forkbeard entered. His face and hair had been rendered a deathly white and his clothes obscured by what was intended as a winding-sheet. Facing the audience, the apparition expressed delight at the death of the sailor and his wife, branding them both thieves and deceivers. His curse, he told the audience, needed no magic or prophesy. He was the proof that all those who resorted to crime and murder, as he had done, would end by tasting the treatment they handed out to others.

There followed a crash and a red flaring light of some kind of firework, a final burst of demonic laughter from off-stage, and the curtain came down. The play was over.

When the company assembled to take their bows, there could be no doubt that the audience had enjoyed their work. Cheers and huzzas greeted the young naval officer, jeers and catcalls the sailor, his wife and Forkbeard (or his ghost). Yet all were accompanied by loud applause and much waving of hats.

The farce which ended the entertainment was exactly as predicted. The company, clearly buoyed up by the success of their principal performance, delivered it with great verve and gaiety. The double meanings came thick and fast, aided by more ribald comments from the back of the audience. The actress playing the (supposed) virgin, took every opportunity to show off her buxom figure. Once or twice, accidentally-on-purpose she even revealed shapely legs. As a result, the evening ended with all in high good humour, including Adam and Capt. Mimms.

The old gentleman had made no show of modesty. Indeed he had been amongst those most ready to raise his quizzing-glass to ensure he missed no display of feminine charms. Adam too, being in male company and far enough from home, had relaxed into the spirit of the evening. Though he mentally advised himself to censor the story he would tell when he arrived home.

Yet even during the amusement of the evening, something nagged at him. He felt he had been offered some insight which he had failed to grasp. The archdeacon's death was always at the back of his mind. That evening's melodrama had shown him people playing one victim off against another. Might that not suggest something? If it did, he could not grasp it. In that puzzle which so obsessed him there was only one victim. Yet...what if that were not so? What if the constable had been playing some deeper game? What if...?

No, he told himself, that is enough. Leave the matter for today. Sleep upon it. Perhaps tomorrow may dawn clear.

AN UNLAMENTED DEATH

Chapter Twenty-nine

The Hunt Begins in Earnest

July and August, 1792, Aylsham

FOR A WHILE, LIFE FOR ADAM RETURNED TO NORMAL. There were patients to be seen, of course. Yet now the recommendations Adam had
received over the past few months meant that he could drop many
of his most onerous tasks. Being freed from the necessity of making
money by any means possible, he could pick and choose. He was well
on his way to establishing his practice amongst the more well-to-do
people of the neighbourhood.

His social life was expanding more slowly. He dined with Lassimer and Lassimer came to him in return. His mother visited, bringing
Miss LaSalle. Adam found the young lady's company most congenial. The three dined with Mr. Jempson and his daughter, Elizabeth, in
their home and made up a happy party. The Jempsons had completed
their move from Norwich and were now well-respected residents of
the town. As Adam might have expected, their house was modest, yet
still a haven of comfort and quiet good taste.

Elisabeth Jempson proved to be both agreeable and well-educated, as befitted a Quaker family. Her father had made sure she had an education rather greater than many women of her time and she had taken full advantage of it. Miss LaSalle was plainly delighted with her company. Before an hour was past, they were calling each other Elizabeth and Sophia, as if they had been childhood friends. If this easy intimacy caused Adam some feelings of envy, he took care to keep them hidden.

Adam admired Elizabeth Jempson's mind and conversation as much as Miss LaSalle did. Yet he could not help noticing her neat, well-proportioned figure, her fine, grey eyes, her sleek hair and her excellent complexion as well. Like her father, Elizabeth dressed in Quaker fashion, though the quality of the cloth of her dress was apparent. It was a good time since Adam's affections had been engaged by a woman. Now, with two in the room who might appeal to any man, he should have been content. He was not, and it had much to do with neither of them being available for a more intimate relationship.

Mr. Jempson had written before their visit to tell Adam that he had informed his daughter of Adam's interest in making contact with Mr. William Ross. She too thought him the person her friend had spoken of. So she had written at once to Birmingham. Yet Mr. Jempson explained to Adam that Elizabeth thought the friend a poor correspondent. She feared it might be some time before she obtained a reply. He would need to be patient.

Yet when the next week the Jempsons dined with Adam and his mother in their turn, she was ready with news. The young man her friend Alice had found so agreeable was indeed Mr. William Ross. He had travelled to Birmingham immediately after his father denied him his own house. There he found the warmth and welcoming friendship he had come to expect from the members of the circle of Dr. Priestley and Mr. Darwin. There was more. Once they heard the details of his situation, some of the most important men in the city had taken swift action to find him a way to earn his living.

Mr. William Ross's prowess with numbers was well known. Now these men of business discovered him to be diligent in his application of his skill to practical use. As a result, a Mr. Bredwardine, a partner in a bank as well as in several manufacturing concerns, had swiftly engaged him as his chief clerk in all financial matters. Mr. Ross enjoyed the work and still found time to pursue further studies in mathematics and science.

It was in connection with Mr. Bredwardine's business interests that Mr. Ross was presently absent from Birmingham. He was visiting various shipowners and traders in the port of Hull. Unable to speak to him directly, Alice had therefore sent him a letter through Mr. Bredwardine. In it she had acquainted him with his mother's contrition and unhappiness, and urged him to make contact with her as soon as he might be able.

This was such good news, and so suitable to Adam's desires in the matter, that his thanks caused Miss Jempson to blush. Her father beamed upon her and added his own praise for her kindness in the matter.

'Let us hope the young man is persuaded to act out of love and sympathy,' Mr. Jempson said. 'The whole service of God consists in kindness towards your fellow men. Without such deeds, the most profound faith and devotion is worthless. Did not St. Paul write that a man that hath not charity is but as a sounding brass or a tinkling cymbal?'

'From all that I have heard,' Adam said, 'I am indeed hopeful that the young Mr. Ross will be as loving towards his mother in her grief and suffering as any man. He has made a most powerful impression on the people with whom he is now living, and I cannot believe that comes solely from his intellect. In my experience, many of those most admired for their powers of reason make but a poor fist of dealing with their fellow human beings. Yet Mr. William Ross has made himself useful and pleasant to the cream of commercial and scientific society in those parts. I cannot doubt he has more to offer than an ample mind.'

Two days later, Adam's mother and her companion went on their way to visit Trundon Hall. Adam went with them. In part this would ease the fatigue of the journey. His brother had also arranged a dinner party to welcome his mother and Miss LaSalle to Trundon. He invited Adam too, saying that several members of prominent local families would be present. They would all have known Mr. Harmsworthy for a good while, he thought, and might well have some useful insights. Of course, this ensured Adam would attend, as Giles knew it would.

While the ladies were present at table, conversation moved amongst conventional topics, but was none the less animated or interesting for that. Only when the ladies retired to the drawing room, the cigars were lit and the port began its endless journey around the table, did Giles bring up the subject of Mr. Harmsworthy. It looked likely to be an evening of considerable drinking. It would thus be well to hear what the others had to say while most were still sober.

'Does anyone know Henry Harmsworthy?' Giles began. 'Adam had something of an odd encounter with him recently. He was quite rude.'

'Not surprised,' Lord Sidestrand said at once. 'Bit of an odd fellow all round. Reclusive. Never heard anything definite against him, you understand, but not the kind of person you would want to welcome into your family.'

Robert Norton-Harvey took up the topic. 'I've heard he can't be found,' he said. 'Left his house and disappeared, no one knows where.

I also heard he has resigned from the bench of magistrates. I wonder if he plans to move away?'

'No great loss,' Sir Daniel Rivers said. 'Not to society anyway. As Sidestrand said, the man is a recluse. You never see him at anyone's house, nor at society events. Not married either. Well, that estate isn't much, so I suspect few mothers have ever had him in mind as a match for a daughter looking to rise in society.'

'If that is the reason,' Norton-Harvey said. 'Odd men like that, you know. Makes you wonder. To be fair though, I haven't heard anything specific to suggest he's the other way inclined. That's the odd thing about him. He's dull of course. But he's also pretty near impossible to get to know.'

Now Braydon Townsend joined in. 'You have to admire what he's done with that estate. When he inherited it, it was worth scarce a thousand a year. It must be worth double that today. I wonder where he got his skill with money? Not from his father, that's for sure.'

'Nor his mother either,' Lord Sidestrand said. 'Not that way, anyhow.' The four of them nodded and laughed at that. Here was something they all knew that Adam did not. So, putting on his most innocent voice, Adam enquired why Mr. Harmsworthy's parents provoked such mirth.

Lord Sidestrand, who had probably consumed the most port, was the first to answer. 'Mr. Harmsworthy senior was an odd fellow,' he said. 'No bottom. All surface polish, but nothing behind it. Never could settle to anything. Start it, spend heavily, then drop it. Even his own father didn't care for him.'

'You must be even more drunk than I am,' Norton-Harvey said. 'I could barely understand a word of that. For goodness' sake, Sidestrand, start at the beginning and try to use complete sentences.' He turned to Adam. 'The answer to your question is in there somewhere, Bascom. It's just been mangled by Sidestrand's mode of speech.'

'So tell him,' Sir Daniel protested. 'Listen to me, Dr. Bascom. Mr. Harmsworthy senior never recovered from going on The Grand Tour. He came back more Italian than the Italians. While he was in Italy, he took up collecting paintings and statues. Of course, when he came back he had nowhere to put them. His father wouldn't have them in the house. So the son sulked in London for several years, learned to lose at the card tables and ran through a whole series of expensive mistresses. He would have ended in a debtors' prison if his father had not died in the nick of time.'

'He got his hands on the estate,' Townsend interrupted, 'but it didn't change his ways. He put up all his paintings and started paying huge sums to architects to rework the house in the latest style. That, a new set of women and even more gambling debts ate up most of the ready cash. Then he married a woman as wild and feckless as himself.'

'Real beauty though', Lord Sidestrand said. 'My father said he'd never seen a lovelier, better-dressed woman. That was something, coming from him, believe me. He'd made a lifetime study of ladies of every kind.'

'Beautiful indeed,' Townsend continued, 'but with the morals of an alley cat. As he grew older, her husband lost interest in women and turned to horses instead. It was said he had the finest stable in the country and she had twice as good a stable of men and rode them twice as hard. They had one child between them—our Henry—and neither took any interest in the lad.'

'He must have been about ten when his father died,' Sir Daniel said. 'His mother then lost all restraint. The paintings, horses, jewels and the like, all gone. There wasn't even much left of the estate to mortgage. Charlotte Harmsworthy did what her kind always do: first she sold whatever she could, then she lived off a succession of elderly fools while continuing to enjoy every stiff, young cock she could find.'

'There was quite a scandal, I believe,' Norton-Harvey added. 'It may even have been at the Dublin Castle. She arrived at a ball wearing a gown cut so low even the gentlemen were shocked.'

Adam had been listening with barely half his attention up to this point. Now he felt as if a spring had jerked his head upright and caused his whole brain to tingle.

'Did you say Dublin?' he said.

'Of course,' Norton-Harvey replied. 'Didn't you know the Harmsworthy's are an Irish family? Not papists, of course. Part of what gets called the Protestant Supremacy. Our Henry was definitely born there.'

'Must have been about the time of the scandal that he left,' Lord Sidestrand said. 'Dublin got too hot for his mother and she went abroad somewhere. Henry was packed off to live with some dreary uncle in Glasgow. Poor boy had nothing. Even the estate was seized by the creditors and sold. Anyone know what happened to Lottie?'

'I believe she died in Italy somewhere,' Sir Daniel said. 'About two years later. You can't keep up that kind of pace and live a long life. You're right about the son. I think he was destined for the Church. It's often the only source of income open to poor sons of good families. What rescued him was the death of his mother's step-brother without issue. He got the estate here and the chance to live like a gentleman again.'

'His rackety upbringing left its mark though,' Townsend said. 'He has never been happy in company. Nor has he ever married.'

'I heard he isn't the marrying type, if you catch my drift,' Lord Sidestrand said. 'There was that fuss about old Merson's son a few years back. He and Henry Harmsworthy were almost inseparable until Merson whisked the young man away.'

'Nothing was proved,' Sir Daniel said, 'though I admit it seemed fishy. The Merson boy was definitely that way. I believe he lived in

241

France until they all went mad there. Half the nobility of France were sodomites … rest were adulterers! Now those who are left are running for their lives over here. Not that we need any more of their sort, if you ask me.'

Ever since the mention of Dublin, Adam's mind had been working at double speed. As a result, he more or less missed a good part of the subsequent discussion. Indeed, he would probably have missed everything else that evening if his brother had not gently touched him on the arm and roused him from his speculations.

'Wake up, brother,' Giles said. 'We're going through to join the ladies now. Was that helpful to you?' Adam could only nod.

As soon as he arrived at his home the next day, Adam wrote at once to Mr. Wicken. He did not trouble that powerful and devious man with news of Mr. William Ross. That would hardly be of much interest to a person he had come to think of as far more than a mere spymaster. Instead he set down a full explanation of his recent actions and thoughts, together with a brief summary of the discussion around the dining table at Trundon Hall.

Chief amongst the points he made was his realisation that he had been most remiss in ignoring the contribution of Mr. Harmsworthy to the affair of the archdeacon's death. The magistrate had appeared open enough about his contact with Dr. Ross on that fateful evening. Yet a fuller consideration revealed that this openness was deceptive. Nor had Adam known of Harmsworthy's connection to Ireland. He was sure Mr. Wicken had told him one of the men taken in the raid was both Irish and a notorious rebel. What did this say of Harmsworthy's actions?

As he set all down for Mr. Wicken, it became even clearer. Mr. Harmsworthy had stated after the inquest that he had taken Dr. Ross to the churchyard at Gressington. There he had left him, never en-quiring the reason for the choice of such a strange destination at that time of the day. But that would not do. Constable Garnet had seen Mr. Harmsworthy and Dr. Ross together. Adam was certain that must be correct. He had been sufficiently alarmed to run away. Mr. Harmswor-thy must have done more than drive into the village, allow Dr. Ross to alight alone, and drive away again.

To this Adam now added the intelligence that Mr. Harmsworthy had Irish connections, had left home at some time close to the raid on the smugglers and had not returned. No one was certain where he had gone. Must that not also be seen as suspicious, he wrote? It was well beyond Adam's means to track Mr. Harmsworthy down, but he was sure that Mr. Wicken's resources would be more than equal to the task. He therefore ended his letter by urging that Mr. Harmsworthy be found as soon as possible. Only then could he be asked to account in detail for his actions—something he had not done in the course of the inquest.

Adam sent the letter by the first available post to London and was gratified to receive a reply within less than four days. Amidst flattering words on Adam's clarity of thought, Mr. Wicken stated that he would at once see what could be done to ascertain Mr. Harmsworthy's cur-rent whereabouts. Once found, the man would be called upon to clari-fy his situation on many points and not just regarding the archdeacon.

'Mr. Harmsworthy is clearly a person of much interest in this case,' Mr. Wicken wrote. 'Had it not been for you, sir, I believe we would all have missed that fact, which was perhaps what the man in-tended. I myself took his assurances at face value, when he said that he had no knowledge of the circumstances surrounding Dr. Ross's death. That is, I assure you, something I do not do often —and will be dili-gent to make sure I never do again.'

That Mr. Wicken had devoted all available effort to finding Mr. Harmsworthy was proved by a second letter Adam received on Wednesday, 15 August, barely a week later. This one came via a special government messenger sent for the purpose.

'When Garnet was taken,' Mr. Wicken wrote, 'the Frenchman taken along with him proved to know little. The Irish traitor refused to speak and so has already received his just reward via the hangman's noose. So I took care to obtain a source of intelligence on Garnet's conversation with those who shared his cell in the prison. My informer has been moved from Newgate to the county gaol in Norwich. He is supposedly awaiting transportation to a prison settlement in Australia. In reality, he will be taken from the gaol and quietly allowed to escape. His continued stay in prison is purely to verify that he will keep his mouth shut about the deal we made. I always have need of suitable spies. In this man's case, there is a further advantage. He can always be retaken and sentence of death imposed again, if he fails to do as he is told.

'His name is Josiah Osman and my intermediary has instructions to take you to him. Will you consent to speak with him? The messenger bearing this letter will return for his answer tomorrow. If you agree, he will arrange conveyance to Norwich at once.'

When the messenger came, Adam indicated his agreement and the meeting with the informer was set for Monday of the week following.

Chapter Thirty

Josiah's Tale

EARLY THAT MORNING, ADAM DRESSED as simply as he might. He had been asked to hide his status as a gentleman lest anyone seeing him where no gentleman should be became suspicious.

He assumed that he would be taken within the castle at Norwich, since it now served as the county gaol. It was not a prospect he thought of with pleasure. All he had heard of it suggested conditions within were squalid. The accommodation for prisoners had, for many years, been a series of fetid shacks and rooms within the ruins of the Norman keep. Of late, the architect Sir John Soane had been engaged to carry out some rebuilding. Whether this had improved the place much, he supposed he would discover.

Promptly at eight, a plain chaise of the kind used by all the inns drew up outside Adam's house. The driver, a faultlessly polite young man called Mr. Henry Gamelion, explained what he could. The man Adam was to meet was a 17-year old thief by the name of Josiah Osman. He, his elder brother, father, and uncle had all been convicted of having entered a house at Costessey in the owner's absence. Once inside, they had, Gamelion said, been remarkably thorough. First they took the clothing left folded in various chests and the linens from the beds. Then they removed all the cutlery, crockery and other household goods. Finally they had stripped the larder of foodstuffs and helped themselves to the householder's ale and a small tub of gin. In total, the value of the goods taken was estimated to be more than ten pounds. That was ample to see them all condemned to death.

From this unhappy family, only Josiah now remained. The judge had, as was customary, petitioned the King for clemency on account of his youth. The rest had already perished on the gallows outside the castle walls.

Since no one must know Josiah Osman was anything but an escaped felon with a price on his head, the meeting was to be held at a secret place. Adam would be denied his visit to the gaol itself, but thus it must be. Osman's future value as a spy depended on it.

Osman had been woken at dawn, Gamelion said. Last evening, the turnkey had been told the prisoner was to be taken at once to a prison hulk at Portsmouth. That would occasion no special interest. From time to time, spaces became available on the next passage to the penal colony of New South Wales. When they did, all the prisons in a given area would be told to supply a certain number of those condemned to death. Some might wait years for a passage. Others could be transported almost as soon as sentence was passed. This morning, a typical cart for prisoners had come to the gaol to collect the boy. It was hoped the turnkey would not even suspect that those who drove it were anything but what they seemed. In reality, they were all Wicken's men.

Once outside the city and away from prying eyes, the cart conveying Osman would leave the highway at an arranged spot. There it would wait, hidden amongst some trees by the river, until the doctor arrived. When he was finished, Osman would continue along his path towards Portsmouth. Whether he would ever get there was not for them to know.

Thus the two set out on the road to Norwich. As their chaise neared the centre part of the city, Gamelion steered it away from the main road and stopped beside the river bank below the cathedral. There Adam was to transfer to a wherry to go down the river to the meeting point. The boat's crew were, Gamelion assured him, all naval men. To-day, of course, they dressed in the typical garb of those who plied the river taking goods between the city and the docks at Yarmouth. To any who watched, it would seem some local merchant was taking the most comfortable route to inspect an incoming shipload of goods.

Mr. Gamelion, as the driver of the chaise, would stay behind to await their return. Adam's new guide was the wherry's captain. This was a solid, cheerful man who introduced himself as Captain Smith, though the broad wink he added made clear that this was far from being his real name. Adam, as instructed by Mr. Gamelion, replied that he was Master Miller of Helmsby. Thus wrapped in their aliases, they proceeded down-river in silence.

By now the sun was warm and the hour not far short of eleven in the morning. So it was not unusual to see a wherry tie up at a riverside inn and the sole occupant make his way within to seek refreshment. Nor would any watcher have considered it odd when two men, labourers or draymen, also made their way to the door. One was carrying two small casks and the other a leather bag with the tops of several bottles showing above the brim.

Once inside, these men were directed to the kitchen with their loads, where they placed them on a table before turning back the way they had entered. Here, however, both made a sharp turn down a narrow passage and entered a small storeroom, empty but for two chairs.

Adam was already seated in one and his visitor immediately took the other. The second man, one of those Mr. Wicken had sent for the purpose, remained outside on watch.

Josiah Osman bore an uncanny resemblance to some species of weasel. He had a narrow face and gingery hair. He also had a nervous habit of licking his tongue over small, sharp teeth. If Adam had not known the details of the crime that had ended in a death sentence, he would have been sure it was something furtive and sly. This young man had not the stature for a highway robber, nor the weather-beaten face and sturdy build of a smuggler. Indeed, he looked younger than his seventeen years. No matter, he was here now and Adam had no wish to prolong this meeting beyond what might be necessary. Osman might be away from the gaol, but the smell of it clung to his clothes and was filling the whole room.

Adam got straight to business. 'Tell me of Garnet,' he said. 'Did he speak freely to you?'

'Indeed 'e did, sir,' Osman said. His accent did not come from Norfolk. Maybe he was a Londoner. 'I couldn't stop 'im. Mortally afeared of the drop 'e was. Not a man cut out for villainy. 'E convinced himself 'e was secure from the law because of 'is position as constable. Now that had failed 'im, 'e was as great a coward as any. 'E would talk to anyone, so 'e would, just to stop 'isself thinking of what lay ahead.'

'Truthfully?'

'Aye, there's the question, sir. At first there was several who gathered around to hear 'is tales of smugglers and the like. 'E liked to boast, that Garnet. Make 'isself out to be stronger and more important than 'e was. A prison's a poor place to play such a game, sir. Too many within 'as seen worse crimes and stronger men. Before long, those who 'ad listened to 'im at first drifted away, for 'is tales owed more to 'is imaginings than to anything 'e might 'ave done. Garnet's gelt ran out too. A bed in that hell-hole costs two shilling a week, if you like to lie alone.

Good food costs that and more. No one came to see Garnet and bring him vittles or more gelt. By the third week, 'e was living mostly on bread and water and sleeping three to a bed for sixpence—when 'e did sleep. Nightmares 'e had, sir, right fearful ones. 'E'd wake up screaming and set everyone by the ears.

'After me brother and me old dad … went … one of the turnkeys told me as I could earn my freedom if I did as I was told and kept me trap shut. I won't pretend I liked the idea at first. No one wants to be a squealer. But, well, dead is dead and going to Australia as good as, they says. You 'as to take your chances in this world, me poor old man told me. Not that 'is words did 'im any good. Nor the rest of us neither.'

'Is your mother left alone?' Adam asked.

'She died when I was born, sir,' Osman replied. 'Never thought as 'ow I would be glad of such a thing, but better she didn't see all 'er menfolk served like they was. We was starving, we was. No work anywhere. What else could we do but steal?'

Adam brought the boy back to the point. 'Did they keep Garnet long before they executed him?' he asked.

'No, sir. You misunderstands me. All this was afore 'is trial. 'E still seemed to have some 'ope of being transported or the like, though the rest of us could never see it. 'E was a murderer. Worse, 'e had murdered a soldier or some such, while trying to get away. There's no chance in 'ell for one such as that. No, 'e was always destined to be turned off and, deep down, 'e knew it.'

'So you took your chance,' Adam said.

'That's right enough. I'd been told I could buy my way out of the passage to Botany Bay, if I would befriend Garnet enough that 'e would talk to me truthfully. That's a powerful reason to do anything, sir. Trouble was, at the start there was always so many around 'im that 'e barely noticed I was there. Besides, if 'e started saying more than 'e should, someone would be sure to stop up 'is mouth. My chance came when the rest were tired of 'im and angry that 'e disturbed their sleep.'

'What did you do then?' Adam asked. He longed for Osman to get to the point, but realised his best hope of hearing all was to allow this wretched boy to talk as he wished. Too much haste now might mar everything.

'I 'ad some money, you see. Those who 'ired me gave me just enough to make my life a mite better, without seeming too flush, if you get my meaning. A woman who said she was me mam would visit me each week with good food and a few pennies.' He laughed. 'As I told you, me real mam died seventeen years ago, but none knew that. Whoever played 'er part did it real well and I wasn't about to let on neither.

'When Garnet was near the limit of what 'e could take, I started to talk to 'im. I even told 'im I 'ad just enough money for a bed on me own, but feeling sorry for 'im like, I was prepared to let 'im share it. I shared my vittles with 'im too. I even gave 'im a drink or two from a flask I kept about me. 'E never seemed to notice I didn't touch it meself. A dose of laudanum each night made 'im sleep. That made me popular with the other prisoners, even if a few suggested I 'ad other ways of making 'im tired enough to sleep properly. If you're young and fair-enough looking, there are plenty in a place like that ready to ask you for certain favours, if you takes my meaning. No, sir, they left 'im and me alone, glad to be rid of 'im and 'aving the opinion of me that I was 'is Molly. It were as well for me I got away now, sir, or I would 'ave 'ad a worse time fighting 'em off me than I did, once Garnet was gone.

'I'd 'ad to suffer a deal of 'is boasting before 'is trial and nothing of use with it, so I reckon I 'ad earned my fee right then. But once 'e had seen that judge put the black cap on 'is 'ead, and knew 'e would be on 'is way to 'ell in a day or so, 'e changed. No more boasting of imaginary deeds, I can tell you. All 'e wanted to do was to lighten the weight on 'is conscience. No minister or priest to talk to 'im about God's forgiveness in there, sir. I 'ad to do instead.'

'Was he so ashamed of all his dishonest deeds?' Adam asked.

'Lord no, sir. None of that. I'd 'eard all about that, again and again, afore 'e went in the dock. No, 'e gloried in most of 'is life. What nagged at 'im was another matter. It seems 'e 'ad brought about the death of a clergyman—not intending to, 'e swore that over and over—but caused it just the same. That's what 'e believed had led the Almighty to see 'im taken and brought to the 'angman. 'E 'ad caused the death of one of God's own. Maybe 'e even thought that by showing remorse 'e might still escape the noose. Who can say? If that was on 'is mind, 'e was mighty soon proved wrong. Just one night 'e 'ad, sir, to tell me all, then they took 'im away and 'e never came back.'

'What did he tell you?' Adam asked. If only he could end this wretched tale and get back to Aylsham. Osman's flicking tongue and high, childish voice were driving him insane.

'It was like this, you see,' Osman began again. 'I believes 'e'd heard this clergyman preach somewhere. All 'ellfire stuff it was, full of God's wrath for sinners and fornicators. Made 'im laugh, 'e said. 'E knew where the greatest fornicators was: sitting pretty in their grand 'ouses and forcing themselves on any girl foolish enough to come within an arm's length. Boys too. In fact, 'e was making good money from just such a bunch of rich sodomites. They paid 'im to smuggle 'em lewd books and pictures from overseas. 'E looked at a few before 'anding them over and they was full of engravings of men being buggered by other men. Aye, and men strutting around showing off their great pricks and bollocks too. Some of them pictures was even hand-coloured, right down to the red knobs on their ... well, I'm sure you sees what I'm saying, anyhow. Made 'im laugh, Garnet said.

'Still, Garnet was always on the look-out for new ways of making gelt. It took a while for the thought to come to 'im, 'e told me, but when it did 'e could see it was one of 'is best ever schemes. 'E arranged somehow to talk in private to this parson-type and tell 'im 'is conscience was troubled by the knowledge 'e 'ad of wicked doings not far from the coast. Imagine that! 'Im claiming to 'ave a conscience! The parson-type fell for it though. Right excited 'e was. Told Garnet 'e could save 'is soul by telling all 'e knew.

'Garnet weren't such a fool as to go along with this. Instead, 'e told the parson 'e 'ad 'eard a group of rich men was meeting at a certain 'ouse. They would eat and drink together, before getting down to the real business of buggering local boys who was paid well to stay silent. According to what Garnet said to the parson, 'e didn't know exactly where these meetings took place. 'Owever, should the parson be able to provide 'im with a certain amount of money, 'e was sure 'e could persuade those who did know to part with the information.

'No sooner said than done, Garnet told me. The clergyman arranged to meet 'im in a churchyard somewhere, late in the afternoon, and 'anded over no less than five guineas. Rich pickings!'

'But how was Garnet going to lead this clergyman to meetings he had made up?' Adam asked.

'Garnet said that was the best trick of all. 'E went to 'is customer for the dirty books and told him 'e 'ad 'eard some churchman was on to what they was doing. That 'e would make their names public, if 'e could once find 'em. What's more, 'e said, the clergyman had come to 'im and offered 'im five guineas to tell all 'e knew. Of course, exactly as 'e knew 'e would, 'is customer offered 'im ten to stay silent. Garnet's plan was to go on as long as 'e could taking money from both sides, each time claiming the other had increased the size of the bribe.'

'Could he have done it?'

'For while 'e could,' Osman said. 'Course, in the end 'e would have to disappoint one or the other. My guess is that 'e planned to give the parson some spot to visit. Then, when nothing was found, 'e would rant and roar that 'is informer 'ad cheated 'im. Of course, once 'e'd made them rich cullies fear 'e might betray their secret, 'e could go on getting money from them for years ahead. It was, you 'as to admit, a neat enough scheme.'

'So what went wrong? Something must have happened to cause the arch…the clergyman to be killed.'

'It seems 'e had set up another meeting at the same place as before. This time, the parson-type was to bring more money and be told the place and time of the next meeting of them madge culls—I means buggerers, sir. Course, according to Garnet, something would cause the meeting not to 'appen, so as 'e could extract still more gelt to reveal where and when it 'ad been moved.'

'And so?' Adam said.

'Went to the churchyard, 'e did, nice and early, and waits. 'E always did this. Although 'e told the parson to come alone, Garnet was mighty cautious. Now 'is caution was proved right an' all. The parson came alright, but 'e 'ad a magistrate with 'im!'

'What did Garnet do then?'

'Took to 'is heels, you may be sure. Thought that was the end of it. But next day, the parson's body is found right there in the churchyard. Garnet 'adn't killed 'im neither. 'E swore that over and over.'

'Did he know, or guess, who had?'

'Said 'e reckoned it must 'ave been one of the sodomites, or someone paid by them. They must have been watching 'im and believed 'e was passing their names to the clergyman. Odd thing, though. No wounds on the body, 'e said, nor any sign of a struggle. What's more, when 'e suggested it must 'ave been some kind of accident, everyone went along with this. Fair puzzled, Garnet was. Why wasn't anyone interested in looking deeper?'

'Did he know why?'

'Not at all, sir. All 'e could imagine was that the rich fornicators had enough power to make sure no awkward questions was asked. It must have been that, 'e said, because some fool doctor started asking all the obvious questions at the inquest and the coroner fell over 'isself to shut 'is mouth.'

'And then?' Adam prompted. How much longer would this take?

'That was pretty much it. Garnet lay low for a few weeks, then started up again. 'E got a message from some smugglers that a party would bring 'im two men to be taken out to their ship, no questions asked. This time, though, the Revenue men caught 'im and, like a fool, 'e tries to fight 'is way out.'

'Did he know anything about the men he took out to the ships?' Adam asked.

'No, 'e did not, sir, and I believed him. Them smugglers are ruthless men. Cross 'em in any way and you'll be food for the fishes. No, Garnet was no fool about that. 'E'd take the money and keep 'is eyes and 'is mouth tight shut.'

So there it was. The archdeacon had not died by Garnet's hand, even though he had been fool enough to pay the man for imaginary information. Well, what could you expect from someone as bigoted as Dr. Ross? Had he hoped to make his name as the man who exposed the next Hellfire Club? For the rest, it was much as Adam had imagined. A clandestine deal gone wrong, leaving the archdeacon in a lonely churchyard in the dark.

Not alone, though! Mr. Harmsworthy had been there. He must be involved. It had to be so.

As he was taken back upstream in the wherry, Adam remained sunk deep in thought. If only he had been cleverer, he told himself, they could have worked nearly all this out for themselves, weeks ago. Now everything depended on Mr. Wicken being able to lay hands on Mr. Harmsworthy. If he escaped, they could go no further.

Thus it was that he met Mr. Gamelion again and was driven back to his home. Wisely, the man didn't press him for news, beyond asking if he had got what he wanted.

'Yes,' Adam said. 'I did. Please send word to Mr. Wicken that I shall write to him at length as soon as I may, but the main mystery remains. It is all up to him now.' With that much, the man had to be content.

AN UNLAMENTED DEATH

Chapter Thirty-one

Night Call

Thursday, 23 August, 1792

EACH EVENING, IT WAS ADAM'S HABIT to take a candle and spend some time alone in his study catching up on his reading. At the same time, he answered correspondence that did not relate to patients or his medical practice. He enjoyed studying and tried to stay in touch with various avenues of knowledge opened by the new scientific methods. He also tried to keep in contact with some at least of the friends he had made during his years of study. He thought too many physicians preferred leisure to learning. Those were the ones whose medical knowledge stopped short the day they qualified. They gained experience, of course, but they rarely strayed from the methods of treatment they had been taught twenty or more years before. He was determined not to be of their cast of mind.

A loud banging at his door late that Thursday evening roused him from his studies. He had been reading of a most interesting case of severe nausea and stomach cramps. This had gripped a party of people who had dined together, so it was clear that something they had eaten had caused the symptoms. What was not clear at all was how to discover what that was. Being questioned, all admitted to having tasted at least something of every dish on the table. The author of the paper had therefore undertaken a series of experiments involving feeding each dish in turn to various dogs. When none of these beasts displayed any symptoms, the experimenter felt he had reached an impasse.

Adam angrily laid his book aside to deal with whoever it was who seemed intent on rousing the whole neighbourhood. Had he been in a better temper, he would probably have gone into the hallway to discover who had come calling. As it was, he stayed where he was and waited for the maid to bring him news.

Adam was still more annoyed when the door to his study was flung open. A stranger entered almost at a run, followed by Hannah, the maidservant, still feebly protesting at such a grave breach of etiquette.

The stranger nodded to him in a perfunctory manner, then demanded to know whether he was Dr. Bascom. Such rudeness effectively silenced poor Hannah. Yet there was something in the stranger's manner and posture—some erectness in his stance and directness in his eyes—that caused Adam to temper his reply.

'Yes, sir,' he said. 'I am Dr. Bascom. May I ask whom I have the honour of addressing?'

'Pardon my haste, doctor, and the lack of manners it forces upon me. My name is Marshall and I am employed by someone whom I think you know: Mr. Wicken. It is on his instruction that I am here. He told me that, should anything arise of an urgent nature that could not wait until he might be reached, I was at once to come to you.'

By now, Adam felt like a hound held tight on the leash and the quarry in plain view. Still, he forced himself to keep his voice calm and even.

'Welcome, Mr. Marshall. I will hear your tale at once.' Then, turning to Hannah, still vibrating with suppressed anger at such an assault upon her master's home, he said merely, 'Thank you, Hannah. You may leave us now.'

By unspoken agreement, Adam and his visitor stayed silent until the servant had left the room and closed the door behind her. Adam could hear Mrs. Brigstone's voice enquiring what had caused such a noise at this hour and Hannah replying that she had left all in the master's hands. The housekeeper knew better than to disturb them. She was used to people arriving at the house at all hours, wanting the doctor to give aid to someone in distress.

As silence returned, Adam sat again in his chair and motioned to Mr. Marshall to take a seat as well.

'Permit me to remain standing, sir,' Marshall said. 'My mission is urgent and I will shortly ask you to accompany me at once to render what assistance may be possible.'

'Very well,' Adam said. 'Give me your report.' His use of this military term was deliberate. When it produced no sign of surprise, he was convinced that the man standing before him, though he wore no uniform, was indeed a member of one of His Majesty's armed forces.

'We have found Mr. Harmsworthy, sir. When we have leisure, I will tell you all you wish to know of the matter, but not now, with your leave, for every moment of delay counts against us. Suffice it to say that he left Lynn at dawn this morning, traveling along the road towards Fakenham. He was making good speed, yet not hurrying unduly. He passed through Fakenham without stopping and began to head for Holt. He may have wished to stop there. It could be he went that way because it is a better road than making his way in the lanes closer to the shore. But now, being once again on familiar ground, he was better able to notice anything unusual about him.

'Of a sudden, he turned in the saddle, appeared to see more people behind him than ought to have been there and urged his horse headlong into a gallop.

'My men gave chase, meaning now to seize him, since he would not lead them anywhere once he knew of their presence. He rode as fast as he could, but our horses are better than most and he must have realised he would be overtaken before many minutes had passed. That was when he drew a pistol from under his cloak and discharged it.'

'At your men? Did they fire back, for I assume they were also armed?'

'They did not fire, sir, being under the strictest instructions to avoid notice if possible. If not, they were to take the quarry alive and unharmed. But I did not make myself clear as I should. Mr. Harmsworthy did not fire his pistol at my men, he fired it at himself.'

'Suicide.' Adam said. 'So, after all this, he has been lost.'

'No, doctor, which is why I am here. It is no easy matter to aim a pistol when riding at full speed, as I know very well. I have done it myself on many occasions and wasted ball and shot on nearly all of them. Even he must have thought that a shot to the head would likely miss, for he pressed the muzzle of the pistol against his chest and fired in that position. Nevertheless, the violent motion of the horse must have caused the muzzle to slip at the last moment. The ball passed through him, sir, right enough, but it failed to cause immediate death. Nor did the fall from his horse, for the poor animal was winded and had slowed almost to a walk by the time its master slid from the saddle.'

'Is he hurt badly?'

'I have seen many men shot on the battlefield, sir,' Marshall replied, 'and I believe I know the signs of a mortal wound. He is gravely hurt, doctor, and may not last long enough for Mr. Wicken to reach here from London. That is why I am here. We took him to an inn in Holt, The King's Head, and have lodged him there under guard. Aye, and the innkeeper is mighty sour at our doing so, though I promised him ample payment. Will you come with me, doctor? You may be able to preserve his life for a little longer. You may even disagree with my view of his wound and be able to save him altogether. Yet, whatever happens, I will have discharged my duty to Mr. Wicken in seeking you out.'

'Of course I will come,' Adam said. 'Allow me but time to put on suitable clothes, speak to my housekeeper and have the groom make ready my horse.'

'With respect, doctor,' Marshall said, 'I doubt your own horse could keep pace with ours when we are in haste. We have a suitable beast ready and saddled outside for you, and an escort to see us safe through the roads at night. As to riding gear, might not a thick cloak be sufficient?'

'It might,' Adam said. 'Still, I would tell my housekeep where I am going in such haste. I will also need to fetch my medical bag. Will you allow me enough time for these?'

'Of course, doctor. One of my men will bear your bag for you. You may need both hands on the reins before this ride is out.'

Adam knew himself to be, at best, an indifferent rider, so he bore this implied judgement of his ability without rancour. He dreaded the ride, if truth were told. Though he believed he could stay in the saddle, barring accidents, he was sure the damage to his backside would be severe. When he finally returned, he would have to bear a good deal of discomfort as a result.

'Two minutes then,' Adam said, and went to find Mrs. Brigstone and his thick cloak, only to discover she had already anticipated his needs. She was standing by the front door with the cloak over her arm and his medical bag in her hand.

Adam would long remember that night's ride to Holt. His own horse, Betty, would never have kept up the pace the others set. Nor would he have relished telling his groom the next day why he had returned with her broken-winded and exhausted. The cavalry horse he had been given was, fortunately for him, a sure-footed and co-opera-tive beast. Yet even getting onto its back had been a challenge, so tall an animal was it.

Now, as they rode into Holt well after midnight, they made a noise such as must rouse every householder in the town. Adam's body had long since become numb with the fearful shaking their pace caused, for they thundered along poor, rutted roads at somewhere between a fast canter and a full-out gallop. Every horse was marked with flecks of foam. Adam's backside was probably scarred for life.

The innkeeper at The King's Head was ready to meet them when they entered his house. 'Who are you?' he demanded of Adam. 'I don't know you. Are you the one in charge, because if you are I demand an end of all this.'

Adam's reply was terse enough to have stopped any sensible per-son from continuing.

'I am a physician,' he said. 'You have a gravely injured man here. Stand aside at once.'

'Stand aside? Stand aside? You aren't the doctor in Holt. We have our own doctor. What cause is there to bring one such as you in from heaven knows where else. And in such a manner! These men turn up here with some wounded criminal, commandeer my best bed, ruining the sheets with blood. Five shillings those sheets cost me! Worse, they keep everyone up half the night, then ride through the town as if all the devils from hell were chasing them. You have woken every Chris-tian soul in the place and caused who knows what stories to spread about my inn. I'm an honest innkeeper, I tell you. I'll have the law on you!'

It was too much. When Adam spoke again, the quietness of his voice and calmness of his manner should have told the innkeeper he was about to regret what he had just said. 'You say you are an honest innkeeper. Very well. Let us prove it. Captain Marshall (he had no idea whether this was truly Marshall's rank, but it sounded right for the purpose), send two of your men into the cellar of this inn. Let them search a little and see if there is anything that could be of interest to the Revenue.'

In an instant, all the colour drained from the innkeeper's face. Vainly he tried to turn aside the terror that had fallen upon him. 'Sir, good sir, I spoke hastily. I did not mean any disrespect. You may have whatever rooms you want in my humble establishment, for you come on His Majesty's service ...'

'Indeed we do,' Marshall said grimly. 'Baker, Sawyer, go into the cellar and report back on to me what you find there. If any stand in your way, use your weapons.'

The two men hurried off to do as they were bid, trying to suppress their grins at the effect all this was having on the pompous landlord. The innkeeper ran after them, still vainly offering apologies. Marshall now turned to Adam. 'How did you guess he has contraband within?'

'We are scarce four miles from the coast, Mr. Marshall. You are unlikely to find one single inn in these parts that does not have regular dealings with the smugglers. No, probably not above half a dozen gentleman's mansions either. It was no guess. Come, take me to my patient. That fool of an innkeeper has wasted time we can ill afford, if what you told me before proves true.'

One look at Mr. Harmsworthy was enough to confirm that Marshall had been accurate enough in his estimation of the wound. The man's face was white as the best paper. His breathing was harsh, irregular and accompanied by specks of moisture on his lips. And his skin, though clammy with cold, was drenched in sweat. Mr. Harmsworthy was dying. Adam doubted he could prevent that. The best he could do would be to ease the pain of his passing a little.

Adam fumbled in his medical bag for the laudanum which might bring sleep and some relief from pain. At that moment, Mr. Harmsworthy's eyes opened and he recognised who was standing over him. 'So, doctor. They have brought you. Do not waste your energy on trying to heal me. I am dying and I know it. Indeed, I welcome it and would have had it come far sooner than this. At least it will release me from the hangman's noose, even if it does not free my family and name from the disgrace I have brought upon them.'

'Hush,' Adam said. 'Do not try to speak. I will prepare a draught to ease your pain in just a moment.'

'Wait, good doctor,' Mr. Harmsworthy said. 'People say confession is good for the soul. I have no time for priests or their cant, sir, nor do I fear entering hell after I die, for I have long been there in this life. Yet I am still vain enough to wish at least one man to know this before I die: though I am a murderer and a traitor, I am not an evil man. What I did, I did from love, though it brought me none in return. Let me speak first, then I will take your potion and pray it may help me die in less pain that I suffer now. I need a clear head to tell my tale—and tell it I will, though it speed my death.'

For a moment, Adam looked at the dying man with nothing in his heart but sympathy and anguish that he should come to this. Then he nodded his head and sat by the bedside, leaning close to hear the quiet voice. A voice that explained how a dull English country squire had come to commit murder and treachery through the demands of love.

'I must perforce start with my childhood,' Mr. Harmsworthy began,' for without understanding that you can understand nothing that happened later...'

Adam interrupted him. 'Nay, save your strength. I know you were born in Ireland. I also know something of your family and circumstances before you came to Norfolk. If you must tell, tell only what is essential.'

'I am amazed,' the dying man said. 'I knew the authorities were on my trail and must have taken care to discover what they could of my past. I had not known they would tell you. Never mind. I will do as you say, for I feel myself sliding into the abyss. Yet there is one part of my youth you will not know, for none do save one, who is dead already. There I shall start.'

It would be tedious to include all the pauses, the periods of gasping for breath and groans of agony that punctuated Mr. Harmsworthy's story. Thus it will be set down here as Adam recalled it later. Telling his tale drained every last reserve of the dying man's strength. Only his utter determination to present the truth at the last kept him alive long enough to finish what he wished to say. It was that experience, of eyes bright with fever, a voice rent with pain, and an icy hand clutching his arm, that burnt Mr. Harmsworthy's words into Adam's memory. Burnt them with such clarity that he could relate them to Mr. Wicken later with near-perfect accuracy.

AN UNLAMENTED DEATH

Chapter Thirty-two

Last Confession

Given verbatim, so far as it could be recalled

I WAS, AS YOU SAY YOU KNOW, BORN IN IRELAND, in a grand house not far from Dublin, and I am an only child. My parents were part of the so-called Protestant Ascendancy: a group of English gentry who owned the best land in the country. Even so, this elite huddled in Dublin itself for fear of the peasants who worked the land on their behalf. My father was a cold and distant man, some years my mother's senior. He had no interest in me, save as the necessary heir.

I worshipped my mother as only a lonely and neglected son could. She was beautiful, fashionable and loving in a random way—when she remembered my existence. For the bulk of her time, she gloried in the many balls, assemblies and routs that took place in that city. My father took no notice of these events, but she never lacked a suitable male companion. He took no notice of that either.

Since I was alone so much, I grew into a withdrawn and solitary boy. None knew, or cared, that this solitariness was my armour against the petty cruelties of my fellows.

When I was ten, my father died leaving little but debts. Under his will, my guardianship and affairs passed into the hands of an uncle, for my mother showed little inclination to take any greater notice of practical matters than she had during her husband's lifetime. She was still under the age of forty, still beautiful and still, it seemed, determined to remain a star of fashionable society. Where she obtained the money I had no idea, though the perpetual parade of different men through her house whenever I was there should have told me. To me, she was still a vision of distant perfection. To the rest of society, she was the merriest of widows. She was also the mistress of a succession of rich, elderly men, the secret lover of a good many younger ones, and a scandal waiting to break.

Thus my life continued until I was sixteen years old. Then, one summer, the world changed for me. I met Michael O'Dowd.

O'Dowd was seventeen and a papist. He was also handsome, charming, witty and athletic; in short, everything that I was not. Why he noticed me I never knew. He talked, I listened and I fell in love. For the first time in my life, I had a friend. Soon I had a lover too.

Of course, before long my uncle found out and his rage was fearful. I think he cared little about my discovery of my true sexual nature. All that mattered was that I was close friends with a papist. O'Dowd was forbidden any further association with me.

Worse was to follow. My uncle arranged to send me away to live with some remote relatives in Glasgow. My mother too was sent abroad. Her affairs had become ever more outrageous until scandal could no longer be averted. We were both cast out from the family to be forgotten. I never saw her again.

Since I had next to nothing, I was to be trained for the church. Nothing else was possible to keep me in the style of a gentleman. Yet fate, so cruel up to now, intervened. My mother's step-brother, a man I had never met, died childless and left me his estate in Norfolk. Thus here I came and here I have been ever since. I believed myself content, if not happy, and thought I should remain thus for whatever period of life was allotted me.

All that changed in April of this year. One day, late in the afternoon, someone came to my door. That itself was unusual, for few ever sought me out. My manservant answered their knocking, then came to tell me that two men were seeking to speak with me. Being curious about who these men might be, I agreed to see them, never imagining that my past should be returning to bring me yet more pain. Into my room that day came none other than Michael O'Dowd. He was older, a little bulkier, but yet the same man I had been torn from in Ireland all those years before.

His tale was soon told. As a result of my uncle's actions, he was seized with the deepest hatred for everyone connected with those who wielded power in Dublin. His father, it seemed, had been blind to the boy's nature. Now he knew, he professed total revulsion. It was too much for O'Dowd and so he ran away from his home. No one tried to find him.

For a time, he wandered, working where he could and begging where he could not. For a while, he was the plaything of a papist bishop, then of a petty local clan chieftain. Eventually, he took up work with a printer and was taught the skills of that trade. And all the time he sought out those whose grudges against the English banded them together. Yet even he could see that they had little chance of turning their wishes for freedom and reform into actions. That was why, when a few years later he heard of the rebellion and revolution in the American colonies, he sailed for the west. There he determined to make a new life for himself, far from Ireland and its bitter history.

For a while, he prospered. He found work again as a printer and bookseller, making enough money to afford a comfortable house and a few servants. He served in the local militia. Yet all the while his heart burned at the injustices he had suffered in his past. He told himself to stay content with what he had, but it was too hard.

At length a sad destiny found him. One day, he fell in with a group of men as eager as he was to bring the same kind of revolution to Ireland as had proved so successful in America. Like them, he believed that since the Americans had succeeded in winning their freedom from English laws and English kings, the Irish might do the same. All that was lacking was money, weapons and leadership. They might prevail upon the French king to furnish the first two, if they could convince him that the native Irish would provide the third.

When revolution gripped France itself, the time seemed ripe at last. Surely the new French republic would help them. It must be time to turn from plotting and scheming to stir up popular revolt amongst the poor and dispossessed of Ireland.

Sadly, most of these Irish patriots had been absent, like O'Dowd, for many years. They too easily mistook their dreams for reality. They saw French peasants bringing down the power of the nobility. They missed noticing the mass of educated, middle-class, professional men who acted as their leaders. In their minds, Ireland was a powder-keg awaiting the spark of their fervour to erupt into rebellion. As Michel now admitted, what he found when he returned was far different. Peasants there were in plenty, but so weighed down by hunger, deprivation and years of hopeless servitude that they no longer had the will to resist. Of a middle class, there seemed little enough sign outside Dublin and The Pale. There he found lawyers and doctors, but few who would risk what they had to help peasants they despised much as the gentry did. Worse, the Irish who had stayed in that island, and suffered the full weight of English attempts to root out rebellion, had no wish to be instructed by those who had left. They had their own groups and hierarchies. These 'Americans' should go back, they said. How could they be trusted when they had already deserted the cause once?

Thus O'Dowd, and the Frenchman who stood alongside him in my house on that day in April, soon found themselves isolated. Alone and confused, they tried to carry on, but someone, maybe a spy or a disgruntled native, betrayed them to the authorities.

Now at last they fled, always but one step ahead of those who pursued, and tried to find some way to reach France and safety. In the end, a group called The United Irishmen offered help. They too rejected O'Dowd 'the American' as an ally, but they would not give the English the satisfaction of capturing him.

O'Dowd said they were directed to travel to England and seek out a man known to the United Irishmen on the east coast. He would take anyone out to a waiting ship on payment of enough gold. Neither had much money, but it was the only chance they had. They pooled their remaining funds and agreed to the plan. In reply, they were told that a smuggling vessel would be waiting for them on a certain night. All they had to do was make their way to a village called Gressington in Norfolk, contact and pay the ferryman and await until the appointed time and tide.

It was chance brought them to me. When they went to the inn, O'Dowd heard someone mention my name. Since it is an unusual one, he questioned how long the man of that name had lived in the area. It was a risk, of course, but had it been a cousin or someone else he did not know, he would have told them he had been mistaken and left it at that. If I was indeed the Henry. Harmsworthy he had known living there, what better place to hide? Who would look for a wanted man in the magistrate's house?

O'Dowd was as persuasive as always, telling me the delay would be no more than a week at the most. If this location proved impossible, they would be told of some other place where the smugglers might meet them. Yet to see him again—to relive for a few days the closeness we had once shared—was enough. I agreed at once to let them stay. I told my servants that one was an old friend from my school days—that at least was true—and the other a French nobleman fleeing persecution by blood-thirsty peasants. My solitary ways now came to their aid and mine, for few ever came to my house and they were safe enough if they remained within.

Then another person came to my door one afternoon: the Archdeacon of Norwich. He was hot on the trail, as he claimed, of some supposed cell of devil-worshippers and sexual deviants who met close by. On his way to Gressington to meet his informant, his chaise had broken an axle, so he could not continue in that way. This meeting was imperative, for he would be given the names of these men. Then he could expose their wickedness to the public gaze. I thought he was mad, yet his words terrified me. The last thing I wanted was to have anyone, even the church authorities, paying close attention to what was happening in the area around my home.

I tried to put him off, but he grew angry and demanded that I take him to Gressington at once. Indeed, with all the righteous zeal of the worst kind of fanatic, he shouted that I must take him. If I refused, he would assume I myself was a member of this group he believed in. Was it not said in these parts that I was odd and reclusive? Was it not a matter of wonder that I had never married?

His wild words grew ever wilder and I had no choice but to agree to his request, taking as long as I could to get ready and have the chaise prepared. Even then, I clung to the hope that along the way I might be able to convince him that no such coven of devil-worshippers existed and he must be the victim of a cruel hoax.

My hopes were, of course, fruitless. At the churchyard, he demanded I waited to bear him away again. I agreed readily enough, for I wished above all things to keep him under observation and see what might result from his meeting. As you know, no one came. Yet far from being aware, as any rational person would have been, that this proved the tale was false, he grew more and more angry. Soon, he was convincing himself that I was indeed part of this Hellfire Club or whatever. I had delayed in leaving my home in order to send word to my associates to waylay his informant and make away with him. All I wished was to stop his ranting lest he bring others to the churchyard. So I stepped towards him to try to calm him down.

At that, he started back and must have caught his heel on something, for he fell full-length upon the ground, striking his head on some stone that was hidden in the grass. I thought he was dead.

Alas, it was soon proved that he still lived. Even as I hesitated, unsure whether to leave him there or try to move the body where it might be better hidden, I heard him groan. Then he started to make feeble efforts to raise himself, muttering something about me trying to murder him.

What I did next will haunt me until my death. It seemed to me that only his death could still his tongue and keep my guilty secret— and O'Dowd—safe. If he died there, people would assume he had been set upon by robbers or smugglers. Few questions would be asked. In a moment, I had wrapped my cloak into a soft bundle and was pressing it down over his face. For a little while, I could feel movement, then all went still and I knew him to be dead indeed.

You will think me an arrant coward, doctor, but all that I could think of was to get away. I went at once to my chaise and set off for home as fast as I could. There I said nothing to anyone. Instead, I spent a sleepless night trying to concoct a story. One that might account for my presence at the churchyard, should anyone have seen me, yet keep me free from suspicion of involvement in the archdeacon's death. By morning I had a feeble tale ready.

I did not need it. The authorities seemed full of eagerness to put the death down as an accident and loath to make any further enquiries at all. I spent a few days in great apprehension—not helped by your attempts at the inquest to ask the exact questions any sane person would turn to at once—then all was quiet. I had escaped, or so I thought.

The rest you know. The authorities let the smugglers feel they were safe. Then they provided the ideal opportunity to carry out illegal activities unmolested. The trap was sprung and all were caught, including O'Dowd and the Frenchman.

Would they betray me? I did not know and I did not wait to find out. Once again I fled, this time back to Ireland, where I hoped to carry news to Michael's family and friends of what had happened to him. It was not to be. None would talk with me. I left cryptic messages and heard nothing in return. I was in despair, wandering around Dublin with neither destination nor purpose.

Thus it was that I started to feel uneasy, as if someone was watching me. Who might this be? I did not know, yet now Dublin felt hostile. I determined to leave as soon as I could find a passage. I sent a letter to my steward to arrange for him to leave a horse for me at Lynn, then made my way back to England, as fast as I might without arousing suspicion.

The feeling of being watched now grew. Worse, I was helpless and alone. I always carry a pistol on the road for my protection, so I determined that I would take my own life rather than face questioning. I knew myself to be a murderer and a traitor to my country. My life would be forfeit in any case. Perhaps I could at least avoid the shame to my family name. If I went to the gallows, I would blight other lives as well as my own.

Now I have failed even in that. When I was certain men were following me, I tried to run, hoping to have time to end my life before they seized me. Have you ever tried to fire a pistol from a galloping horse, doctor? It is far harder that I believed. Even with the muzzle pressed to my side, I managed to fail in ending my life there and then. I have ended it, of that I am sure now, but not as I had wished.

There, my tale is ended. Give me your potion, for God's sake. Bring me oblivion, for I am in great agony of body and spirit and wish for nothing but to find death as soon as I may. I am the most reluctant murderer. I killed, but never wished or meant to do so. And whether what I have told you convinces you or no, it is the truth. There is no more that I can do.

AN UNLAMENTED DEATH

Chapter Thirty-three

Loose Ends

HENRY HARMSWORTHY CLUNG TO LIFE until shortly after five in the morning. During his last hours, he was unconscious and Adam remained by his bedside the whole time. Once Marshall joined him, Adam used some of this time to complete the picture in his mind.

'Mr. Wicken has, as I believe you know, been searching for this Mr. Harmsworthy,' Marshall began, in answer to Adam's questions. 'I understand it was in connection with events that took place in these parts a short time ago. At first, no trace of him could be found. Then, to our surprise, one of our regular watchers reported seeing a stranger who matched Harmsworthy's description. This man seemed to be trying to make contact with a group of people well known to us, sir. A group suspected of planning various treasonable activities.'

'Where was this?' Adam asked.

'It was as I believe you had surmised. It was in Ireland, sir. To be precise, in an area of Dublin known to be the haunt of all manner of felons and rebellious rogues.'

'Indeed so, in Ireland then.' Adam was gratified that his ideas had so quickly been proved correct.

'Yes, sir. Now, thanks to you, we knew where to look, we found him easily enough. In fact, some of our men had seen him earlier, for he seemed to be trying to make contact with a nest of rebels well known to us. The United Irishmen they call themselves and they are desperate men. Our agents had reported seeing a stranger seeking these traitors out. Yet not knowing his identity, or any of his recent actions, they gave their report no particular prominence. In fact, he was so inept that they guessed that he was a writer or a journalist trying to find material for his writing. Only when the description of the man we sought reached them did they realise he had already been seen.'

'What was his actual purpose in seeking these persons out? Did you discover?'

'We did not, I fear. It was clear he was not known to them, for they turned him away and would not exchange words with him at all. I imagine they suspected him of being one of our men, come to try to tempt them into some indiscretion and provoke their arrest. These fellows have learned to be wary of strangers, sir.'

'As I imagine they should be,' Adam said. 'Go on, please.' He could have enlightened Mr. Marshall on this subject, but chose to stay silent, judging it best to present his latest discoveries first to Mr. Wicken. Let him decide who else should be told.

'Our people judged correctly that Mr. Harmsworthy was new to this game. He somehow knew enough to be able to find the right people, but was at a loss when they would not speak with him. For a week or more, he simply wandered around Dublin. Again, he seemed to know the city, yet showed neither sense of purpose in his wanderings nor any delight in them.

'By this time, our people were on full alert and had sent an urgent message to Mr. Wicken seeking instructions. When the reply came, it was clear they must on no account lose sight of the man, but should not interfere in any other way. He might have led us to persons we did not know, sir. The fact that he had first sought out some notorious rebels had to mean that he had some knowledge of them and their activities.

'Our team watched and waited. Four days passed. Then, on a sudden, the quarry seemed to make up his mind what to do next. In a flurry, he left the inn where he had been staying and made all haste to find a berth on a ship traveling back to England.'

'How long ago was this?' Adam asked. Mr. Wicken must have known something was afoot when he asked Adam to meet Josiah Osman, yet had made no mention of it. Perhaps he too was confused by the randomness of Mr. Harmsworthy's actions. Or was he was loath to mention the man had been found until he was sure what to make of the reports reaching him?

'Tuesday of last week, sir,' Marshall said. 'One watcher followed Mr. Harmsworthy aboard. For the rest, as soon as we knew the man was in Ireland, the watch on all the ports where ships arrive from those parts had been increased. Thus it was easy enough to pick up observation of Mr. Harmsworthy when the ship bearing him came into harbour at Liverpool on Saturday morning's tide.

'Where he had been aimless before, he was now firm in his purpose. He went first to discover where he might board a stagecoach to London and when the next one departed. That was near dawn on Monday morning and Mr. Harmsworthy was on it. What he did not know was that one of our watchers had been substituted for the regular guard on the coach. That coach makes several stops before reaching the capital and we were determined not to lose him along the way.'

'Did he go to London?' Adam asked. If he had, he could see no reason why he should be acting as Mr. Wicken's substitute in this way.

'No, sir. At Oxford, he went to an inn and ordered a post chaise to take him onward the next morning—yesterday—to Lynn. We were surprised at that and had to change our own plans in great haste. He left at dawn and travelled as hard as the driver would let him, so that he arrived at Lynn late that same evening.

'You will understand, sir, that we all have the greatest respect for Mr. Wicken. His ability to anticipate the actions of desperate people is almost uncanny, and never more so than in this instance. It seems that, as soon as he heard Mr. Harmsworthy had crossed back to England, he ordered that a close watch be set on his house. Thus it was that his steward was detected leaving home on Tuesday, leading a spare horse. His master must have sent him a message as soon as he reached Liverpool, though none of our watchers saw him do it.

'Anyway, the steward took the horse to the stables of an inn at Lynn, then returned home alone. Mr. Harmsworthy had himself taken to that same inn as soon as he arrived.'

'So he had his own horse to use yesterday morning,' Adam said. 'And was returning to his house.' At that time he must have been quite unaware of his watchers, or he would never have taken so bold a step.

There it was. Over at last, all questions answered. Yet Adam could feel neither satisfaction in this knowledge, nor joy at being proved right in so many ways. Beside him a man lay dying: a good man, a dutiful man, who had done his best to live without harm to any. Yet in the end, he had been unable to escape the cruelness of an undeserved fate. Out of love, he had betrayed his country and murdered a man of a far more blameworthy character than his own.

Now Adam and Marshall sat watching and waiting, as so many must do at bedsides when no more is possible. If it was Mr. Harmsworthy's destiny to die by his own hand, he should not die alone. When, soon after the sun had risen, Mr. Harmsworthy's life reached its end at last, Adam and Marshall both stood, heads bowed, while the doctor gently raised the sheet to cover the face of the corpse. For a moment, they stayed silent, looking down at the shape in the bed. No words of prayer were said, yet it seemed neither man was willing to let the magistrate's death pass unmarked by any ceremony, however brief. At length they turned away together and left the room.

Adam felt near overcome by exhaustion. Whether it was from the wild ride, the emotions of the magistrate's confession and passing, or his own inability to do more than ease the man's agonies, he did not know. Whatever the cause, he needed sleep and a return to normality. Thus it was that he asked Marshall to have him taken to his brother's house at Trundon. One of Marshall's men readied the inn's chaise and Adam, once more heavily cloaked against the morning chill—and prying eyes—left Holt before nine.

Giles was used to his brother arriving unannounced and travel-worn, usually after spending a long night at the bedside of some patient. He was not therefore surprised when Adam came. Nor did he question the simple statement that his brother had been called out to a dying man, and had asked to be brought to the nearest source of a soft bed and relaxing company. Though he was not the imaginative type, Giles understood that being so often close to suffering and death must leave you drained to the uttermost.

After taking a simple breakfast, Adam retired to bed at once. And though Amelia gave firm instructions to servants and children to make no noises that might disturb his rest, it would not have mattered. Had a regiment of dragoons been manoeuvring outside, he would have heard nothing. He slept for nigh on eighteen hours and woke feeling ready for more.

For a while, Adam stayed abed, but hunger eventually drove him to rise. When he had washed and shaved enough to appear respectable, he went downstairs, finding the servants preparing for breakfast. His brother and Amelia seemed determined to avoid any subjects of conversation but the lightest, though they must have been agog to know what had caused him such weariness. In its way, this was almost more unsettling that a barrage of questions might have been, but Adam was much moved by their concern. And so, politely declining an invitation to stay once he had breakfasted, he begged his brother for loan of a carriage to take him home. It would be some time, he told himself, before he would again subject his backside to contact with a saddle.

As he was making his farewells, Giles put a letter into his hand, telling him it had arrived early that morning. He had kept it aside lest it should prove bad news of any kind. Now he was free to read it along the way or keep it until he was safely back in Aylsham.

Adam could not, of course, wait so long to open the paper, so he began to read as soon as the carriage was moving down the drive from the Hall.

It proved to be a letter from Mr. Wicken, saying that he had arrived in Holt late on that Friday evening and needed to deal with certain matters. He would then take some rest in his lodging at the White Lion before calling on Adam. Would it be convenient for him to come to Adam's house on Sunday morning?

Mr. Wicken arrived at about ten on Sunday morning. Despite one night's sleep, the effect of a long journey, undertaken at high speed, still showed. He was not quite his normal urbane and elegant self.

Hannah ushered him into Adam's study, where her master waited. Then, as Adam had arranged earlier, she brought a jug of punch and a pot of good coffee, with both glasses and cups, then left, closing the door firmly behind her.

Mr. Wicken tasted the coffee, sighed in appreciation and stretched out his long legs. 'You have no idea how good it feels to be in a fine room like this, drinking your excellent coffee, with no one coming in or out asking for direction,' he said. 'I cannot thank you enough for responding at once to my man's summons, doctor. You impressed all by your calmness in taking charge of a most confused situation. And before you berate yourself for not having saved Mr. Harmsworthy, let me assure you I am fully aware you did all you could. Marshall was a soldier before he entered my service. An experienced officer too. He told me that he knew from the start Mr. Harmsworthy was far beyond the help of any physician.'

'All I could do was hear what he termed his confession and try to ease his last hours,' Adam said. 'I still feel the greatest sympathy for the man. He admitted to killing the archdeacon and harbouring a wanted rebel and a French spy, yet I cannot bring myself to call him murderer or traitor.'

'We will return to that matter in a little while,' Mr. Wicken said. 'Tell me first what he related in his so-called confession.'

Adam did as he was bid, speaking in Harmsworthy's own words with as much accuracy as he could. To do thus brought back much of the pain of the first hearing. Yet he believed he owed it to the dead man to let him speak in his own voice to those who would judge him.

When he had finished, they sat in silence. At length, Mr. Wicken spoke his thoughts. 'There is something of the Greek tragedy about poor Harmsworthy's life,' he said. 'From all you have told me, it is clear he was caught in the meshes of a most unhappy fate. Is this your judgement too?'

'It is,' Adam said. 'I have spent many hours since the man's death wondering what should be done next. My power to influence events is small indeed, but I feel bound to tell you my conclusions.'

Mr. Wicken smiled. 'You may have more sway in these matters that you think, doctor. Since you are the only witness to Harmsworthy's words, none can act upon them without your co-operation. But that is of no matter for the moment. Tell me your conclusions and I will see if they match with mine.'

'Let me make it clear that my concern is for the living, not the dead,' Adam began. 'First, I am of the opinion that making it public that Dr. Ross, the archdeacon, was murdered can bring no benefit to any. For a start, in my medical opinion, the blow to his head would have killed him anyway. That seems indeed to have been an accident. We have no proof other than Harmsworthy's words that the man was then smothered while lying on the ground. If he was, it but hastened what must have come about anyway. Mrs. Ross and her family have begun to come to terms with the events of April. To upset them again for no real reason seems to me cruel and unnecessary.'

'So far we are in complete agreement,' Mr. Wicken said. 'The affair of Dr. Ross has only ever been a sideshow in relation to my concerns. Let us allow him, and his family, to rest in peace.'

'Thank you,' Adam said. 'You have eased my mind a good deal. Yet it may not be so easy for us to agree on the rest. To brand Mr. Harmsworthy a traitor to his country for his actions would be just, I agree. There is no doubt of that. He knew O'Dowd was a wanted rebel. He knew the Frenchman ...'

'Monsieur Alphonse Baudet de Harnoncourt, a notorious agent provocateur,' Mr. Wicken interposed.

'... the Frenchman,' Adam continued, 'was a spy sent to try to bring about rebellion in our land. Still, he gave them shelter and did what he could to see them on their way to safety. That makes him a traitor without any doubt. However, he is beyond all our justice and the other two are taken ...'

'One is dead,' Mr. Wicken said, 'hanged as he richly deserved. The other says little, but probably knows less. No one trusted him in Ireland.'

'What remains,' Adam said, refusing to be led away from his argument, 'is this. If we make known that Mr. Harmsworthy was a traitor, his whole family will suffer shame and likely ostracism from society. By his own words, none but he was involved in this treachery. I would not see them thus branded and ruined for the sake of his crime.'

Mr. Wicken smiled at this. 'It should not surprise you, doctor, to find we are also of the same mind in this area. Your motives are purer and more worthy than mine, but we reach the same point by our different routes. To make public what Mr. Harmsworthy told you would serve only to alert our enemies to the true extent of our ability to keep watch on them. I wish to avoid that, for obvious reasons.

'Let me tell you what I have done already. I could not wait to speak with you in detail, for which I apologise. Some actions must be taken on the instant for them to stand any chance of success.

'You showed great presence of mind, doctor, in not identifying yourself at the inn in Holt. That has helped me a good deal and I thank you for it. Your little game with the innkeeper and the contraband in his cellar was also perfect. By the time I arrived, the man was so frightened by the prospect of a visit from Revenue officers that he was ready to agree to anything I asked—only let him have the time to hide the evidence! He has already begun to spread abroad the story I told him. Indeed, he is saying it so often and so loudly that I do not doubt he will, in time, come to believe it is the truth. Much of it is, of course. I have found that a strong mixture of truth with the lies and distortions makes for a better result.

'Here is the tale then. As before, a trap was being planned for more smugglers along this coast. Men in the service of the authorities were moving about in small parties, spying out the land and judging where the smuggling trade was most active. It was one such group that came last Thursday night to The King's Head, bearing a severely wounded man.

'That man now has a name. It was Mr. Henry Harmsworthy, a well-known and respected magistrate in these parts. It seems Mr. Harmsworthy had been overseas, visiting old friends and conducting some business (which is true, in a way). His man had left a horse for him at Lynn, where he was due to return. (No mention of Ireland, you see. It is best if certain people do not know we ever traced him there.) His return to Lynn must have been later than he thought, for he was nearing his home only late in the afternoon. Thus it was that he was set upon by several thieves or ruffians. In the melée that followed, he suffered a severe wound to his chest from the discharge of a pistol.

'Hearing shouts and a shot, a party of government men hurried towards the noise, but were too late. The ruffians had fled at the sound of the approaching horses and poor Mr. Harmsworthy was lying where they left him. At once, most of the rescuers bore him away to the nearest town, where they found him a room at the first inn they came to. Others rushed to summon an eminent physician, a specialist in battlefield wounds, who had been asked to spend a few days in the vicinity. Since men had been killed in the last seizure of smugglers, the authorities wished to be prepared for the next.

'The physician came and did his best—none could have done better—but all was to no avail. Mr. Harmsworthy died. Now a substantial reward is being offered for the apprehending of his killers. It is also likely that a troop of dragoons will be billeted in Holt in the near future. The extent of smuggling along the coast between Wells and

Cromer has reached such a point that the Revenue men alone cannot cope.

'Well, doctor, does my story seem a good one to you? Will it convince people?'

'I am sure it will,' Adam said. 'You have done this before, Mr. Wicken. That is plain. Lies there are, but remarkably few. A few things are made to seem otherwise that the reality. Yet all will convince, since nearly all is simple truth. I am amazed.'

'In the work that I do,' Mr. Wicken said, not bothering to conceal his pleasure at Adam's words, 'it is as often necessary to explain public events away as it is to conceal others. Yet you gave me a good start, doctor. Without that, I would have needed to lie more and thus take a greater risk of the truth becoming known.'

'I do have one complaint,' Adam said.

Mr. Wicken frowned. 'Tell me,' he said. 'I will put it right if I can, I assure you.'

'Your tale includes an eminent physician, well-experienced in dealing with woundings. That, sir, is the most blatant falsehood I ever heard!'

'Not at all, good doctor,' Mr. Wicken replied, laughing now. ' I have done nought but bring forward what will sure to be true one day. I have no doubt of your future eminence. In what precise field … there I might, I own, be somewhat wider of the mark.'

Since there was no more to discuss after that, Mr. Wicken said that he must take his leave. He was, as always, needed back in London as quickly as possible. He might even be there by late that same evening, if he went at once.

As Adam was walking to the door with him, Mr. Wicken stopped. 'My good doctor,' he said, 'I had almost forgot your fee for attending our patient, and I brought a banker's draft with me expressly for that purpose.'

Adam took the document Mr. Wicken gave him and would have set it aside until after, had not Mr. Wicken urged him to check that it was all in order. What he opened was a banker's draft, drawn on The Bank of England, no less. The amount startled him and he looked up at once, only to find Mr. Wicken smiling happily.

'But sir,' Adam protested, 'this is far too great an amount!'

'For such an eminent physician? I think not. Besides, it is well below the worth you have been to me,' Mr. Wicken replied. 'Hush, doctor. I will not take it back. Now, I must go, leaving you with my thanks as always and a certain belief that we will meet again —maybe sooner that you think.' And with that, he stepped quickly out through the door to where his chaise, coachman and a discrete escort were waiting, leaving Adam standing open-mouthed in surprise.

Chapter Thirty-four

The Story Elaborated

Wednesday 29 August 1792, Aylsham

ADAM HAD BEEN ABSENT A good deal from his practice and patients of late. It behoved him to remember that he was, first and foremost, a doctor. Not a servant of the Alien Office, nor a rich man able to spend his time freely on whatever he wished. He thus devoted two full days to business and medical matters, ignoring all distractions. Only after that was done, and order restored to his life and work, would he allow himself some leisure. Thus it was Wednesday morning before he came at length to visit Lassimer's apothecary shop nearby.

Luck was with him. His friend was not visiting patients, nor was the shop full of customers. As soon as he entered, Lassimer pointed to the door of his compounding room, saying that he would take but a moment to finish his current task and close the shop for a while. Then they could speak in private and at length, for there was much news.

Lassimer did not join Adam quite as soon as he had promised. That was explained by the arrival of the lovely Anne, bearing a jug of good ale and a beaming smile for the doctor. Quite why she proved so disconcerting to Adam when she did this he did not know. It was plain though that she was well aware of the effect she could have on him at will and enjoyed seeing him flustered and embarrassed.

Coming into the room behind her, Lassimer saw what was happening in an instant and came to Adam's rescue.

'Be off with you, you baggage,' he said to her. 'I will not countenance such shameful behaviour under my roof … save with me, of course. Our good doctor's mind is on higher things. You must not expect him to notice a servant-girl's charms, however pleasing.' Then he gave the lie to his pretence of disapproval by fetching her a sound slap on the backside. She went, as ordered, but she was still smiling.

'Ignore her,' he said to Adam. 'She is all too knowing of the effect she produces in unwary males—especially those who deny themselves the proper exercise of their masculine nature on a regular basis. Now, what have you been doing, my friend—other than going out late at night in the company of a group of desperate-looking men?'

He laughed at the startled look on Adam's face. 'Come, doctor. You must know by now that everything that happens in this little town is soon reported to my shop, sometimes within the hour.'

'I was called to a patient in need,' Adam said, thinking furiously. 'As to the messengers who came to me, my patient had been entertaining a group of friends. They came together partly for protection and partly because none knew the road well.'

Adam need not have worried. Lassimer was far too eager to impart his own news to inquire too deeply into anything else.

'Well,' he said, 'unless you were in Holt, you missed all the excitement. Our Mr. Harmsworthy—that same magistrate whose actions we so suspected —is dead! What do you think of that? No, I see you

290

are not surprised. You knew already! But you have scarcely been out of your house since Friday. Maybe that strange gentleman who visited you on Sunday morning brought you news.'

This was all tending uncomfortably close to the truth. Fortunately, Adam had brought with him a simple way out of the problem.

'I suppose I should be flattered that the town deems my coming and goings so important,' he said. 'In reality, I find it tiresome. Still, the answer to your question is simple. I know about the matters that took place last week in Holt because I received a long letter from Capt. Mimms only this morning. He seems as excited as you are about what took place there.'

Lassimer was crestfallen. 'I had forgotten Capt. Mimms,' he said. 'Now, I suppose my news is stale.'

'How shall I know until I hear it?' Adam said. 'What Capt. Mimms wrote seems incredible enough. Detachments of dragoons. Highwaymen on the road beyond Letheringsett. Pistols fired in a desperate melée. The local inn thrown into confusion in the middle of the night. I think he has taken too much of his own excellent wine.'

'Then you are wrong,' Lassimer said, once again excited at the opportunity to share his own knowledge of the events. 'All that is true … aye, and more!'

'Capt. Mimms writes that Mr. Harmsworthy was killed by footpads,' Adam said. 'Then a group of men happened upon him lying by the road and brought him to Holt seeking medical help. A physician was called, but it was too late. Mr. Harmsworthy died before dawn came.'

'Hah!' Lassimer said. 'Capt. Mimms is a dull old stick indeed. He has left out much and reduced the rest to the most boring recitation of facts. He has even made serious errors in his relation. My own information comes from those who were close to being eye-witnesses.'

'How close?' Adam asked, but Lassimer seemed not to hear.

'Listen,' he said. 'I will tell you how things really went.' Thus he launched into his own tale.

According to this, the authorities had planned another significant assault on the smuggling gangs, much as before. It was to involve detachments of dragoons, Revenue Riding Officers and others. A group of local magistrates had also been summoned to assemble in Holt, ready to dispense immediate justice. All those captured would thus be on their way to prison in Norwich without delay.

One such magistrate was Mr. Harmsworthy. He, it seemed, had only the day before arrived back at Lynn from the Netherlands, where he had been pursuing his business interests. By the time the summons reached him, the hour to assemble was close. He could not delay. In his haste, he was unwise enough to ride out alone to join up with the others. Either that, or he expected to meet with a suitable escort before he had gone far. Whatever the reason, he rode alone, protected only by a brace of pistols at his saddle. That was when he was set upon by a murderous band of those same smugglers he was expecting to commit to the assize. They had an especial hatred for him, for they blamed him for the capture and punishment of so many of their number.

'They must have been watching his home,' Lassimer said. 'When he rode out, they knew at once that they could fulfil their design. All that was needed was to come upon him before others were about on the same road.'

'I imagine they had been studying the methods of the people of Aylsham,' Adam said. 'Maybe they even had an apothecary in their number.'

Lassimer rewarded this witticism with a glare, but refused to be turned aside when in full flow.

'However they accomplished it, they caught Mr. Harmsworthy alone on a deserted stretch of the road,' he continued. 'There followed a terrific chase, with many shots fired by both the pursuers and their quarry. The sounds of galloping horses and pistols being fired woke people from Field Dalling to Letheringsett and beyond. Of course, there were too many of them for Mr. Harmsworthy to fight off. They had come to murder him. Now they fulfilled their purpose.

'As soon as they saw him fall from his horse, mortally wounded, they rode off, leaving him lying in the road. As luck would have it, a small detachment of Revenue men had also hear the noise of shooting and hurried to see what was going on. They found Mr. Harmsworthy, but it was too late. He was already dead.

'Fearing lest the smugglers should return, these men took up the body and went as swiftly as they could to Holt, where they lodged the corpse in The King's Head Inn. The innkeeper, so I am told, is in excellent repute with the Revenue on account of his refusal to deal with smugglers in any way. Thus he was trusted to provide a secure refuge, should the smugglers be so bold as to come to carry the body off.

'Just in case the Revenue men had been wrong, the innkeeper sent at once for a most eminent retired naval surgeon—a personal friend—who, alas, certified death.'

'Doubtless they reasoned they did not have time to find an apothecary,' Adam said. 'To search the bedrooms of all the widows in those parts in hope of discovering where one might be would have occupied them to the morning.'

'You are in a strange mood today, Bascom,' Lassimer complained. 'If I were not so fond of you, I would take such words amiss.'

'Ignore me,' Adam said at once, for he did not wish to upset his friend. 'I do not mean to mock you. It is just that your tale is so serious that I felt in need of a moment of levity.'

'Hmm,' Lassimer replied. 'I judge you would be well-served by resisting such urges in future. Others might not be as understanding as I am.'

'Your pardon,' Adam said. 'It was a most foolish and unnecessary remark and I withdraw it at once. Please continue with your tale. You are indeed telling me much I neither know nor could ever guess at.' The worth of Wicken's remark about mixing a good measure of the truth into a lie was now proved in ample measure. Much mollified, Lassimer continued.

'My story is almost complete,' he said. 'With Mr. Harmsworthy dead, the authorities called off their plan and turned at once to trying to secure his killers. To kill a magistrate is a most serious crime. The reward offered is thus in proportion. I do not doubt it will prove more than enough to persuade someone in the gang to implicate the rest.'

'What is the reward?' Adam asked.

'A thousand guineas! Imagine that. Why, it is more money that most honest men would expect to see in seven years.'

'It is indeed a princely sum,' Adam agreed. Of course, Mr. Wicken could have offered even more, had he wished, since none would ever claim it. Still, he has calculated well, Adam said to himself. It is enough to provoke great interest and discussion, yet not so much as to occasion total disbelief.

'Of course,' Lassimer continued, 'the worst of all—at least for us—is that we cannot now know what part Mr. Harmsworthy played in the death of Dr. Ross, the archdeacon.'

'Indeed,' Adam said. 'I expect no more about that affair will ever be brought to light.' Enough, he told himself, you are enjoying this too much. He had not realised how easy it was to speak the truth purely to mislead.

They sat in silence for a few moments, then Lassimer spoke again. 'So, it is over at last. I am almost sad. I enjoyed puzzling over things with you —and setting you right on several occasions, as I recall.'

Adam smiled at this. He did not begrudge Lassimer his moments of triumph. What his friend said was true. Without him—and Capt.

Mimms, Mr. Jempson and even Miss LaSalle at the end—he might well have failed to get anywhere.

'All that you say is true, Lassimer,' he said. 'I too feel somewhat sad that our quest has ended. And I admit most readily that you found more solutions that I did. All of which proves, once again, that apothecaries have the most devious and calculating minds. Physicians, on the other hand, are much too honest and straightforward to do well in such murky waters.'

At once, the old sparring between them began again and they spent another hour in that amicable state of teasing that is such an important part of true friendship. It did indeed seem as if both of them should return wholly to their respective businesses and leave the solving of crime aside. Yet they were to be proved quite wrong about this before too many months had passed.

AN UNLAMENTED DEATH

Chapter Thirty-five

Postscript

A Letter from Mrs. Bascom to her son, Norwich, 28 August, 1792

My Dear Son,

I should be gratified to find myself at present much in demand amongst the better society of this city. Alas, it is not my wit or conversation that causes so many invitations to be sent. Nor does the blizzard of calling cards in the hallway signify anything about me. It is not even curiosity to meet dear Sophia, richly though she deserves it.

No, what draws all attention is the simple fact that I have a son. Not any kind of son, you understand. This one is hailed as 'a young man of infinite promise', 'the best ornament of the medical profession in these parts' and 'saintly in his care for his patients'. I am assured on all sides that he is 'quite the thing'. People pester me with questions about him. Certain ladies amongst my acquaintance have derived much repute from having met this amazing young man 'in the flesh', in a manner of speaking—though I am certain more than one of them (and none more so than Miss Jane Labelior) would dearly like to turn that saying into reality.

Who can this man be? I have but two sons. One is a country squire, with no connection to medicine. The other is a physician it is true. But I know him only as a most retiring and scholarly person. Admittedly, he is sometimes drawn into all kinds of madcap actions through a most over-developed curiosity, but no more.

Yet, I am assured, this is the one. Mrs. Ross, the wife of the late archdeacon, sings your praises more sweetly than the choir in the cathedral sing their anthems. Amongst the Quakers of this place, of which there are many, your name is held out as a paragon of bravery and good sense. Even the bishop's chaplain, I hear, has been moved to refer to you as 'an excellent person'. That is a great compliment indeed, coming from him. He is well-known to be critical of all who are not relatives of His Lordship, the Bishop, or members of the higher ranks of the peerage.

On the subject of Mrs. Ross, I imagine you know that she and her son are now reconciled. He is living in Birmingham at present, I understand, where he has found eminent men in commerce and banking closely interested in furthering his career. All thought Mrs. Ross would leave Norwich, but she assures us it is not so. She has left the Archdeacon's residence in the Close, of course. Yet her son intends to return to this city in due time. It seems that he has good hopes of entering into a partnership with one or more of his patrons from Birmingham and starting a business here of banking. In the meantime, he has rented a suitable property for his mother. Since, we are told, his father did not manage to cut off his inheritance in the legal sense— dying before that could be done—he has sufficient wealth to establish himself in business when he is ready.

I would ask you when you next intend to visit me, but you might do better to stay in Aylsham until the fuss has died down. Unless, of course, you relish the idea of being pestered by every eligible young woman (and a good many not so young) with long accounts of their ailments. I think Sophia and I will come again to visit you instead. Then we can go on to Trundon as we did on the last occasion.

Sophia and I get along wonderfully together. She is quite the most tactful and delightful of companions. When we wish, we attend the theatre and other sundry entertainments, where she seems always to draw a small crowd of attentive young men. Sad to say, they depart unsatisfied, for she is resolute that she will never marry. Instead, she spends her time with several close female friends of her own age. They are gaining the status of bluestockings, I fear, for they occupy themselves mostly in reading, study and scientific experiments most unsuitable for young ladies. I do not interfere. What is judged acceptable for the young of our sex has always seemed to me to be too dull to contemplate.

What she thinks of you she will not tell me. Make of this what you will. I suspect she harbours a certain tendresse, but will not admit it. But then, I am a silly, sentimental old woman. It is just as likely that she rarely thinks of you at all.

So, my dear boy, expect us to visit during the last two weeks of September, if that is convenient for you.

Until then, I remain your most loving and devoted mother,

Mrs. Eleanor Bascom.

Printed in Great Britain
by Amazon

27710528R00175